David Storey

A Temporary Life

Penguin Books

Penguin Books Ltd,
Harmondsworth, Middlesex, England
Penguin Books, 625 Madison Avenue,
New York, New York 10022, U.S.A.
Penguin Books Australia Ltd,
Ringwood, Victoria, Australia
Penguin Books Canada Ltd,
2801 John Street, Markham, Ontario, Canada L3R 1B4
Penguin Books (N.Z.) Ltd,
182–190 Wairau Road, Auckland 10, New Zealand

First published by Allen Lane 1973
Published in Penguin Books 1978
Copyright © David Storey, 1973
All rights reserved

Made and printed in Great Britain by
Richard Clay (The Chaucer Press) Ltd, Bungay, Suffolk
Set in Linotype Plantin

For Sean

Part One

I

Hendricks says,
  'On the same latitude as what?'
  'Omsk,' I tell him.
  'Anywhere else?' he says.
  'A place I can't pronounce,' I add, 'in Khabarovsk.'
I pause.
  'In North America, of course,' I tell him, 'Queen Charlotte's Island ... Goose Bay.'
  'And longitude?' he says.
  'Saragossa. Cartagena. Oran in North Africa. Timbuctoo.'
  Tall, fair-haired, with a fair moustache, attired in white shorts and a white sweater, in white plimsolls and short white ankle socks – folded neatly over at the top, immediately above the uniformly fastened laces – Hendricks leans back in his canvas chair. He's drinking from a glass of lemonade which I've just brought him from the cafeteria further along the path of the municipal park. Behind us, the man who's responsible for letting out the courts, for supervising the putting as well as the bowling greens, for raising and lowering the tennis nets, is locking up his shop.
  The park now is almost deserted. The sun has begun to set, sinking down behind the trees to where the ducks still quack, the geese still honk, the pigeons in the municipal aviary still coo. The cafeteria too, it seems, is closing up. No doubt it's already night in Omsk, and in that unpronounceable city in Khabarovsk. Ships in their respective oceans will be waiting for the sun to set, to rise, to grow stronger, to grow more faint. Together, Hendricks and I have watched it for an hour.
  'And all the while,' he says, 'we're sitting here.'

'Fifty-three degrees and thirty minutes north, one degree and thirty minutes west.'

I catch a glimpse of myself in the window of the hut behind, the dark hair cut short, the scarred, thick-boned brows projecting above dark and rather melancholic eyes, the broken nose. I have a rather listless look; my arms hang down, limply, over the edges of the chair. Rust, from the wire-netting fronting the courts, has stained my shirt; damp patches show beneath my arms and round my chest. I ease one leg, cautiously, across the other. The chair is altogether too small for my ample frame. It creaks.

The man emerging from the hut looks up.

'Will you be finished here?' he says.

'Just about,' I tell him. 'Almost done.'

I get up quickly.

The chair, relieved of its burden, has suddenly collapsed.

Hendricks laughs.

'What was the score?' he says.

'Two sets to one.'

'I should think, for one thing, Freestone, you need more exercise,' he says, and adds, 'And as for another, a little more skill wouldn't go astray.'

'More skill. More exercise.' I begin to fold the chair.

'Walk back? Or do you want a lift?' he says.

'Walk, I think.'

I lean the chair up against the hut.

Hendricks stoops down: he fastens the string bag containing the tennis balls to the handle of his racket. He tightens up the screws on his metal press.

He seems altogether unmoved, in fact, by the scene before us, the darkening trees, the lengthening shadows, the faint mist which has crept up from the direction of the river. He folds up his chair, hands it to the waiting attendant, then, his racket in one hand and the now empty glass in the other, steps down to the path.

'Sure about the lift?' he says.

'Sure,' I say. I fasten my jacket. 'Cooler now,' I add. 'And stiff.'

'If you did it every day you'd feel much better.'

'Sure,' I tell him. 'I think I would.'

He leaves the glass on one of the metal tables at the front of the cafeteria and walks on towards the gates. One or two other figures can be seen moving off beneath the trees. The nets in the court have already been lowered; the wooden gate leading to the bowling-green is locked. The jaw bones of a whale stand up in a pointed arch above the path.

Our faces, for a moment, fall in its shadow.

'Cape Cod. Antarctica. Greenland's icy shore.'

Hendricks is gazing off towards the gates where, in the shadow of the trees, his car is parked.

'I suppose we ought to play again,' he says.

'Anytime,' I tell him.

'I'll fix it up,' he says.

He swings off the path, feeling in his pocket.

'See you tomorrow, then,' he says.

'All being well,' I tell him.

He waves.

Moments later a dark blue shape slips out from beneath the trees; a white clad arm is raised then lowered.

The path I've taken leads directly to a hill standing in the centre of the park. Its lower slopes are wooded; a belt of trees is drawn out in a thin arc around its summit. When I reach the intervening area of grass I can see the tennis courts and the bowling-green stretched out immediately below like panes of glass, smooth, their regular shapes half-buried now by shadow. Beyond stands the outer wall of the park itself, the retaining wall to the grounds of an old brick mansion whose tall black chimneys and blackened balustrade are visible, starkly silhouetted, over the furthest slope of an adjoining hill.

As I move higher up the slope the area beyond the park comes into view: hedged fields broken up by odd clumps of trees and the darker outline of isolated buildings rising, some distance off, to the line of hills that mark off the southern limits of the valley.

The mist has thickened; the shadows of the trees have been moulded into a single shape. A band of shadow rises, like water, across the contour of the hill.

I come out, finally, into an open space immediately below the summit. To my right, the valley broadens to a darkening vista of wooded plain and hill-land; to my left it narrows to a silhouetted gorge. Behind me, to the south, lies the shadowed area of tennis-courts and greens and, beyond those, the hedged fields lining the valley bottom. To the north, immediately ahead, appears the sun-lit, emblazoned outline of the city.

I've been conscious for some time of the strange, inferno-like presence of the hill above my head, of the bursting, sun-lit mass of trees, of the encroaching mass of shadow; then, suddenly, as if it might have sprung from the ground itself, I see immediately before me the flame-like structure of the town, the domes and steeples, the vast, brick-fronted towers, caught now by the last, horizontal rays, a glowing, reddened edifice shot here and there with sudden gleams and flashes and lit, along its crest, by a strip of golden light.

Even as I watch the light begins to fade. The darkness creeps up the separate blocks and towers. I feel the dew against my face, and the sudden chilling of the air as the hill itself falls into shadow.

Birds have settled in the trees. Odd shapes are flung up, briefly, against the silhouetted leaves and branches.

I start off down the hill. It's as if an aperture has opened; odd sighs and groans come up from its furthest depths. Above, the last pinnacles of the town still catch the light, long, orange fissures let into the blueness overhead. As I reach the bottom of the hill they too begin to fade; new lights, with fresh shadows, spring up from the growing darkness. Soon only a faint glow, somewhere to the west, remains.

2

'If you drop a line vertically, from the thorax, it should reach a point somewhere near the centre of her left ankle. Providing that her weight,' I add, 'is entirely on that side.'

The model sways. She draws her weight over, wearily, onto her other foot.

'In practice, of course,' I say, 'you may find it's somewhat different.'

I get up from the wooden stool, gaze down at the drawing for a moment longer, then move over to the second stool and wait for the student there to rise.

'Is it time for a rest?' the model says.

She scarcely speaks above a whisper.

'Do you feel like a rest?' I ask.

Her feet are red; her ankles, it seems, are slightly swollen.

'I'm feeling hot,' she says.

'Have five minutes, then,' I tell her.

I get out a cigarette, light it, remember the rule about smoking in the life room, stub it out and cross over to the window. The model shakes her legs, forces her feet into her slippers and climbs down from the platform. Most of the students stay near their stools; one or two lean down, rub out some offending limb or feature, or begin to shade in the bits they like. Outside I can hear Wilcox complaining about some recent damage to the paintwork. 'The damn thing's not been painted a couple of weeks. Do you behave like this at home?' A faint murmur runs through the room as the students wait.

'That's been done by a bloody chisel.'

A fainter, less uncertain voice replies.

'Accident? That's no accident. A mark like that's not done by chance.'

The answering voice replies again.

A door is slammed. The voices fade.

I smell the smoke from a cigarette and look up in time to see a faint blue cloud rise above the curtain drawn across the front of the model's cubicle. The rule about smoking, strangely, I've never questioned; has it got something to do with etiquette – one never smokes, perhaps, in the presence of a naked woman – or with Wilcox's reverential feelings for the room itself: the last bastion of art, as he once described it?

Mentally, I wander off into the adjoining rooms: the library with its shelves of untouched and virtually untouchable books – 'If you want any books apply in writing and, if I think it's worth your while, I'll let you have the keys,' – beyond that, the room with the lithographic presses, the printing presses, the etching baths and etching presses, a foul, fume-ridden place – acids, inks and washing-fluids – for which I have no feeling of any sort at all. Neither have I much feeling for what goes on in the room beyond: dress-design and needle-craft; groups of thin, emaciated girls and fat, broad-chested women pinning strands of coloured cloth to dummies or sitting, round-shouldered, in front of black, foot-pedalled sewing-machines – 'Damned exercise'll do 'em good. Teach 'em to be economic. Won't put a seam in until they're certain,' – laughter – 'How much does that cotton cost a bobbin?'

Wilcox's presence permeates the entire building, like a cloud of smoke, an atmosphere into which one ascends on arrival – up either wing of the bifurcated stairs – and which seems to seep into one's very pores, until you find yourself on leaving taking on the identity of the man himself, thick-necked, broad-chested, delving into cracks and fissures, hauling out a pencil or the stub of somebody's half-smoked cigarette: *'Is there no end to this bleeding rubbish?'*

Beyond the dress-designers and embroiderers comes the largest room of all, its interior divided up by a series of paint-encrusted screens. Behind the screens a variety of activities are carried on: lettering, designing, illustration, pictorial composition, anatomy, the study of antiques, still-lifes and plants. Here a certain amount of smoking is allowed simply because Wilcox can't be behind all the screens at once; neither can he be in the lithographic and etching department when he is in the life room; neither can he be in the life room when he's bawling out some student on the stairs.

I'm brought back to the present, in fact, by the sound of the Principal's voice. 'Someone,' he says, having come into the room unnoticed, 'is damn-well smoking. And that, mind you, when that certain someone knows that smoking in this room is damn-well not allowed.'

The faint blue cloud above the model's cubicle drifts slowly off. Perhaps Wilcox is unaware, has failed to notice, that the model is no longer standing on the throne. He strides directly to the centre of the room. 'Ash. Is that ash I can see on there?'

'No, sir. It's from my rubber.'

'Rubber? Rubber? That looks like cigarettes to me.'

He dabs his fingers at the mess.

'Good God.'

He gazes over at the chalk-marks where the model's feet have been, then at the students, then, with increasing dismay, he glances at myself.

'See here,' he says. 'What's happened to the model, Freestone?'

'I'm afraid,' I tell him, 'she isn't feeling well.'

'Well? Not feeling well?' He glances round as if he's never encountered this condition in his life before.

'She said she'd carry on,' I tell him.

'Carry on?'

'Which is very good of her,' I add.

'Good of her?'

The model reappears. She climbs onto the platform, glances down at her chalk-marks, then, fixing her gaze on a point a few inches above the Principal's head, resumes her pose.

'You'll be fetching her cups of tea in next.'

He glances round him once again.

'Somebody's been smoking in here. I don't suppose you've noticed.'

'That's me, I'm afraid,' I tell him. I indicate the cigarette, stubbed out, which I'm holding in my hand. 'A momentary aberration.'

'Aberration?' Wilcox gazes at my hand for several seconds. 'You know the rule about smoking, then, I take it? If we can't set an example ourselves I don't know who damn well can. I spend half my time going round trying to keep this building tidy.'

'More,' I tell him.

'More. That's right,' he says.

Perhaps it's the association of cigarettes, drifting clouds of smoke and the body of a naked woman that Wilcox instinctively recoils from. Almost absent-mindedly I withdraw my fingers from the cigarette and leave it equidistant between us on the window-ledge. I turn my gaze to the window, see, faintly, the Principal's face reflected in the glass, and concentrate my attention on the view outside.

It comprises, very largely, that area of the town with which as yet I'm least familiar. The college, a prominent, square-shaped building, stands near the centre of the town, looking out over the roofs of the nearest buildings towards the park. Hedged fields, low hillocks, clumps of trees and odd, isolated copses, stretch out in a broad perspective towards a distant line of heath and hills.

'It's not only the smoking,' Wilcox says. 'Somebody's been scratching at the paint outside.'

Clearly, he's come to a decision about the cigarette. I can even feel a certain amount of sympathy for him when I consider the effort required on the Principal's part not to snatch at the offending object – a certain degree of violence invariably accompanies the disposal by Wilcox of a piece of rubbish – crush it, and drop it in his pocket.

'I've a damn good idea it's been done by one of these damn chisels. They come up here at home-time and put them in their lockers. They know damn well they're supposed to stay downstairs.'

He pauses, in illustration, listening for any sounds from the sculpture room below.

My own thoughts move on, first to the pottery room beyond, then to the room beyond that given over to the gas-fired kiln, then to the room and passageway beyond that given over, on certain afternoons and evenings, to sign-writing and interior decorating.

'The damn building'll drop to bits if I don't keep going round,' he says. 'As it is we don't come very high on the priority list of that so-called – though I don't know why – education committee over yonder.' He gestures at the window now himself.

'It needs someone to keep them on their toes,' I say.

'Toes? Bloody backsides I should think's more like it. When it comes down to it there's not one in here, or over there, that does a proper job of work.'

He pauses again. The silence of the room is undisturbed, save, that is, for the scratching of the students' pencils, the odd sighs of frustration, the thudding of a rubber against a board.

'It's the time they take over the work. Not to mention the work itself. Spend two minutes on a bit of hardboard – never mind your canvas – and think they've done a Mona Lisa. Two hours with a bit of wire and plaster and you'd think they'd turned out a John the Baptist.'

'Yes,' I say. I nod my head.

'Too hot, is it,' he says, 'or cold?' He indicates the model's heater: two rectangular metal sheets set one above the other on a metal stand.

'Warm enough, I think,' I tell him.

The model nods.

'Think on about the smoking. I don't mind it in the staff room. I draw a line at it in here.'

He glances over at the model, coughs, lengthily, as if overwhelmed entirely by the atmosphere of the room, and then, still coughing, crosses to the door.

He lets it shut behind him.

A murmur of relief runs through the room.

'Thanks, Mr Freestone, for getting me off the cigarette,' the model says.

'That's all right,' I tell her. I hold up the one I've started smoking. 'My mistake as well.'

'Dying for a smoke,' she says, swaying now, wearily, from one foot to the other.

I cross over to the nearest stool, wait for the student there to rise, sit down and gaze at the drawing on the pad before me.

It's comprised almost entirely of irregular triangles. They begin at the top of the paper and run down with increasing boldness to the bottom. The feet of the figure are clad in what look like an enormous pair of metal boots.

'The idea, really, was to sort of indicate the masses. And to sort of counterpoint the main areas and shapes.'

'Yes,' I say. I nod my head.

A hand comes down, casual, wistful, as if about to bring the metallic shape to life.

I glance over at the model.

Odd shadows have appeared at the corners of her mouth.

Cramp, I think. Or pins and needles.

'Sort of projecting, I suppose, the principal masses.'

'Yes,' I say.

I ease my legs against the stool.

I glance over, idly, to the drawing on my right.

From a distance of three or four feet the figure there looks uncommonly like a peeled banana. To my left, the Black Hole of

Calcutta: a mass of erasures, scratches, crossings-out; beyond that, an armature-like construction – arms and legs reduced to matches – and on the other side a figure constructed from what look like motor car inner tubes and tyres.

'Perhaps you can shade a few of these in.'

'Yes?'

'Give the figure,' I say, 'some sort of context.'

'Context?'

'Give it some relief.'

'The idea, really, is to get the masses.'

'Yes,' I say. 'I see.'

The hand comes down again. I'm attracted immediately by the neatness of the nails, like petals, pink and smooth. A girl.

'To keep it two-dimensional,' she says.

'Yes,' I say.

Her hair is dark. It hangs around her face in a shallow cowl. Her eyes are grey. A thin line of black mascara strengthens the already pronounced effect of her thick black lashes. The lips, too, in profile, remind me of a flower: the texture of her skin, smooth, unblemished, brings back the image of a petal. I smell her scent.

'I wondered if you'd look at one or two drawings I have,' she says.

'Yes,' I say. I lift the pad.

'Not here,' she says.

'Perhaps I could see them when we have a rest,' I tell her.

'I haven't got them here,' she says.

'Bring them tomorrow, then,' I tell her.

I get up from the stool.

'Shall I carry on?' she says.

'Yes,' I tell her and cross over to the door, hear Wilcox's voice in the corridor outside, and move back slowly towards the window.

I glance over at the girl. Fletcher? Newman. Christian name? Begins with 'R'.

She wears a white sweater and a short grey skirt; her leg's outlined against the profile of the stool.

I look back towards the window. *Wil cox be in fashion this year?* someone has written on the paintwork.

'Tennis tonight, or something else?'

Hendricks has come into the room on soft-soled shoes – lunch-time spent playing Badminton in the gymnasium of the Technical College across the way – and now stands by my elbow gazing at the view.

'Spend more time looking out of there than looking at anything else, I think.'

'Yes,' I tell him.

'How about the tennis?'

'Will the weather hold?' I ask.

'Should think so. Still autumn, not winter. Five-thirty, old man? I've booked a court.'

He glances at the model.

'What's she like?' he says.

'All right.'

'Might come in and do a plate or so myself,' he tells me.

Hendricks teaches lithography and etching.

'Heard who's disappeared this morning, then?' he says.

'No,' I tell him. I shake my head.

'Freddy. Gone and vanished. Been searching high and low,' he says.

He takes out a comb and runs it through his hair, ducking down so that he can see his face reflected in a framed print of the 'Discobolus' on the wall.

'Hell of a temper. Been into every room,' he says.

'Came in here. Never mentioned it,' I tell him.

'Preliminary inquiries. Search everybody, I suppose. Won't commit himself too soon. Bide his time, old man. Then pounce.'

Freddy is a yellowing, much-fingered plaster cherub used, perhaps in Wilcox's earliest days, for drawing from the antique. Recently, several other casts have disappeared, integral parts of their anatomy having, over the months, preceded them. Freddy's own single dismembered piece lies invariably on the pedestal by his side.

'How's it feel?'

'Feel?'

'Arms ache?'

'A bit.'

'A few more games: you'll feel all right.'

He glances over at the model: he gives his comb a final shake.

'Do you want a lift, or shall I meet you there,' he says.

'See you there, I think,' I tell him.

'Okey-doke,' he says.

He gazes round at the students, crosses to the door, waves, then disappears.

'Rest,' I say and watch, abstracted, as the model eases first one foot then the other, then, breasts trembling, climbs down from the throne.

She pushes her feet inside her slippers, eases her back then, glancing first in my direction then at the door, walks over to the drawings.

She examines the Michelin tyre-man first, frowning, her head held slightly to one side.

Still frowning, she moves over to the armature, then to the Black Hole of Calcutta, gazes for several seconds at what is, plainly, an indecipherable mass of scrawls and whirls, then moves on, more slowly, to the triangulated frost-man. From there her eyes pass on, perplexed, to the peeled banana. As if some error of judgement on her part is involved, she glances back along the row; peeled banana, frost-man, black-hole/coal-hole, wire-man, tyre-man; she glances up, smiles, stretches, then comes over to the window.

'I used to be interested in drawing.'

'Really?'

'Years ago.'

'Not now?'

'Never find the time.'

I examine the skin around her shoulder. The white line left by a strap runs down through an area of suntan to the white skin above her breasts.

'I don't suppose if I had the time I'd be much good in any case. Not nowadays,' she says.

'Why's that?'

'Not with this modern stuff,' she tells me.

She points back towards the drawings.

'I don't understand half of it,' she says.

'Same here.'

She smiles again.

'*You*'re supposed to be a specialist,' she says.

I can see our two figures reflected in the framed print of the 'Discobolus', a broad, stocky, dark-haired man: secondhand, fawn jacket, white shirt and blackened collar; and the pale, pink, glowing figure of a light-haired woman. She runs her hand across her chest.

'Think I'm boiling. These heaters are stronger than you think.'

I feel her arm.

'I'll switch them off,' I tell her.

'Too cold. Even with one on it gets too cold. And with two on, of course, it gets too hot.'

'Better too hot,' I say, 'than cold.'

'That's what I think, love!' she tells me.

She glances back towards the throne. Beads of sweat have run down beneath her arm. Her feet are still inflamed; her ankles, perhaps, are always swollen.

'At this other place I go to the heaters are always breaking down,' she says. 'It's like standing in an ice-box.'

'At least one or two things work here,' I say.

'Thanks, I think, to Mr Wilcox.'

'Thanks to Mr Wilcox. Yes,' I add.

She begins to laugh.

Behind her I can see the Newman girl. She's standing with her back to the wall, her hands clasped behind her, pushing herself off from the wall then letting herself fall back against it, laughing, listening to the small, squat, black-haired boy who has produced the peeled banana.

'In some schools they hardly draw from the model anymore.'

'Be doing you out of a job,' I tell her.

'If it wasn't this I'd probably find something else,' she says.

'Such as?' I say.

'Worked in a factory once,' she says and adds, 'Sewing buttons.'

She lifts my tie.

'Don't you have anyone to sew them on?' she asks me.

'No,' I say. I shake my head.

'That's how it is nowadays,' she says. 'Don't think marriage, *looking after* somebody comes into it anymore. Not like it used to.' She runs her hand across her chest. 'Think I'll go get dressed,' she adds.

The Newman girl has left the wall; she's walking along the

row of stools, glancing at the drawings, her hands behind her back, stooping, pausing here and there, her feet astride, her chin thrust out: she glances up at one point and sees me by the window. She shakes her head, smiles, then, flushing slightly, moves on around the stools.

3

I go through to the staff room before the class is finished. Pollard is sitting at the table drinking coffee and reading a midday paper. Small, red-faced, fair-haired, attired in a patched jacket and light-coloured corduroys, he leaps to his feet and makes some attempt to hide the cup.

'O my God,' he says. 'I thought it was the Skipper.'

He takes out a lighted cigarette from the pocket of his jacket.

'Only me,' I tell him. I go over to the cupboard where the register is kept.

'Back Methuselah,' he says, 'or Genghis Khan?'

'Neither,' I tell him. I shake my head.

'Methuselah's a damn good bet,' he says. 'Nine to four against. Can't lose.'

'What lost yesterday?' I ask him.

'Dope-test, old man. They had it from the jockey.'

He folds up the paper, finishes the coffee, and goes over to the door.

'Heard about the tool-less cherub?'

'Gone absent, Hendricks says.'

'Third one in as many weeks,' he says. He adds, 'When de Milo goes, and that prickless wonder with his discus, we're going to be bereft of all antiques.'

'Who's taking them?' I ask him.

'Madman. Bound to be,' he says. He shakes his head. 'Can't get rid of them. Not even to the rag-man.'

Pollard teaches design and lettering. At one time, according to Hendricks, he's been a lightweight amateur boxer: his legs are slightly bowed and his arms, when he walks, swing out on either side like the handles of a jug. The students call him Major. He has, though I've never seen them, seven children. In the evenings he can be seen occasionally in the town driving about in an open-top prewar Austin Seven with several of his offspring in the back.

'Who's the girl with dark hair and light grey eyes?' I ask him.

'Who is she indeed, then?' Pollard says.

'In my class, by the name of Newman, I believe,' I tell him.

'Rebecca is her name,' he says.

'Have you seen her work?' I ask.

'All I wish to see of it,' he says.

'Don't think much to it, then?' I say.

'Not paid to think, old man,' he tells me.

I take down the register, remove the notice which says, *'I'd like this register down a little bit sooner if somebody can be bothered to sign it. Signed: R. N. Wilcox'*, and open it at the page devoted to first year entries.

'What's "N" in Wilcox stand for, then?'

'Norman,' Pollard says.

'Robert or Norman: which does he prefer?' I ask him.

'Neither,' Pollard says.

Pollard, I've noticed, always addresses the Principal as 'sir', Hendricks as 'Principal'. I haven't, as yet, decided which I ought to use myself. Occasionally I've addressed him as 'Mr Wilcox', but on the whole I avoid talking to him directly unless Wilcox comes up and actually starts a conversation. On these occasions there's never been any need to call him anything at all.

'Rebecca Kathleen Elizabeth Newman. Born ... Address ... Previous education:' here follows a list of schools so long that I give up reading. She's travelled, evidently, half way round the world.

'That's where he gets his nickname from.'

Pollard is still standing by the door: it looks out directly onto the design room. Beyond one of the screens I can see the skeleton, used in anatomy, being waved as a signal, slowly, to and fro.

'R. N. Hence: "Skipper",' Pollard says. He adds, 'Anything of interest, then?'

Wilcox's voice comes boldly from the corridor outside.

'*Who's in charge,*' it says, '*in here?*'

Pollard douses his cigarette, drops the butt into his jacket pocket, pointing at the kettle. 'Be a chap,' he says.

'*Damn racket. Can hear it in me room. Who's teaching, or has he gone on holiday, then?*'

The door has closed.

A moment later I can hear Pollard's voice as if at the end of some hour long peroration droning on behind the screens.

I pour the remaining water from the kettle, pour in cold water, rinse it out, then do the same with Pollard's cup.

The door has opened.

Wilcox puts his head inside.

'What's going on in here, then? Mothers' meeting?'

'Checking on the register,' I tell him.

'That's a bloody miracle,' Wilcox says.

He crosses to the sink.

'Been brewing up, then, have they, lad?'

'Don't think so. No.' I shake my head.

Wilcox crosses to the kettle, feels it: he glances about him at the room.

Two windows look down onto the yard at the back of the college: onto piles of coke and the broken roof of a bicycle shed.

'Cool it down and think I never notice. But somebody's been drinking coffee. Don't you worry.'

'It could easily be the paint,' I tell him.

The smell of paint from a recent bout of midsummer decorating still lingers in the building, fighting a rearguard action with Wilcox's Personal Deodorant – a smell of senna pods and weakened tea – and the more indigenous smells from Hendrick's acid baths and lithographic plates.

'Know coffee when I smell it. Ought to. Had a lifelong aversion to the bloody stuff. Shortens your life, keeps you awake, encourages indigestion.'

He opens the cupboard, feels the other cups, then comes over to the table.

'I'll catch them one day. Mark my bloody words. It's not the drinking I object to, as the example that they set.'

I fold the register, return it to the cupboard, then move over to the door.

'Who's been missing, then?' he says.

'I was looking up a name,' I tell him.

'A name?'

He waits.

'Don't need names in this place. You, you and you. That's always been my motto.'

I wonder, not for the first time, if Wilcox mightn't be deranged; if he's not in need of some sort of medical attention.

'I'll get back to the class,' I tell him.

He nods. 'Cold do you think?' he says. 'Or warmer?'

'Warm enough.' I look about me at the room.

'Not in here. The life room,' Wilcox says.

'To warm, if anything,' I tell him.

'Always complain,' he says. 'The models.' He adds, 'Always complain if they get a chance.' He looks over to the window. 'Belly-ache to me, but who do I have to belly-ache to?'

'Yes,' I tell him.

Behind me, faintly, I can still hear Pollard's voice.

'Not a day goes by but somebody doesn't start.'

'It's a difficult situation.'

'Situation?' He glances over at the kettle, at Pollard's cup, at the copies of *Art Review* and *Studio International*, months if not years now out of date. He looks across. 'You've heard about the plaster-cast, I take it?' He waits, momentarily, for this to be confirmed. 'I'll come up here one of these days and find the entire place has disappeared.'

He pulls out a chair, sits down, and lowers his head between his hands.

He gazes down for a while into the bottom of Pollard's cup.

'Land of the Philistines, round here.' He coughs. 'Nothing but technicians. Don't think we've got an artist in the place.'

He coughs again. The skin on the top of his head has reddened.

'Same down there.' He nods at the floor. 'Sculpture? More like a rag and bone shop. When you think of Phidias and Donatello it makes you wonder what you've got.'

Through the wall, from the direction of the life room, comes the sound of several cries and shouts.

'I better be getting back,' I tell him.

'Back?'

Wilcox rubs his head.

On top he's completely bald. A thin reef of greying hair circles the craggy contour of his skull.

'In the old days you had a set of rules. Standards. Things you could rely on. Laws. These days you've got hardly anything at all.'

The cries from the life room have grown a little louder. Wilcox raises his head.

'It's not often I open up,' he says. He watches me, sharply, out of the corner of his eye.

'One evening, if you're free,' he adds, 'come up to dinner.' He gets up from the table.

'Dinner?'

'Not often I have anybody back.'

He glances round him once again.

'Better get back to that racket. I can hear them through the bloody wall.'

I close the door, cross the design room, see Pollard's head raised, inquiringly, beyond the screens, then pass on to the corridor outside.

When I open the door of the life room two of the students are dancing on the throne.

The shouting fades. The two get down.

'I don't think we'll have that again,' I tell them.

The model shakes her head.

'I don't mind it, love,' she says.

The Newman girl is still sitting on her stool, drawing. She's scarcely raised her head.

I cross over to the window. The room itself grows quiet.

I gaze out, abstracted, to the distant line of trees and hills. Odd clouds of smoke and steam have risen from the valley bottom, dull and heavy, bulbous, flung up against the lightness overhead.

4

'I wondered,' she says, 'if you'd like to come and see them. It might be easier than bringing them all up here.'

'Come and see them where?' I ask her.

'At home.'

She points off, vaguely, in the direction of the town.

'I don't think I've got the time,' I tell her.

'Not now,' she says, and adds, 'Perhaps one week-end.'

She's been waiting in the hall. Beneath her arm she holds a leather pouch, tight, bulging. The leather is stained here and there with blobs of coloured ink.

'It's not very far,' she says, and adds, 'I can always pick you up. I have a car.'

'Are you old enough to drive?' I ask her.

'Just about.'

She winds a strap from the pouch around her arm.

'I'll see when I can fit it in,' I tell her.

'I'd be grateful if you could,' she says. She adds, 'I shall have to dash. I'm being picked up myself in town.'

She runs across the hall, waves, then disappears to the street outside.

I can hear her running from the steps, the sound flung up against the buildings. When I reach the street I see not her but Pollard, walking along, arms swinging, his attention not on her but on a car which has just drawn out from the kerb a little way ahead. Bright pink, almost crimson, it turns into the stream of traffic, swings round, and disappears towards the town.

'Told you,' Pollard says when I catch him up. 'Came fourth. Should have known. Not a favourite's won today.'

He folds up an evening paper and puts it in his pocket.

'Four certainties. One week. I can't believe it.' He adds, 'What did Wilcox want?'

'He's invited me to dinner.'

'Didn't ask you for a fiver, then, as well?' he says.

'Just the invitation. Nothing else.'

'Last bloke he had to dinner, Skipper sent him to the fish

shop. "Salt *and* vinegar," he says. Asks him what it comes to. Nods. Never pays him. Asks him, when he's leaving, if he'd like to come again.'

'Who was in the car?' I ask him.

'Never noticed, boy,' he says. 'Your friend the Newman girl got in. Apart from that, too dazzled by the colour.'

We reach the corner of the street. The centre of the town opens out before us, the corner of the cathedral close, the adjacent row of shops, a garden, the façade of a recently constructed hotel with glazed windows opening onto the street itself, a small edifice with the inscription mounted above the door, 'Bingo Now Five Nights a Week'.

'How are you making out?' he says. 'Flat, have you found yourself, boy? Or got yourself some digs?'

'Flat,' I tell him.

'Wilcox-recommended, or otherwise?' he says.

'Otherwise,' I tell him.

He laughs.

'I went into Wilcox-recommended rooms when I first came here. I think he takes a cut, or, if given the choice, is allowed to decorate the walls himself. Nubile peasants, mules and treey vistas. Quite a Pre-Raphaelite in his way is Skip.'

'Come and have a look,' I tell him.

'Wife would never allow it, boy,' he says. 'Hour late: seen nothing like it. Has a municipal timetable, trains *and* buses, pinned up beside the sink.'

'Could send a telegram,' I tell him.

'Horses, boy, and an occasional run in a pre-war banger: that's all this married man's allowed.'

He winks, as if this limitation to his life is a well kept secret, turns, waves, calls, 'See you, sonny,' and sets off down the street.

I watch him to the corner: he joins the queue for a local bus, disappears for a moment in the mass of bodies as the bus draws up, then, reappearing, shuffles forward.

He climbs aboard; I see him at a window. The bus sweeps past: he doesn't look up.

'I suppose, Hendricks, you didn't make a mistake in coming

here?' I say, later, sitting on the balcony at the front of the park attendant's hut.

'Coming here,' Hendricks says, 'in particular, or coming here in general?'

I gesture at the courts and then, more vaguely, in the direction of the town.

'Coming here in general.'

'I have a philosophy,' Hendricks says, 'which, amongst other things, embraces the belief that no one makes mistakes, merely that one does some things that are less interesting than others.'

He screws back the top of his thermos and returns the flask to his canvas hold-all.

'For example, I might have gone abroad,' he says. 'Or stayed in London. And yet if – as I suspect – life is nothing more than an irrelevance, then to have pursued a purely rational, opportunistic course would have been to fly in the very face of what I, personally, have come to recognize as reason.'

His face is flushed; beads of sweat run down from his blond hair across his brow. Rust, from some recent fracas with the wire-netting surrounding the tennis court, has stained his shirt: damage which he obviates now by pulling on his sweater. It too is white, like his shorts, his socks and his court-stained plimsolls. On the front of the sweater is embroidered a yellow crest comprising two horizontal scimitars surmounted by a star. He leans down, slots his racket into its press, then tightens up the screws.

'In any case, what're *you* doing here?' he says.

'I've no idea.'

'Your parents still alive?'

'No,' I say. I shake my head.

'Your wife?'

'She's not on the scene, as they say, at present.'

'Dead?'

'Not exactly.'

'Divorced?'

'Not that either, I'm afraid,' I tell him.

'Separated.'

He gazes off, abstracted, to where the sun-lit trees are fading into shadow.

'There's nothing really to keep you, then.'

'I only got the job,' I say, 'for a year.'

'A year?'

'I didn't tell Wilcox that, of course.'

'The Skipper's quite a decent man,' he says. 'Providing, of course, that you treat him right.'

'He's invited me to dinner.'

'What?'

I can already see the words on Hendricks's lips: 'He's never invited *me*. All the years I've known him. The service I've put in,' etc.

'I gather he's notoriously remiss in ordering food on these occasions.'

'Really?'

'So I gather.'

'I'm not familiar with his domestic habits.' He fastens the string bag containing his tennis balls to the handle of his racket. 'Ready?'

'Sure,' I say.

I add,

'Would you mind, by the way, if I had a lift?'

It seems he would; he says nothing for a while.

We step down to the path together.

'I can drop you off in town if you like.' He looks at his watch. 'I've got an appointment,' he says, 'in half an hour.'

'That'll suit me fine,' I tell him.

'I thought, as it was, you usually walked.'

'Usually I do,' I tell him. 'But not tonight. I'm feeling tired.'

He swings the balls from the handle of his racket. We reach the car. I climb inside.

It's like, for a moment, dropping off a cliff.

We drive out, in silence, between the gates.

'I don't intend staying for long, in any case,' he says. We turn towards the town. A tree-lined boulevard opens out before us. 'With a job like this, nowadays, I find, if you wish, you can always move around.'

'Flexibility.'

'It has.'

'Like tennis.'

'Like most things, if you look at them,' he says.

We overtake a car: the news about Wilcox has, very slightly, set him back. We pass a second car. A motor-cycle overtakes us. Hendricks's knees have reddened. His views, concerning the irrelevance of all decisions, appear for a moment to have been forgotten. The town, a mass of sun-lit towers and steeples, appears like a blur on the horizon immediately before us: scarcely has it registered, however, than a second motor-cyclist, attired in a policeman's uniform, materializes by Hendricks's elbow; a white-clad hand is raised and lowered.

The car slows down.

'My God. All the times,' Hendricks says, 'I've been along this road.'

The policeman, as the car stops, dismounts a little way ahead.

'The one time,' Hendricks adds, 'I go over the limit.'

'Tell him,' I say, 'you were only doing twenty-five.'

'Good God, Freestone,' he says, 'it was nearer sixty.'

'Say twenty-five was all you saw.'

The policeman, removing his whitened gauntlet, is walking back towards the car.

He stoops down for a moment, examines the number plate, then, more attentively, the licence, then straightening, glances directly through the windscreen at Hendricks's sweater, at the scimitar crest, and then at Hendricks's racket with the bag of balls still fastened to its handle.

'Got a sporting appointment, have you, sir?'

Hendricks shakes his head. 'We've just been playing tennis, officer,' he says.

'Tennis?'

He looks at the car again.

'Here? Or abroad was that?'

'Here.' He gestures behind us to the park.

'Going that fast, sir, o'course, it might have been another country.'

'I was only doing twenty-five.'

'Twenty-five?' The policeman, as if antagonized, removes his other glove. 'O'course, if you'd come out with a straight confession I might have let you off. As it is, could I see your licence, sir?' he says.

Hendricks groans.

He glances condemningly in my direction.

'If you multiply twenty-five by two, and add one or two digits, sir, I think you'd get a fair appraisal,' the policeman adds.

'Twenty-five,' Hendricks says, 'was all I saw.'

'Twenty-five you might, sir. But not when I was doing seventy to try and catch you up.'

'I haven't got my licence,' Hendricks says.

'In that case, sir,' the policeman says, 'could I have your name and address?'

Hendricks spells it out.

The policeman writes it down.

'Honesty is the best policy.' He looks across.

'That's right,' I tell him. I nod my head.

'You'll be hearing from us in due course,' the policeman says. He sets off back towards his bike.

'My God, all the times I've been along this road.'

'You should have insisted,' I tell him, 'on the twenty-five.'

'My God, Freestone, what else could I have done? He might have booked me for something else.'

'Always insist you're right.'

'You can see where your policy's got me now.'

'On the other hand,' I tell him, 'assuming that no one makes mistakes but merely that one does some things that are less interesting than others, you could say that that encounter was, in one sense, an unqualified success.'

'Where do I drop you off?' he says.

A small red shooting-brake is parked almost opposite the door. As I draw abreast, the door of the car itself is opened. The Newman girl gets out. She's wearing jeans and a dark-blue jacket. There's someone else in the car beside her though, since it's almost dark, I can't see who this is.

'I thought I might catch you,' she says, 'if I waited here.'

'Not too long, I hope,' I tell her.

'Just one or two minutes.' She gestures at the door: the house, the central one of a terrace of nine, looks out over a dilapidated garden across the street to the slope of the valley immediately below the town; ancient Georgian squares and terraces fall, in symmetrical array, towards the concrete towers standing by the river.

'I was wondering if next week-end might be convenient,' she says.

'For what?'

'For seeing my work.' She gestures to the car. 'Saturday afternoon would suit me fine.'

'Saturday afternoon,' I tell her, 'is a difficult time.'

'I could pick you up in the car,' she says.

'Since I don't know when I'm free, it might be better if I made my own way there,' I tell her.

'Whichever's more convenient.' She shakes her head. 'I've written the address,' she adds, 'on this.'

She gives me a slip of paper, glances over once more towards the house, the crumbled brickwork, the peeling paint-work, then turns back to the car and climbs inside.

'Till next Saturday,' she says.

'Till next Saturday,' I tell her.

She waves.

The door is closed. With something of a lurch the car gets under way; veering from one side of the road to the other, it disappears towards the town.

I turn back to the house.

I get the key, find the door already open and, inside, a man with a red moustache waiting in the lighted hall. The door to the ground-floor flat is standing open; the sound of a gramophone floods out to the hall itself.

He nods his head, waits for some return or greeting and, getting none, watches with a look of quiet dismay as I mount up to the second landing. He coughs, lengthily, as I climb the stairs; then, after a moment's silence, the door below is closed and the music fades.

I unlock my room and step inside.

It's dark. Through the rear window I can see the black, silhouetted bulk of the cathedral spire, the glowing clock face set in the tower below it, and one or two odd street lights glowing, between the buildings in an adjoining street. Through the window at the front, a view of the town is revealed not dissimilar to the one glimpsed earlier that day from the life room window: the roofs of the buildings lower down the slope, interspersed with dark, silhouetted chimneys, fall in oblique, strangely angled steps to the tall concrete tenements standing by the river.

I drop the racket, cross over to the bed, lie down and, gazing at the yellowish face of the cathedral clock, with its roman numerals and black, elongated-diamond hands, soon fall asleep and, but for a vague recollection of the red-moustached figure in the hall below, joined in some curious way with that of the helmeted policeman gazing in through Hendricks's sports car window, remember nothing, it seems, for several hours.

5

The gates themselves have long since been removed: the hinges still remain, and the rust which has stained the inside of the posts, a layer of ochrish-brown against the black.

From the drive itself it's impossible to see the house, or any of its numerous shed-like extensions. To my left is a playing field owned, reputedly, by the local council: pitches have been marked out and posts set down, and, at the very centre, stands a brick pavilion, blackened by soot and falling into ruin. At the far side of the field a line of trees stands up, faintly, against a low bank of mist and cloud.

To my right the view's completely obscured by a tall brick wall, a hedge and several trees. The drive itself runs straight ahead; I've never followed it, in fact, to its furthest end; it comes out, allegedly, by a shallow stream and from a wooden bench, according to Yvonne, you can gaze out, across the river and the fields, towards the town.

The drive broadens to my right: white lines have been drawn across the tarmac; parking places, marked out and numbered. Only two of the places are occupied today. Directly ahead appears the entrance to the house, an architraved porch set at the top of a flight of steps. A man with a broom is working on a lawn at the side of the house; a mound of leaves he's swept up is being loaded by a tall, broad-shouldered man into a wooden barrow.

I let the glass door bang to behind.

On each visit I remind myself to close the door behind me; each time, forgetting, I let it crash, wincing, half-turning to see the view outside – the drive, the trees, the vista opening to the field – tremble as the glass vibrates in the loose, ill-fitting, wooden frame.

I nod to the receptionist behind her counter and turn off, to my right, along the corridor leading to the ward itself.

The floor, evidently, has just been polished: it reflects the bowls of flowers standing in the window-bays, chrysanthemums, irises, a bunch of roses; I can hear the music from a wireless, a concert, coming from one of the private rooms.

The corridor, beyond a wooden door, opens out directly into a dining-room. It's set out like a small cafeteria, with yellow, plastic-covered tables and yellow, plastic-covered chairs. A nurse, in a white apron and a blue dress, is setting the tables: she looks up, smiles, and nods towards the door leading, past the kitchen and the matron's office, to the common-room.

'Watching telly.'

A woman is lying on a couch, opposite the kitchen door, her head propped on her hand. In the common-room beyond, a crowd of women are gathered round the television set. I catch a glimpse of several horses, hear the commentator's voice, then see Yvonne, tall, slender, walking up and down in the corridor which leads through from the common-room to the ward itself.

She's smoking, her head bowed, gazing at the floor. A nurse, in a white apron and a blue dress, is fastening up a cupboard on the wall.

'There's your husband here now, Mrs Freestone,' the nurse has said.

She closes the cupboard door: it has two locks, one in the centre of the door, exactly like a safe. The shelves inside, I notice, before the door clicks to, are full of transparent plastic boxes, each one labelled with a name, and containing a variety of coloured pills and capsules.

Yvonne looks up, nods, her gaze abstracted.

'Is it today you were coming, then?' she says.

I glance over to the nurse. 'Is it all right if we go out for a meal?' I ask.

'Not today.' The nurse has returned the keys of the cupboard to the pocket of her apron. 'I can ask if you like. Your wife was asking this morning. We thought it best she stayed today.'

'It doesn't bother me,' Yvonne has said. She continues pacing up and down. Through the window of the ward beyond I can see the lawn at the front of the house and the man with the broom sweeping up the leaves and the tall, broad-shouldered man loading up the barrow.

'You can have a spot of dinner here,' the nurse has said. 'I'll fix it up. We'll put you on the table at the end.' She adds this to Yvonne, stooping slightly so that she can see into her face. 'Would you like that, Mrs Freestone? Have a spot of lunch with your husband, then?'

'It doesn't bother me,' Yvonne has said.

'She'll be after it like a shot, once she gets the smell.' The nurse has laughed. She jangles the keys inside her pocket.

'We'll have a walk round, then,' I tell her. 'If that'll be all right.'

'Work up an appetite.' The nurse gestures at Yvonne. 'She could do with putting a bit of stuff inside. Turned her nose up, you know, the last few times.'

Yvonne has stubbed out her cigarette. She's gone over to a mirror on the wall while the nurse is talking. She runs a lipstick round her mouth, lightly, lifting her head, gazing into the mirror which is set on the wall directly opposite the cupboard. For a while, the lipstick poised, she examines her own expression: the dark eyes set wide apart, the mouth still parted, the broad cheeks, the hair combed down, loosely, across her brow. It's almost, oddly, a girl's expression, frank, ingenuous, inquiring. It's only when the nurse takes the lipstick and asks her if she's finished that she looks away.

'I've brought you some cigarettes.' I hold out the packet. 'I'll put them in your locker.'

'Oh,' she says. She nods her head.

I go through to the ward. Her scarf and beret are lying on the bed. Her locker door is open. Inside is a carrier bag, a nightgown, a skirt, a blouse, some underwear, several bits of paper, and the torn-up remnants of several cigarette packets.

I put the two full packets on top of the nightdress and close the door.

I pick up her beret and scarf, push her slippers, which are

lying in the middle of the floor, under the bed, then go back down the ward.

The nurse has gone. Yvonne has returned to pacing up and down.

'Have you got your coat?' I ask.

She's lit another cigarette. She glances across at me, still dazed. 'What?'

'Your coat.'

'I don't need a coat.'

'Don't you want to have a walk?' I say.

'Anything. Anything that'll get me out of here.'

She carries the cigarette with the lighted end turned in towards her palm. She twists her hand round as she puts the cigarette to her mouth, as if she were coughing onto the back of her hand, or yawning; then she turns to the annexe and the toilets where her coat and her jacket are usually kept.

Outside a faint drizzle is falling. 'Don't go far,' the matron says, calling, from the door of her office. 'Dinner soon.'

Yvonne doesn't answer. I doubt if she even hears.

'Don't walk her too far,' the matron says.

'Do you mind the rain?' I ask her when we get outside. She walks a little way ahead, her hands in the pockets of her coat. Her head is bowed, her beret pulled over to one side. 'Do you mind the rain?' I ask again.

I catch her up.

'I don't mind anything.' She glances round. 'Did they say we could go out?' she says.

'Not today.' I shake my head.

She nods.

We turn off along a footpath that leads away from the drive and the main building, past the extensions, to the garden area beyond.

I can feel the drizzle against my cheeks. I have no hat; I pull up my collar and, like Yvonne, push my hands inside my pockets. She walks ahead, her dark hair sticking out from beneath the beret, neat, slim, compact, absurdly self-possessed.

'I wish I could get out of here,' she says, suddenly, pausing, so that I hear her clearly as I catch her up. She takes out a cigarette, searching for her lighter.

She flicks up the flame, shielding it with one hand. In

moments of distress, like this, it seems strange she can light a cigarette at all. It's like putting on the lipstick: odd activities, casual, almost incidental, which, because of their casualness, show up the turmoil going on inside. At first, during my early visits, she'd cried. She'd cried the first time, coming out of the door of the ward, smiling, red-faced, as she might have come out of a room at home, pleased, talking to the nurse; then, the next moment, with the same casualness, as I grasped her arm, she'd begun to weep, hardly aware, like a child, her words lost in a strangled, half-suffocating wail. She'd cried too when I'd begun to leave, standing in the porch, her face inflamed, her dark eyes wet, expressionless. She'd cried then, almost out of habit, at the beginning of every visit, as if she were presenting me her grief, a credential to reassure me that she had, after all, come to the proper place.

I walk with her more slowly up and down the path. A few vegetables stick up from the clayey, greyish earth; most of the garden has recently been dug. To one side a pile of manure has been spread along the bed of a narrow trench.

'I've got a job.'

'What?'

'Teaching.'

'What?'

She walks ahead.

It's like walking out a dog.

'I thought I'd get the job ...'

'What?'

'To keep me occupied.'

'What?'

'I thought I'd get a bit of money while I had the chance.'

'Yes.'

'We'll need it.'

'Yes.'

'Three days a week.'

'Three.'

'I said I'd never go there when I saw it. Remember?'

'Yes.'

'The art school.'

'Yes.'

'The rest of the time I've been playing tennis.'

'The women are the worst.'

'Why mix with them?' I ask.

'You have to. If you want a cup of tea.'

'Can't you wait till meal-time, then?'

'It's hours.'

I shake my head. Yvonne is gazing round her once again. Her eyes are nervously alight; it's as if she expects a woman to leap out from the ground itself.

'As soon as you take out a cigarette, round they come. Ask to buy one and they haven't any money. You give them all away then you don't have one yourself.'

I wonder, in any case, whether she gives the things away. It's like her to; and then, having done so, it's like her to complain.

'Same with tea. Buy a cup and they ask you if you'll lend them twopence.'

'Twopence?'

'That's what tea costs,' she says, 'round here.'

She looks up at me, curious, as if she finds it strange I don't know about the price of tea; as if some integral part of her pain has been ignored or overlooked.

'Twopence. It's not much. But they never have it.'

We walk on to the end of the path, turn, pause; Yvonne starts off again.

'Marking time.'

Yvonne, however, scarcely listens.

'How's my mother?'

'All right.'

'It's her I feel most for.'

'She's all right. She's fine.'

'I could stick it if it wasn't for her.'

Her mother visits her on Wednesdays.

'Shall we walk on a bit?' I ask.

'It's all the same.' She shakes her head.

The cloud, if anything, is thickening. I can see the rain glistening on the top of her beret and along the shoulder of her coat, fine beads of moisture caught by the strands of cloth.

'Should be dinner-time soon.'

'Grand meals they have in here. I'll grant you that.'

'Do you want to go in, or do you prefer to stay out here?'

'Stay out. The longer I'm out of there the better.'

For a moment, in fact, she appears quite normal. The look, however, scarcely lasts.

'Maybe next week we can go out and get a meal.'

I wonder what has happened during the week to make them feel it's wiser that she stays inside. Perhaps she's argued with her mother, or grown unduly distressed at seeing her leave. With her, frequently, she behaves exactly like a child, clinging to her, her head hidden against her shoulder while her mother pats her back and tries to kiss her cheek.

'It's a hell-place, this.'

'Today's not so good. When the sun's out it's always different.'

'You don't realize. Some of the people. You wouldn't understand. The sooner I get out of here the better.' She looks across, almost with the same expression she uses on her mother. 'They haven't given you a date, then, have they?'

'They don't. Not until you're ready. They usually tell you the day before.'

'Yes.'

She nods.

Most of the things I tell her she disbelieves, exaggerating her helplessness at times, as if to press the responsibility for her being here directly onto me.

'If they told me to jump off the roof I'd do it. Anything they tell me; anything they tell me to get me out of here.'

She stresses continually her willingness to co-operate: pills, tests, exercise, meals. At the beginning, she'd done everything they'd asked her. Only recently has there been a slowing down, a faint distrust, as if somewhere her real complaint, her real anguish, has gone unnoticed.

'I'll never get out of here,' she says.

'Don't worry. Just think: all the time, it's getting nearer.'

'It's getting near; but it's not getting out of here that's getting near.'

I turn her attention to the plants.

'Do you remember the sprouts we used to grow? We'd go out and get them on a Christmas morning.' Yvonne moves on again; when I catch her up I see she's started weeping. 'Let's be making tracks. A good meal'll make all the difference.'

She nods. We're walking away from the house. From beyond the trees comes the dull, dual-tone hooting of an engine. The bare trees enclosing the garden are shrouded now in mist. I try to imagine the room, Hendricks, Wilcox; anyone, that is, not concerned with this. My mind, briefly, moves on to the girl.

I take her arm. I feel her strange compactness.

We've turned towards the house. It's like holding a piece of stone; I can feel the hardness beneath the coat.

'I've felt lost ever since I got up this morning.'

'Let's get out of the rain and have a bite to eat.'

'It comes on you. I don't know why. Nothing matters any more.'

'We'll be all right.'

She nods. 'I'd give ought to get out of here, you know. Things go on here I couldn't describe.'

We walk on, my arm around her, back towards the house.

6

'You never came.'

'I had an appointment somewhere else.'

'You never said.'

'I didn't remember.'

I can see the car, lurking, some distance up the street. It's like a salmon, but with the proportions of a whale. There's some other figure behind the wheel. It wears a chauffeur's hat.

'We called at the house.'

'House?'

'Your flat.'

It's almost dusk; pools of bluish light illuminate the street beyond. Nearer, closer to the flat, the ancient gas-lights erupt like yellow flares.

'I'm sorry about that.'

'I had the drawings ready.'

'Don't you think you could bring them in?'

'In?'

'To the college.'

'You could have rung.'

Her face seems older in the evening light; the grey eyes now have an almost malignant, harried look, the thin-boned features taut and hard, the mouth pulled back in a kind of snarl.

She's dressed in a blue windcheater, unzipped, and jeans.

'I don't suppose there's much point in bringing them to the college.'

'I don't see why.'

'With all the others? It's better you see them on their own.'

The car, I realize, has crept a little nearer. The chauffeur, a thin-faced man, is gazing over in the girl's direction. Perhaps he's been waiting there some time.

'What about an evening, then?'

'I play tennis in the evenings.'

'What?'

For a moment, absurdly, I feel I'm with Yvonne.

'We've waited hours.'

The car after some further hesitation, has drawn abreast.

'It's like an aeroplane; its dashboard lights are on: the glow illuminates the chauffeur's face. He looks across: long-nosed, the eyes like buttons pressed in on either side. The mouth is thin and wide. His hands are gloved. The breast-pocket of his suit has a narrow pleat.

'I thought if I came myself I could drag you out.'

Something of the girl returns; unsure, she glances at the car.

'All right.'

'What?'

'I'll come.'

'No tennis?'

'Not tonight.' I gesture round. 'In any case,' I add, 'it's dark.'

Perhaps it's the chauffeur who makes the choice, compelling decisions by his look alone.

'Bennings,' she says, 'I think we're off.'

He seems uncertain whether he'll get out of the car. The girl resolves his dilemma by opening the back door herself then waiting while I climb inside. 'It won't take long. And Bennings can easily drive you back.'

I'm not sure, from my view of the back of Bennings's head, whether, in principle, he approves of this. He doesn't look round.

The car moves off.

'How long have you been living here?' she says.

She gestures at the house as the car sweeps past.

'Not long.'

'Your wife?'

'Is not at home.' I shake my head.

She settles back.

It's as if the interior's hermetically sealed from everything around: the pale lights of the town flash past.

The road dips down. The buildings darken. We cross the river, pass the point, unmolested, where Hendricks met his fate, and sweep on, through the suburbs, towards the hill-land to the south. The buildings give way to fields, the fields to copses; finally, the road rising, we move out, silently, across a heath.

'How long have you been living here?' I ask.

'Not long.'

'Your first year at the college, then?'

'That's right.'

I suffer at odd moments, from the impression that this journey, this conversation, is a natural extension of the dialogue I've had earlier with Yvonne; at any moment, it seems, the girl might cry, or the car transform itself into that solemn, silent room, with ghosts and gestures that echo, absurdly, some memory of a former life outside. The dashboard light fills the interior with an eerie glow. In the distance, silhouetted against the fading light, a row of mounted figures moves in a dipping line across the heath.

'There's quite a view of the town,' she says.

She turns round in the seat and gazes back.

Apart from a blur of lights, however, there's little to be seen.

'Yeh,' I say. 'I remember it well.'

She laughs.

'You've not been at the college long?'

'A matter of weeks.'

'Do you like it, then?'

'It's better than working, I suppose,' I say.

'What did you do before you came here, then?'

The eyes, gleaming, turn to mine.

'Nothing.'

'Nothing? Didn't you have to earn a living, then?'

'That's right.'

The driver's head has stiffened.

The girl leans back. She gazes out at the darkening heath; somewhere, close to its summit, a row of lights appears.

'The subjects are sort of horses.'

'What?'

'And buildings. The sort of things you see around.'

Several large buildings, dark, unlighted, have in fact loomed up like bluffs of rock beyond the profile of the heath.

'You've been up here, I suppose, before?'

'Often.'

'Often?'

'Once or twice.'

She laughs.

Like boulders, the buildings move in towards the road; one or two are sheathed by trees, their shapes now like elongated heads, the twigs and branches thrust up like hair.

'At night it gets quite eerie up here,' she says.

'I never knew anyone lived up here,' I say.

'*We* do. And one or two more.' She laughs.

Lights appear some distance from the road.

The lights of the car, in response, come on. For a moment, the road before us disappears. I gaze out at an illuminated patch of ground against which, in silhouette, are poised the head and shoulders of the man in front.

'If you'd come this afternoon you could have seen around.'

A pair of metal gates appear.

She straightens up.

'It's a bit confusing, coming up at night.'

A drive sweeps up, curving, towards a lighted porch. The car has slowed. From somewhere close by comes the barking of a dog.

'We'll see you later, Bennings,' the girl has said.

She opens the door as the car pulls up. I stretch across, climb out. The car moves off. A low black edifice confronts us either side of the lighted porch. We climb a flight of steps, the girl in front.

'Do you fancy a drink?' she says.

'A drink,' I tell her, 'would suit me fine.'

'It gets colder up here as well at night.'

'And windy.'

'Oh, the winds haven't really started yet.'

She opens the door; a panelled hall is revealed beyond. A bowl of flowers stands on an ancient table in the middle of the floor.

'Most of the house, you see, is old. There are one or two new bits, the kitchen mainly, fastened on the back.'

A panelled staircase sweeps up, glistening, from the panelled hall.

'If you want a drink we can go through here.'

The renewed barking of a dog is taken up by several more.

'We've got three or four,' she says. 'They're really Mummy's though, not mine.'

We enter a long, broad room, similarly panelled, which opens directly from the hall. A coal fire is burning in a low stone grate. 'We keep that going just to look at really, I suppose,' she says.

The furniture of the room reminds me of a club; large chairs and sofas, orientated, vaguely, around the fire.

'Whisky?'

She crosses to a cabinet behind the door.

'What're you going to have yourself?'

'I'll have a gin.'

She pours it out.

The barking, after a while, dies down. Other bowls of flowers are scattered round the room. On a low table are set out several magazines: *Home and Beauty*, *Woman's World*, *House and Garden*. Over the fireplace hangs a 'View of Delft' several inches larger than the original itself.

'It's quite a house.'

'Do you like it?' She brings across the glass. 'I've put in soda. I hope it'll be all right.'

She watches while I drink.

'I think it's far too large.' She gestures round. 'The house.'

'Enough to be going on with, I suppose,' I say.

'More than enough,' she says and laughs.

She carries her own glass between her hands. She's scarcely drunk from it at all.

'Do you want to sit down here or go upstairs?'

'Upstairs?'

'I've got them in my room.' She waves her arm, vaguely, above her head.

'If you think it'll be all right.'

'What's that?'

'Shouldn't I meet your parents first?'

'They're away,' she says. She shakes her head. 'If you like,' she adds, 'I can bring them down. It'll take me ages, I suppose.' She looks around. 'It's not really the sort of place to see them in.'

We go upstairs. Apart from the dogs, there's no sign of life in the house at all.

At the end of a landing a window looks down to a shadowed mass of trees.

'I have this room at the top,' she says. 'It's quieter there. I get more done.'

She hasn't as yet taken off her jacket. Her glass, half-full, she's left behind. She kicks off her shoes as we mount the stairs. At the end of a landing a second light goes on.

'No one had lived up here for years.' She gestures round. Doors open off from the landing on either side. In her hand, I notice, she's brought the Scotch. 'The things we found in some of the rooms.'

'And now?'

'Oh,' she says. 'They're not there now.'

She opens a door: a cat comes out. A moment later she steps inside.

There's a crash of drawers; a chair, or perhaps some heavier weight, is dragged across the floor. I hear a groan: some other object, it seems, is lifted up. A second later, with a crash, it's lowered.

'Come in.'

She's taken off her jacket. Underneath she wears a sweater. She pulls it down as I step inside.

'You've brought your drink?'

'That's right.'

She looks around. Drawings have been pinned across one wall; several more are scattered on the bed. One or two more are lying on the floor. A window, with its curtains undrawn, looks out, I presume, towards the heath.

'These are some of them,' she says.

She steps aside. I cross over to the wall.

The room is small; in its proportions it's not unlike a cell: there's room for a bed, a chest of drawers, a chair. There's no sign of things you might normally find in a woman's room; no mirror, no bottles, jars, combs, pins, brushes. There's a tin of paints, a pencil, a piece broken from a rubber and a book, *The Life of Modigliani*, lying on the chair itself.

The drawings on the wall are virtually identical to the one I've seen already at the college: triangulated trees and buildings stand amidst triangulated fields, divided up, here and there, by triangulated hedges. A self-portrait, inscribed as such, shows a triangulated face broken up by triangulated features; on the floor there are sketches of a triangulated horse, of several triangulated houses, and a triangulated figure, female, sitting in a triangulated chair.

'What do you think?'

I narrow my eyes; I incline my head.

Before I need to answer she starts to fill my glass.

'Jack Daniels,' I tell her.

'Daddy brought it from America.'

'My favourite.'

'Really.'

'When I can get it.'

'We've got two or three more downstairs. You can take it with you if you like.'

'I wouldn't want to put you out.'

'Honestly,' she says. 'He wouldn't mind.'

I glance once more towards the wall.

I step back, as far as the width of the room allows; I narrow my eyes again, incline my head.

'I like their consistency,' I tell her.

She gazes at the wall herself, intent.

'You seemed to feel at the college it was too formalized,' she says.

'Yes?'

'The drawing.'

'Now I can see quite a few of them, I can see the sort of thing you mean.'

'Mean?'

'Projecting,' I add, 'the principal areas and masses.'

'Yes.'

She inclines her head herself, narrows her eyes: her body is still heaving from running up the stairs.

'It's damn good Scotch.'

'You like it?'

'Whisky really, I suppose,' I tell her.

'Tennessee.'

'Better, I suppose, than Scotch.'

'I forgot to bring my gin.'

She seems disinclined to go back down.

'I wondered if you could shade a few of them in?'

'Yes?'

'The squares.'

'The triangles.'

'The triangular masses.'

'I've thought about that since you mentioned it.'

'It might give some variation. To the surface of the picture-plane,' I add.

'I've started on one or two,' she says.

She opens one of the drawers beside the bed. Inside, I can see, are several folders, not to mention a number of sheets of drawn-on paper.

She's set the bottle on the floor. Having tipped back the glass, I fill it up again. Visions of Yvonne begin to fade.

The girl draws out a folder, unfastens a string and allows two or three sheets to drift out on the bed.

As she's already intimated, the shapes in these drawings – or the greater part of them – have been shaded in: dark, triangular masses recede into a general background of pencilled finger-prints and smears. A triangular tree, with triangular leaves, droops, in a triangular fashion, above triangulated eaves: in the sky a triangulated sun is partly obscured by triangulated clouds. A flock of triangular birds are about to alight on a triangulated roof. Triangular, shaded smoke streams out from a tall, triangulated chimney.

'Dramatic.'

'What?'

'With the shading, I suppose, it's more dramatic.'

'Yes.'

I empty the glass.

'Have you thought of drawing with rectangular shapes?' I ask.

'Square?'

'Rectangular, I suppose, is best.'

'Less uniform.'

'That's right.'

She shakes her head.

'Or just drawing the forms,' I say, 'directly.'

'Directly?'

'As you see them.'

'But I see them all,' she says, 'like this.'

Below, suddenly, a door is closed. There's a sound of footsteps; another door is closed.

'A triangular shape,' she adds, 'has greater variation. That's why Picasso used it, I suppose, and Braque.'

'Mondrian, of course, used squares.'

'And lines.'

'And lines.'

She sees the empty glass.

She lifts the bottle. With her tongue between her teeth she pours it out.

'I suppose it'd be too much to ask for one?' I tell her.

'What?'

'A drawing.'

'Really?'

The drink has spilt. We crouch down. Our heads collide; with a handkerchief she's produced we mop it up.

'Honestly. Would you like one, then?' she says.

'I'd have to forgo paying for it, I'm afraid,' I tell her.

'I wouldn't dream of it,' she says. 'Honestly. It's the first time anyone's asked for one,' she adds.

The glass replenished, she watches, smiling, while I pick one out.

I choose, in the end, a triangulated house.

'Is there any reason for picking that particular one?' she says.

'It's representative, I suppose,' I tell her. 'It'll remind me,' I add, 'of all the rest.'

'It's super of you to ask for one,' she says.

'It's good of you to let one go.'

'Oh, I've any amount. Mummy and Daddy won't let me hang them up downstairs.'

'Perhaps you could show a few to Mr Wilcox. Mr Pollard, I know, is very keen.'

'Keen?'

'On acquiring work.'

'I suppose I could take a few of them to college.' She looks across. A line of mascara accentuates the darkness of her lashes. 'I find schools of art are very backward places, in any case,' she says.

'They provide one or two people with a living, I suppose,' I tell her.

'Is that how you look at them?' she asks.

'Anything else, in the form of tuition, is a sort of extra.'

'They say at the college you're always drunk.'

'Drunk?'

Her gaze, it seems, has scarcely changed.

'That your work is so modern that Mr Wilcox won't even look at it,' she says.

'It's so modern that it's practically invisible,' I tell her.

She laughs.

'Honestly.' She shakes her head. 'They say, at the college, your wife's gone mad.'

'In a manner of speaking, I suppose she has.'

She waits, patiently, for whatever other confessions might be forthcoming.

'I suppose, in reality,' I add, 'it's time I left.'

'Left?'

'Here.'

'Oh,' she says. She shakes her head.

'It was good of you,' I tell her, 'to let me come.'

'In the day-time, you see, they'd have looked much better.' She gestures to the window.

I start to collect the drawings from the bed.

'I'll put them all away,' she says. 'You can leave them there for now.' She produces a cardboard folder, her name written on it in capital letters, and puts the drawing I've chosen carefully inside.

'It's a tiny room.'

'Yes.'

'Don't you fancy anything larger?'

'Than this?' Perhaps for the first time she looks around.

'I suppose you've bigger rooms than this.'

'Oh, much bigger.' She gazes at the wall beyond my head. 'I suppose I feel safer, being in here,' she says.

I take the glass. As an afterthought she takes the bottle.

We go back down. Faintly, from below, comes the barking of the dogs; a door is closed. The barking fades.

On the landing below she takes my arm.

'If you like,' she says, 'you can look at this.'

She opens a door almost opposite the stairs.

The room beyond, as she enters, is flooded with light.

A red-curtained, four-poster bed stands against one wall. White curtains, undrawn, drape the room's four windows.

'This is Mummy's and Daddy's room,' she says.

A photograph of a blond-haired man, genial, relaxed, smiling, stands on a table beside the bed. *To Ann, with all my love, N.* is scrawled across the bottom. He looks like a middle-weight boxer, his expression that of someone caught in the midst of some appeal.

'They'll be coming back, I suppose, next week.'

'On holiday?' I say and add, 'I mean, just now?'

She shakes her head. 'Daddy's working. Mummy went with him. Though usually,' she says, 'she stays behind. Unless all of us go, that is, as well.'

'How many are there in your family, then?'

'Oh,' she says, and adds, 'Just me.'

She puts out the light.

'Just look at the view.'

Having moved to the window she steps aside.

In the distance, beyond the darkness of the heath, are the lights of the town: the sky, to some extent, has cleared. The lights give the impression of some vessel out at sea.

'In daylight,' she says, 'it's quite a view.'

I'm aware of her vaguely as she moves across the room; seconds later she's standing at the door.

Outside, as we reach the stairs, she adds, 'Would you like another drink? We could have a meal. Or watch the telly.'

'I ought to be getting back,' I tell her.

'For tennis.'

'A bit too late, I think, for that.'

She disappears towards the back of the house as we reach the hall.

There's the sound of a woman's voice, a laugh; a moment later the girl, smiling, has reappeared.

'Bennings'll take you back,' she says.

She holds out a bottle as she comes across.

'Jack Daniels,' she says, and lifts it up. 'The other, it seems, you've almost finished.'

'Like time.'

'Gone before you've noticed. Yes.'

I give her the glass. She regards, broodingly, the folder in my hand.

'I've quite a few more, as a matter of fact.' She adds, 'In a different style. They're sort of expressionist, I suppose you'd call them. Yes.'

'I'll look forward to seeing them,' I say, 'another time.'

'If you'd ever like a meal. We could even play some tennis. We've got a court, you know, at the back.'

'I play, usually, in the municipal park.'

'I haven't played for about a year,' she says.

A car horn, like a trombone held to a single note, sounds moodily from the drive outside.

As we move to the porch a door at the end of the hall is opened and a stout, middle-aged woman gazes out. White-smocked, red-faced, she looks across; then, without any comment, the door is closed.

The car stands in the drive below the porch. The thin-faced chauffeur gazes up, the rear door open.

'I've told him where to drop you off.'

She holds out her hand.

I move the bottle and the folder to my other arm.

'It was very kind of you to come,' she says.

'See you at the college, then.'

I shake her hand.

She ducks her head as I climb inside the car.

She stands waving, silhouetted against the light as the car, soundlessly, descends the drive.

I look back at the house as we reach the road; but for the lighted porch, however, it's obscured by trees.

Half-way down the heath I'm suddenly aware of the chauffeur's eyes: they gleam back at me from the mirror by his head. As soon as I look they glance away.

'Not much life here after dark.'

'Dark?'

'Night-time, sir.' He gestures round.

'None at all. After six-thirty each evening the entire population subsides,' I tell him, 'into a kind of coma.'

'I suppose, if you know the place, there are one or two spots.'

'Spots?'

'Where there's still a bit of life,' he says.

'There's an evening life class at the college.'

He laughs. The eyes, briefly, meet mine as he glances in the mirror.

'How long have the Newmans been living here?' I ask.

'Mr Newman's been here almost since the spring,' he says.

'You travel with them?'

'I've been with Mr and Mrs Newman for the past five years,' he says.

'I gather he's away at present.'

'That's right.'

He concentrates for a while on the road ahead.

We reach the river: the road sweeps up, steeply, towards the town.

'Then again, I suppose, there are one or two clubs,' he says.

'Clubs?'

'Singing. Drinking.'

'Strip-tease. Any amount of those,' I tell him.

His gaze drifts up, dreamily, towards the mirror.

'But then, a comatose condition is necessary even there.'

The eyes, narrowed, examine mine.

'In a place like this, immobility, frequently, is one's passport to a better life.'

'You have few illusions about the place,' he says.

'It's a kind of grave. A morgue. Inhabited by zombies.'

I can feel the Jack Daniels heating up my chest; it's like, after its first mellow prickling, a steady fire.

'I suppose we'll have to hope we won't be here for long.'

His eyes, now, revert to a more familiar look: a bird's eyes, a fox's, a weasel's; a predator's before it strikes.

'What does Mr Newman do?' I add.

'He travels quite a lot,' he says.

'What does he travel in?' I ask.

'Usually in aeroplanes,' he says.

The street comes into view. It's as if, for fifteen minutes, I've been sitting in a room.

When the car has stopped and he opens the door I can feel the disillusioning rush of air outside.

'Thanks for the lift.'

'Thank you, sir,' he says, and adds, 'Good night,' calling again, then, as I reach the door, holding the folder, 'Sir,' he says, 'you've forgotten this.'

I move the Jack Daniels to my other hand, nod, take it, and, without another word, climb slowly to my room. By the time I reach it the fire has died.

Part Two

I

'If you hadn't have come back,' she says, 'I don't know what I would have done.' She rocks briefly in her chair, then drinks her tea. 'I've no one else to turn to now.'

Visible, through the rear window of the room, is a tiny yard. Beyond, stand the brick supports of a railway viaduct. Even as she talks a train starts passing by: there's the panting of the diesel, the rattle of the trucks. I only hear the last few words: '... for you to come up here, that is.'

'She wanted to go mad at home,' I add, or think I add for above the noise I'm not sure that she's heard. In any case, she never listens; like artists with their pictures, so mothers with a child: it's the tone of voice that counts.

'The doctors wondered what it was.'

'What?'

'This feeling of guilt.'

'I don't think they bother, really, over that.'

'There's one doctor there ...' She taps her head.

'Lennox.'

'Doctor Lennox.'

It seems crazy in any case that a woman of sixty-seven or eight, white-haired, thin-cheeked, dark-eyed, should, at the ending of her days, be worried about the madness of a child; the child, after all, in its madness, is safer than she is herself.

'Doctor Lennox seems to feel it's connected with the child.' She looks across. 'With losing it, I mean.'

'Women lose children all the time.'

'Yes.'

'And this one,' I tell her, 'wasn't even born.'

'Yes.'

'It was more like an abortion than anything else.'

'She was four months gone.'

'Lennox doesn't think at all. The baby, you know, is propaganda.'

'What?'

'She'll be out again in three months' time. It's like having a headache. An arm broken. You just need time for the bits to mend.'

'The mind, you know: it's not like anything else.'

'It's made up of flesh and blood and gristle. Jab in the right ingredients: like baking bread.'

I don't know why I adopt this attitude with her; it's something to do with the place itself. She's lived here, I suppose, for fifty years; here a child was born, here her husband died; apart from that, endless meals, endless nights, endless wakenings, nothing has happened in this place at all: she grows here like a tree, aimless, uncomprehending. One day they'll come along and chop it down.

'Yvonne always talks of you,' she says.

'I know.'

'If it wasn't for you she wouldn't be alive, she says.'

'She might say the same of you,' I add.

'Yes,' she says. She sighs.

The house itself is a kind of tomb: it's damp; you can smell the river, despite the fumes – and the food she's recently cooked and, it seems, through some kind of natural absentmindedness, has burnt. You can smell the trains; you can smell clothing which hasn't been touched, used, washed, disturbed for years; you can smell the sink: you can smell that harsh industrial inertia which everywhere leaves, inside and out, a kind of filth. You can smell the decay, the neglect of life itself.

Through the front window is visible the street outside: terrace houses identical to her own, two up, two down; nothing to denote, on a Sunday afternoon, that they contain any sort of life at all. They might be ovens, or cupboards, with strange, unwantable things inside.

'It's the crying I find the worst.'

'If she didn't cry, you'd need to be worried more,' I say.

'I couldn't be worried more,' she says.

Worry in any case, I can see, is a kind of food down here;

worry is one of the indispensable ingredients of life. Yvonne herself is full of worries, Vietnam, China, India, Africa; children without food, women without men; men with nothing else to do but fight; napalm, insecticides, pollution: vast abstractions that overwhelm her mind, rendering her incapable of dealing with anything at all. When finally she confronts a person she gazes at them with ever-widening eyes, unable to focus her attention, through this fog of abstraction, on their particular identity or problem: people aren't people any more, they're indecipherable elements of some hopelessly confusing cosmic enterprise, engineered, manipulated, directed by forces beyond her comprehension. Instead of flesh and blood, and fuck and cunt, everything is terror, annihilation, anonymity, and death.

'I've never seen her like this before. Not even as a child,' Mrs Sherman says. 'I can't understand, you know, how it all began.'

'One woman in six,' I tell her, 'at some point in her life goes mad.'

'She worked so hard. We gave her all we had. She went to college. Her degree: they said they'd never seen anything like it quite, before.'

'Conscientious.'

'She cares so much.'

She gets up from the chair; she pokes the fire. From overhead, once again, comes the rumbling of a train. It's like living in an underworld, beneath a stone. I try to imagine Yvonne as a child, coming home, from school, trying to do her work: the smell of the river at the end of the street, the noise of engines thumping, rhythmically, above her head, her father, in overalls and boots, sitting by the fire; and try to create some image that might absorb all this, some vision that might enable her, sitting in this room, to transcend the inertia in which she finds herself. Enter Africa, India, China, Vietnam; enter war and pestilence and fire and famine; enter holocaust and ruin; enter abstraction: enter things that no longer smell and lie: enter dreams of salvation that will take her out of this: enter Yvonne a year before our marriage as I greet her with a kiss, wide-eyed, St George's or Don Quixote's wife, she's not sure which.

'What I was wondering was, how long you'll be able to stay,' her mother says.

'I've got a job.'

'A job?'

'Teaching.'

'Enough,' she says, 'to keep yourself?'

'I'm putting some by for when Yvonne comes out.'

'You've been so good to her,' she says.

'She wanted to go mad, you see, at home,' I add and wonder, briefly, if I've said this once before.

'Have they said how long she'll be inside?'

'They never tell you anything,' I say.

'It's strange. She was always full of hope,' she says.

She wipes her eyes. She turns back to the chair.

'What I can't understand are some of the people they put them with. I'm sure, seeing some of them, it only makes her worse.'

'I was talking to this patient,' I tell her, 'the other day. I was thinking, listening to her rattle on, *"She's going to be in here, you know, for years."* Acquired all the characteristics, tone of voice. Next minute another patient calls out, *"Nurse!"* The one I'm talking to turns round and says, *"Don't worry, now. I shan't be a minute!"*'

She doesn't laugh; the frown, if anything, has deepened.

'I don't like going to the place, in any case,' she says. 'I'm sure it doesn't do them any good putting them all together. I mean, there's a woman in Yvonne's ward who's tried to kill herself.' She pauses, thinks about this, then adds, 'Three times.'

She sighs.

'There's another one who's been on drugs. They say she'll only have another year to live. Eighteen.' She shakes her head. 'Eighteen years old. It makes you think.'

The rocking of the chair has ceased.

Faintly, from further down the street, comes the shouting of a child.

Mrs Sherman gets up; there's a complacency, a composure about her existence in the house, like a dog reclining in its kennel. This is the place she's been told to keep: this is, in a word, her situation. It's only the limits, unquestioned, that set the tone; morality, after all, is a question of money.

'There's one woman there who's been in eight times. You wonder what it is that keeps them going.'

'A sort of machine, I suppose,' I tell her.

'What?'

'A sort of mechanism.'

I have fantasies about this house myself; namely, that Mrs Sherman is already dead: that it's a kind of superstition on my part which makes me insist that she's still alive, that she's sitting in that chair still talking or – as now – standing by the fire and, with a kind of groan, reaching for the poker and banging it against the coal.

'They have lovely flowers.'

'Flowers?'

'I'll grant them that.'

She gestures upwards, backwards, towards the town.

'At the hospital,' she adds. 'And pictures.' She sighs again. 'I've looked at them, you know, for hours.'

'They've even taken off the gates.'

'I noticed that.'

'I never know whether it's because they're broken, or whether it's a political gesture.'

'Political?'

'"*You too can go crazy: step inside.*" A piece of diplomacy, propaganda.'

'I don't understand half the things you say.'

'That's right.'

She might, conceivably, have gone over to the window; she turns, instead, towards the sink: she begins to wash up the cups from the tea we've drunk.

I pick up a cloth.

'I mean, the amusing thing is, the ones who go inside go inside because they're crazy: they've seen the world for what it is.'

'Yes,' she says. She takes a cup.

'Those gates, you see, are a sign to me of the hospital's own feelings of paranoia.'

'Yes,' she says. She nods her head.

'I must say, I've no great sympathy with this contemporary cult of making madness an everyday event. "A malady that can be cured like any other." I think these mental health authorities who foster that belief are really going to pieces, succumbing to a kind of dementia even more profound than the one allegedly, they're trying to "cure". I mean, the fact is, people like Yvonne have been driven there, and to insist, once they get inside, that the place has got no doors – or only half a door – is surely placing on them the kind of burden they shouldn't really have to bear. All that those empty gates imply is that their anguish, their torment, is a kind of delusion: they are, after all, still a part of the world outside – the world, that is, that has actually driven them mad. Those gates to me, Mrs Sherman, are an evil sign.'

Perhaps it's her name that suddenly recalls her: she's been gazing for several seconds, fixated, at the wall.

'I mean, fancy putting a mental hospital in someone's ancestral home. Anyone suffering from delusions of grandeur is bound to find it going directly to their heads.'

'Yes,' she says.

I dry the cup. I stack the saucer.

'I've always felt that mental homes should be bare and spartan places. Not the back of the Bastille, exactly, but simple, white, severe, undecorated, unrelieved. The moment you start to make them cosy – all those cafeteria curtains, pots of flowers – they've even got television in Yvonne's, God help her – you begin to place burdens on the patients which they shouldn't have to bear. I'm sure most of it's there, in any case, to try and reassure the staff, or people like ourselves, that the kind of suburban taste these interiors reflect are what everybody, really, ought to strive for – functional furniture, contemporary fabrics, the odd reproduction of some modern master – the standards of the very world which, in the first place, has driven the poor old patient crazy.'

She's beginning to look at me with some misgivings: I can see her thinking, 'God help me, there's going to be *two* of them in there before we've done.' She finishes off the second cup.

'I mean, I find these insipid decorations a tawdry bolstering-up of the doctors' own delusions.'

She doesn't look up: she hands over a second cup with a kind of backward gesture. No doubt she's heard some of this from Yvonne herself.

'At least, that's my opinion, for what it's worth.'

'Yes,' she says.

'It takes all sorts to make a world.'

'That's right,' she says. 'I think it does.'

The washing-up completed she finds she's nothing else to do. She moves back, instinctively, towards the rocking-chair. Once there, however, she looks across.

'I mean, they know what they're doing,' she says, 'or they wouldn't be there.'

'It depends what you mean,' I say, 'by "know".'

'I mean, they've been to college. They've got degrees.'

Her world, or her aspirations for it, are qualified by 'education'. Education, after all, is what they struggled to give Yvonne; to raise her, that is, to a better life: yet without any awareness that, when you resurrect the dead, you've got to provide them with something to go on living for. A first-class degree, as Yvonne has said, is about as high as Yvonne can ever go: after all, once you're 'qualified' there's nothing else to do; except exploit it in whatever way you can. Education, after all, is the philosophy of the old.

'You never went to school,' she says.

'Not after the legal age,' I say. 'That's right.'

'I mean, if you haven't had the education you can't really tell.'

'We're both in the same boat, it seems,' I tell her. 'Us on the outside, without it, level-headed; Yvonne, who's had it, on the inside, fastened up.'

'Don't tell me you don't believe in it,' she says. She adds, 'Education,' with a slow motion of her hand. It's as if she offers the room, the house itself, as some indication of where, without it, you might end up.

'It's the way the half-baked indoctrinate the uninformed. Like the hospital gates,' I tell her. 'It's propaganda.'

She's beginning to wonder whether – despite Yvonne's protestations to the contrary – her only child hasn't been indoctrinated by what, in other contexts – she's a regular attender at a spiritualist church – she might describe as 'an evil influence'.

'I mean, what things have you done with your life?' she says, still quietly, almost gently now.

'I've had a career.'

'As a professional boxer.' She might, in different circumstances, have begun to laugh. 'How long were you at it, then?'

'About four years.'

'And you gave it up.'

'I felt the audience on the whole were getting more out of it than I was myself. I don't believe, you see, in exploitation.'

'And then you were an artist, after that.'

'I've always been an artist, I suppose,' I tell her. 'It's like having a club-foot. However hard you try, you can never quite disguise it.'

'I thought "art" was very popular,' she says. No doubt she's thinking of the reproductions on the hospital walls.

'It depends what you mean by art,' I add.

'I wonder, with the amount of talking you do, that you never got on.'

'I've got a job as one,' I tell her.

'And by "talking", I can bet.'

'It's true,' I say, and add, 'You're right.'

For a while, unhinged by the thought of education, she wanders on. It's like seeing a train, derailed, steaming on, aimlessly, across the countryside. The image, of a derailed but mobile train, often comes to me when I see Yvonne: the machinery's all right; they forgot the tracks.

'If her father could see her now he'd be upset. He spent hours working overtime to send her to that college. He worked his heart out for Yvonne. When she got her degree he couldn't believe it. "A daughter of mine," he said. I can see him now.' She gazes abstractedly to the door itself. It seems strange, looking back, to think that Mr Sherman lived here too: there's no sign that he existed in this room at all. A photograph on a cupboard against the wall shows a fair-haired man, with a fair moustache, pale-eyed, thin-cheeked: clearly, for a man like that, working in a mill must have been too hard: you can see the unconscious supposition in his eyes: 'I was born to be this: so it *must* be right.'

'He never had a holiday, you know. "My ray of sunshine": that's what he called Yvonne. "If I can't get out of here," he said, "there's one ray of sunlight that always shall." '

She wipes her eyes; in a curious way, Yvonne's collapse has caught her unprepared; a broken arm, a broken leg; even a miscarriage she might, given time, have taken in her stride: the snail's pace, in time, encompasseth all. But going crazy: it's removed, as it were, the filament from the lamp itself; the current's on, the juice is there, the vacuum in the bulb is right; – she flicks the switch, it seems, again; the glow they guaranteed has died.

'I can't understand it happening to a girl like that. So sensible. Well-balanced. She took an interest in so many things. She's helped old people: she's organized charities, you know, for all sorts of causes.' It's as if, now, she's reproaching God: 'Look what she's done for You, you *sod*.' 'She's been on marches; she's been to Russia. She was even arrested in Moscow for demonstrating outside the palace there.'

'She's been a great one for causes, I'll grant you that.'

'She said she wanted to give back some of the things she's had herself. To her own people. To the working-class.'

'She's given it back to them, all right,' I add.

She shakes her head. 'I don't know what'll happen to her after this.' Clearly, for her, Yvonne will never be the same again: an arm might have been mended, a leg straightened, a second child been born; but once they've gone crazy – out in the open again you can't be sure.

'I'll have to be going, in any case,' I tell her.

'It was very good of you to call,' she says. 'I don't see anyone now, you know.'

She gestures to the door.

'The people I used to know round here have gone.'

She gets up from the chair.

'You wonder, sometimes, if there's any point.'

'Yvonne,' I say, 'is still a point.'

'I suppose that's right.'

But that too, it seems, is going too far. She doesn't look up.

'Give my love to Yvonne when you see her next.'

'I shall.'

'Tell her I'll bring her clean clothes *ironed*.'

'I'll tell her that.'

'I was wondering whether to give her any money.'

'She's enough for the present, I believe,' I say.

'She gives it away, you know.' She might have added, then, 'She's mad.' 'Giving it all away, I mean, it's not as if she's ever had a lot.'

She takes out her handkerchief and wipes her eyes.

'It would have broken her father's heart, would this.'

'Let's hope it doesn't break Yvonne's,' I say.

'That's right.' She waits. 'A good job he didn't see it, I suppose,' she adds.

She stands at the door.

'If there's anything else I can do, you'll let me know.'

The street, cobbled, runs down to the warehouses that flank the river. Windowless façades, dark, sooted, loom above the roofs. A chimney, presumably of the mill where Mr Sherman worked, filters out a strand of smoke. Some of the houses have been boarded up: on one or two the roofs have gone.

'They keep saying we're going to be moved. Where to,' she says, 'I've no idea. They've stopped building houses here, you know, unless you've money of your own, that is.'

Her eyes, once again, are full of tears. The handkerchief, for a moment, conceals her face.

'I can't make any sense of it. We had such hopes. It ends like this.'

She leans across; I kiss her cheek; her hand, briefly, clutches at my arm.

'If there's anything you can do, you'll let me know.'

'If there's anything at all,' I say.

'If you've any spare time, you know, I'm always here. I can always cook you a meal,' she says.

I glance back, briefly, from the corner of the street.

She's standing at the door; she waves.

When I raise my arm she waves again, and waits, still waving, until I disappear.

2

A piece of clay, as I open the door, thuds into the wall above my head. A moment later the light goes out. There are several screams, a shout: a stool falls over, then a metal stand.

When the light goes on there's silence in the room.

'What's going on in here?'

'One of the stands fell over,' someone says.

'We thought the lights had fused.'

'Some of the clay got spilled.'

'That's right.'

The model, red-cheeked, red finger-marked, I now see, around her chest and thighs, has smiled; she looks down at the chalk-marks on the floor: the upturned stand is set back on its legs: the tiny clay effigy on top has taken on a lop-sided stance, like a figure pressed up against a pane of glass.

Similar clay effigies, built around wire armatures, are mounted on the stands around the room. Blobs of clay, like excrement, are spattered on the wall. Smeared with grey clay, the students return to their respective stands.

'Could you look at my figure, sir?'

An arm, thicker than a leg, has fallen off. A head, as large as the abdomen itself, is on the point of following it: gargantuan features leer out from the massive, square-shaped skull.

'It seems you've become absorbed in too many details; and lost your initial conception of the figure as a whole.'

'Hole?'

'If you forget about the eyes and nose, the fingers, elbows, knees and toes, and think instead of the figure as a whole: a tall cylindrical shape, dividing into two cylindrical shapes below and surmounted by a sort of ball . . .'

'Yeh.'

'When you've got the overall shape you can start putting in the individual features. The arm, for instance, if you look at it, is scarcely thicker than the leg.'

Dull, red-veined eyes look over at the model; they survey it reproachfully from head to toe.

'In any case, each arm should have an armature,' I add. 'You better put one in.'

'Yeh.'

'I should get the clay out of your hair as well.'

'Oh.'

'And when you do the head keep the clay against the arma-ture: otherwise you'll find that'll start falling off as well.'

'Yeh.'

'Anything else?'

'What?'

'I'll leave you to it.'

'Oh.'

I move on, speculatively, to the adjoining stand. The student there is attired in an American Army combat jacket; he wears a pair of jeans patched at the knees, and a pair of American Army combat boots. His clay's been moulded into a single elongated cube, the corners meticulously squared, the top rounded slightly; across its upper surface have been plaited what look like individual strands of hair.

'Do you intend to cut into the clay?' I ask.

'What for?'

'That's the shape you intend to finish with?'

'I don't intend to finish with anything. I work from an empirical point of view.'

'I see.'

'You start with an original reaction, and go on,' he says, 'from that.'

He sticks his tongue out, briefly, between his teeth; the modelling tool travels smoothly down the edges of the cube.

'Modelling from real life, in any case, is a bit irrelevant.'

'Irrelevant?'

'Who paints from life, for instance, any more?'

'I do.'

'You do.'

He glances over, briefly, in my direction.

The student behind me has begun to whistle, quietly; a moment later he begins to sing.

'*Love me,*
there is no other;
love me,
for I love you.'

'I don't make up the curriculum,' I tell him.

'That's the trouble. The ones who ought to are never consulted.'

'And the ones who do, I suppose, have no idea.'

'Look at this, for instance.'

He cuts off a sliver of clay; he crouches, looks along the surface of the cube; then, with one eye closed, he removes another.

'Love me,
I am your mother;
love me,
your father, too.'
'Perhaps you could ask Wilcox.'
'To stop all this?'
'If he'd mind you being consulted.'
'He'd have a fit.'
'You could burn the studio down if he didn't agree.'
He looks across.
'Love me,
I am your brother;
love me,
your sister, too.'
'If he refused then, you could ask him to resign.'
'Why don't *you* do something, then?'
'I'm not being taught.'
'You're doing the teaching, though.'
'I haven't taught you anything. Only advised you,' I tell him, 'to burn the art school down.'
'And that's what you're here to teach?' he says.
'I wouldn't advise it of everyone,' I tell him. 'Only of those,' I add, 'who might put it to some use.'
'Do I look like an incendiarist?' he says.
'Love me,
I am your teacher;
love me,
your follower, too.
Love me,
I am life's preacher;
love me,
Love's seeker, too.'
'I'd say, perhaps, the figure was over-generalized,' I tell him. 'It might be more interesting, as a next step, to break it down into its individual parts. All works of art, I'd say, on the whole, adhere to the principle of – for want of a better term – reciprocating parts.'
'I see.'
He glances at the clay again.

'The paraffin's kept in the caretaker's store. Next to the pottery room. I've seen it there myself.'

'I'll look into it,' he says.

He doesn't look up.

'Radical feeling in this country is compromised,' I tell him, 'from the very start. They want a piece of the cake, yet, to get it, they won't even forgo the jam.'

Love me,
there is no other;
love me,
for I love you.

'I forgo the jam, and never have the cake. You youngsters nowadays,' I tell him, 'may stand a better chance.'

The you
I see is me;
the me
I see is you.

'What privations did you have to undergo?' He looks across.

'My radicalism is treated as insanity; with you it's the idealism of the young. People, in the end, are afraid of paranoia. Idealists, if they're young enough, can get away with almost anything.'

He cuts slowly into the walls of the cube.

'And would you say the same to Wilcox, then?'

'He'll burn the building down himself.'

'Himself?'

'Or get someone like you to do it for him.'

I move over to the adjoining stand. A gargantuan girl with dark hair, cut short, and a spotty face is constructing a figure as immodest in its proportions as she is herself; arms like inflated rubber tyres are suspended beneath a gigantic, mongol-featured head: a pendulous abdomen, hacked at frustratedly on either side, overhangs a pair of stubby, bulbous legs.

I look over at the model; the finger-marks around her breasts have faded; the whiteness of her figure stands out against the faded whiteness of the wall behind.

'Perhaps we've been over-generous.'

She regards her figure with a frown.

'Not only with the clay, but with the proportions of the thing itself.'

'Yes.'

'The head, normally, goes about eight times into the overall height of the body.'

'Mine doesn't.'

'No.'

'It goes about twice.'

She contemplates the model as if, in this respect, it's let her down; as if its proportions change, habitually, the moment I arrive.

'I'm not very keen on these evening classes, in any case,' she says.

'Why's that?'

'The light's all different.'

'It can't distort proportions; only their effect.'

'It's the effect I'm aiming for,' she says.

'More subjective.'

'I don't know,' she says. She shakes her head.

'Is the body normally half as broad as it's tall?' I ask.

'Some bodies are,' she says.

'But not the ones you model from,' I tell her.

'That's not the one I'm doing, necessarily,' she says.

'Isn't that the object of the class? After all, a figure like that you could do at home.'

'I haven't got any clay at home,' she says.

I say, 'Take some with you. I'll lend you some.'

'I'm supposed to do it here,' she says.

'There's no compulsion to do one here,' I tell her.

'What would you suggest?' she says.

I take her modelling tool; I whittle off the clay: I'm aware, in fact, for a while, of nothing else. The broad, grey wedges disappear; a slender, sylph-like shape emerges, as if by magic, from the centre of the clay. The other students, after a while, have gathered round.

'It's a sort of formula, I suppose,' the jacketed youth has said. 'Like throwing pots: a kind of craft.'

'That's what you're here to study, I suppose,' I tell him.

'Form creates emotion, and emotion its own form,' he says.

I'm aware, suddenly, of the Newman girl; she's standing at the rear of the group, her eyes narrowed, regarding the figure on the stand as she might some object she particularly covets in the window of a shop.

'Anything else,' the student says, 'is a kind of illustration. A set of rules, a gimmick; something applied externally to a given situation.'

'Like paraffin,' I add.

'You're figure's like paraffin,' he says.

'Is it time for a rest?' the model asks.

Her green, hazel-coloured eyes meet mine.

'It's five minutes past,' the whistling student says.

The model steps down.

'Anyone want a humbug, then?' she says. She retrieves a dressing-gown from a nearby stool and takes out a bag of sweets from one of its pockets.

'They're all Philistines here,' the Newman girl has said. She runs her hand across her hair.

'I didn't think you were in this class,' I tell her.

'History of Architecture.' She gestures back, vaguely, in the direction of the college. 'It's break. I thought I'd wander down.'

A wireless has gone on across the room; someone, beside the model's cubicle, has begun to smoke. The model herself, her dressing-gown undone, is dancing, lamely, with the whistling youth.

'I thought you despised all this,' she says.

'That's right.'

'Why do it, then?'

'I've no idea.'

She runs her hand, once more, across her hair. She's dressed in a short grey skirt, pleated, and a yellow blouse; her hair is fastened back beneath a yellow ribbon.

'I find them, on the whole, more stimulating than the rest.'

'That's one way of looking at it, I suppose,' she says.

She leans against the wall, then shakes her head.

'You don't give a damn about anything,' she says.

'I don't suppose that's true,' I tell her.

She laughs. She glances idly along the row of figures.

'Isn't modelling from life, in any case, an irrelevance. Like painting from life, I suppose,' she says.

68

The jacketed youth has come across.

'Love they say
is blind,
but love to strangers
more than kind.'

'Has he got you on this incendiarist kick?' the youth has said.

'Incendiarist?' The girl has flushed.

'He's encouraging me to burn the building down.'

'I offered it, empirically, as a point of view. In a specific instance, you understand,' I tell him.

'I find this class an irrelevance, in any case,' the student says. 'If I didn't come,' he adds, 'they'd stop my grant. Between irrelevance and ineffectiveness I have no choice.'

'The only thing to do,' I tell him, 'instead of complaining, is to exploit the exploiters as often as you can. In the end, you'll find, they'll come to you.'

'For what?'

'They're suckers for punishment of any kind,' I say. He glances at the girl.

'Is anyone taking you home?' he says.

'I suppose they are.' She nods her head.

'I thought I'd ask.' He turns away.

A voice, somewhere by the door, has said, *'Is this a mothers' meeting, then? Or, if they're barmy enough, can anybody join?'*

The dance tune stops; it starts again, stops, comes back, then fades away. The model, like a balloon, collapses on a chair. The whistling youth sits down as well.

Wilcox, red-faced, is standing in the door; his fists are clenched. He gazes round.

'Started a dance-club, have we? I thought this was where the Donatellos and the Verrocchios of the future were supposed to start. Where they learnt first principles, that is, if nothing else.'

His eyes, as he advances, travel along the row of stands. His gaze, finally, is arrested by the fat girl's figure.

'Who's done this?'

'That's mine,' the fat girl says.

'Did you do that?' He seems amazed.

'Sir did it for me, sir,' she says.

For the first time he's aware of my figure by the wall.

'And how much of it's yours?' he says.

'I did some of the bottom bit,' she says.

'Bottom, anatomically speaking, or bottom, figuratively speaking?' Wilcox says.

'I started some of it off,' she says.

She's about to break into tears, it seems.

Wilcox, nonplussed, has come across.

'I make no rules about teaching, as you know,' he says. 'But if a student's work it is, Freestone, a student's work it ought to remain. What would an inspector think,' he adds, 'if he suddenly came on this?'

He lifts his head.

'Is someone smoking in here?'

He looks around.

'It's not you again, then, Freestone?'

'I think it was here when we first came in.'

He narrows his eyes. Pale clouds of smoke, thin, scarcely visible, drift slowly past the electric light.

'There must be an invisible man in here. Nearly every room I go into I find there's been somebody smoking before anybody else arrives. I think he must come in, you know, when everybody else is out.'

He sees, suddenly, with widening eyes, the elongated cube.

'What's this?'

The skin on the top of his head has reddened.

'That's mine,' the jacketed youth has said.

'What's it for?'

The youth has stepped across.

'It's not for anything,' he says.

'Not for somebody's tombstone, then?'

'It's a simple unequivocal form,' the student says.

'It might be unequivocal, and it might be a form. You could say the same about my bloody boot.' The Principal laughs. 'And my boot,' he adds, 'I don't need to tell you, isn't a work of art.'

'Of that you can't be sure,' the student says.

'If I put it up your backside you'd be bloody sure,' the Principal says. 'Good God: you don't have to come here to do stuff like that; you can do all that, tha knows, at home. Without the presence,' he adds, 'of a living model.'

He looks at me.

'It's supposed to be a rest, then, is it?'

The model, as if inflated, suddenly gets up.

'The rests round here get longer every day. Longer even than the bloody classes. We'll be paying them soon for supping tea.'

The model steps over to the chalk-marks on the floor.

'Could I have a word with you,' he says, 'outside?'

He waits for the model to resume her pose.

'I don't see much challenge, you know, in that. One leg forward, one leg back: she ought to have her arms stretched out, or one like this, above her head.'

He stands, one arm raised, inside the door.

The arm still raised, he steps outside.

The air in the yard is cool. A light at the top of a flight of steps marks the rear entrance to the college. Piles of coke occupy one corner of the yard; beside them stands a large parked car, Wilcox's, a fawn-coloured Armstrong Siddeley. Hendrick's dark blue sports car is parked further away, towards the gate.

'I was wondering if you were free one evening.' His arm, as he glances round the yard, is suddenly lowered. 'I told my good lady I'd invite you back. She suggested Monday evening might be the best. First day of the week, that is.' His gaze, slowly, turns towards the car; from there, as if mentally pacing off the distance, it wanders over to Hendrick's by the gate; then, more quickly, he looks at me.

'What time on Monday evening, then?'

'We normally eat at seven,' he says. 'If I'm not at the college, that is. You've no evening class, I take it, then?'

'None.'

'I'll pick you up here,' he says, 'if that's all right.' He looks about him once again. 'The house, you see, is hard to find.'

He starts off, briskly, across the yard.

'By the way,' he says. 'We better make it half-past six. Then it gives us time.' He looks across. 'To find the house, I mean,' he adds.

I close the door of the studio; a moment later, as if suspecting he might return, I open it again. Wilcox is standing by his car: the boot is open. He's picking up pieces of coke, one by one, and placing them, with an absurd, almost ceremonial air inside the boot.

I step out briskly across the yard. The boot slams shut: there's the sound of his feet as he scrambles round the pile.

'Puncture.'

'What?'

'The tyre.'

'It seems all right.'

'It's probably the light.' He bends his back; his head for a moment disappears. 'What're you doing out here, in any case?'

'Register.'

'Register?'

His head comes up.

'Should have been marked, you know, by now.'

'I'm sorry about that,' I tell him.

'Registration's about the most important thing. Next to smoking and the general conduct of a class,' he adds.

I go over to the door.

When I come back down he's disappeared: the light is on in the modelling room: the model, red-faced, is turned towards the door; finger-marks, like red petals, bloom once more around her breasts and thighs.

'Any problems?'

'No, sir.'

'None.'

I lean against the wall and sigh.

The car, fish-like, pink, gleaming beneath the lights from the college windows, glides soundlessly towards the porch: the girl emerges on the steps outside. She stoops to the car; a second head appears. As I set off down the street the car draws up.

A face, not unlike the girl's, peers out, slim-featured, dark-haired, the eyes concealed by a pair of tinted glasses.

'Mr Freestone?'

The glasses are removed.

Grey eyes, dark-lashed, lined by mascara, gaze out from the shadow behind the wheel.

'This is my mother,' the girl has said.

The door has opened.

'I'm Elizabeth Newman,' the woman says.

A hand appears.

'I wanted to thank you for all the trouble you took with Bec.'

I shake the hand.

'It was very kind of you,' she says.

'It was no trouble. None at all,' I say.

'Can we give you a lift?' the girl has said.

'I thought, with the evening being so fine, I'd walk.' Both heads look up, it seems, towards the sky.

'It doesn't seem so fine to me.' The woman replaces her glasses: she looks across.

'I think he'd prefer to walk,' the girl has said.

I can see, briefly, the profile of the woman's head, the sharpness of the nose, the jaw.

Her scent, briefly, drifts out from the car.

'He doesn't like signs of affluence,' the girl has said.

'This isn't affluence, it's just vulgarity,' the woman says.

'The two, for Mr Freestone, are synonymous,' the girl has said.

'I don't think taste and affluence are necessarily incompatible,' I tell her.

The woman looks across again.

'What are you doing on Saturday?' she says.

'He's going out.' The girl has smiled.

'How do you know so much about his movements, then?'

'I know some things, Mummy,' the girl has said.

'Come up to the house,' she says. 'I'm sure, if you try, you can find the time.'

The head stoops down.

'Can we commit you to that?' she says.

'He'll come if he wants to,' the girl has said.

The face, its expression concealed by the glasses, still gazes up at mine.

'Come in the afternoon,' she says.

I wait.

'Yes,' I say.

'At two,' she adds.

'Yes,' I say. I add, 'All right.'

'We'll look forward to seeing you, then,' she says.

I see the smile; the car moves off: I can see the silhouette of the girl inside.

An arm is raised; the car dips down: like a pink suffusion, formless, huge, it blends with the traffic that infests the town.

3

'It may be the sound of a lot of old hens to you, but to me,' she says, 'it's like the music of the stars.'

The room is panelled to almost shoulder height; above that the walls are hung with armorial shields. Gnarled wooden beams project from the ceiling overhead. Each one of the surrounding tables is occupied by women. There's not another man in the room as far as I can tell.

Something in Yvonne's appearance has attracted their attention; that, it seems, and the loudness of her voice.

I watch her now; she eats her food like she smokes her cigarettes, unaware, uncaring.

'It's lovely chicken.'

'Do you like it?'

'We don't get food, you know, like this.'

'I thought you liked the food in there.'

'It's all right,' she says, 'for what it is.'

It's like a game; a certain eccentricity, it seems, is demanded of her: she presents it, at times, as if to reassure herself, and me: 'If I act like this I *must* be mad.'

'It was good of them to let you out.'

'I haven't been out for about three weeks.'

She eats quickly, as if she suspected that the food, if she doesn't instantly consume it, will be taken away.

'I've had these terrible headaches the last two weeks.'

'You never mentioned it,' I tell her.

'They give you these pills. I don't like taking them,' she says. 'If you grow to rely on them,' she adds, 'what are you in the end?'

'If you don't take them you have the headache, so why not take them and get rid of it?' I tell her.

'There was a woman broke out the other night. They lock the doors, you know, at eight.'

The women at the adjoining tables lift their heads.

'She smashed a window. They found her, four hours later, walking round the town.'

'They always bring you back,' I say.

'Suppose you got hidden, though?' she asks.

'And where would you hide that they couldn't find you in the end?'

'I could go to my mother's.'

'That'd be one of the first places they'd go and look,' I tell her.

'In any case, I'm better off,' she says, 'in there.' She shakes her head. 'I realize that. The longer I can stick it, the sooner I'll be out.'

I can see another man's head across the room; small, red-cheeked, fair-haired, the face relieved by a light-moustache. It gazes round: a hand is raised, a small, portly figure comes across, arms swinging out on either side.

'Hello, old man. Fancy finding you in here.'

Pollard bows slightly, then glances at Yvonne.

A woman at Pollard's side, with glaring eyes and a red beret-shaped hat, is glancing disapprovingly round the room for an empty chair.

'There's nowhere else to sit. They sent us here.' Pollard adds this with another bow. 'I suppose they thought you'd finished then.'

'This is my wife Yvonne,' I say.

'My dear, this is Mr Freestone, who teaches at the college,' Pollard says. 'My wife, Mrs Freestone: Mrs Freestone, my wife.'

'This is Mr and Mrs Pollard,' I tell Yvonne.

She doesn't look up; in fact she appears to assume that the Pollards have something to do with the restaurant itself: the pace of her eating has suddenly quickened.

I get up from the table, draw out a chair: after glancing at Pollard himself, his wife sits down.

'This is very decent of you,' Pollard says.

'No children with you, then?' I look around.

'Skipped off to Jenny's mother.' He gestures at his wife.

'We thought we'd eat in town,' his wife has said.

'Make a day of it.' He looks around.

'Are you two from the home, then?' Yvonne has said.

'Home?' Mrs Pollard says. She looks across.

'From the hospital,' Yvonne has said.

'We've *come* from home,' Mrs Pollard says.

'Make a day of it. Why cook a dinner?' Pollard says.

'It's the first week-end they've let me out,' Yvonne has said.

'For the past few weeks, that is,' I say.

'Once they get you in they'll not often let you out,' she says.

'What hospital is that, then?' Pollard says.

'Westfield.'

'Isn't that . . . ?' he says. He shakes his head.

'It's for lunatics,' Yvonne has said.

The waitress comes across.

Pollard picks up the menu; having opened it, he hands it to his wife.

'A la carte or fixed luncheon?' the waitress says.

'I liked the chicken,' Yvonne has said.

'That's nice,' the waitress says. She smiles.

'I could eat another one, I think!'

'Two for the price of one.' The waitress laughs.

'You don't know what it's like to eat good food.'

'We try and do our best,' the waitress says.

'Where I come from they get it out of tins.'

'Still, some good food, I suppose, you get from tins.'

'It's mainly for dogs and cats. Once they've cooked it, you know, it's hard to tell.'

'All the food in here, of course, is fresh.'

'What have you got for pudding?' Yvonne has said.

Mrs Pollard chooses from the menu: the waitress writes it down. Pollard examines the menu for a while himself: he consults the waitress.

'There's a sultana pudding, or various ice creams,' the waitress says. 'The fresh fruit, of course, is very nice.'

'Is it out of tins?' Yvonne has said.

'Fresh out of tins. That's right,' she says.

'I'll have sultana pudding,' Yvonne has said.

Pollard, returning to the menu, dictates his choice.

'And you?' the waitress says.

'I'll have the sultana pudding, too,' I add.

'Two sultana puddings,' the waitress says.

'And coffee.'

'And coffee.'

'I'll have tea,' Yvonne has said.

'One tea, one coffee,' the waitress says.

She glances at the Pollards, glances at Yvonne, then goes off, briskly, across the room.

'We left it a bit late, thinking it wouldn't be so crowded,' Mrs Pollard says.

'Saturday,' Pollard says, 'we might have known.'

'Backed any horses today?' I ask.

Pollard ducks his head; it's as if, briefly, I've trodden on his toes.

'Nothing of any note,' he says.

'Are you backing horses still?' his wife has said.

'Nothing above a pound,' I tell her.

'A pound.'

'That's Freestone. He's got no kids. With me, it's never above a shilling,' Pollard says.

'Wilcox insists, you see,' I tell her.

'Insists?'

Yvonne, her empty plate before her, gazes fixedly at Mrs Pollard's hat.

'It's a sort of gesture of faith, you see, amongst the staff.'

'Community feeling,' Pollard says. 'He's the same about smoking, of course,' he adds.

'Where I am, there's a woman taking drugs,' Yvonne has said. 'She broke up the kitchen the other night.'

The heads at the surrounding tables turn.

'All the plates. The cups. You could hear them from the ward. By the time the nurse got there there was nothing left.'

'How long have you been in Westfield?' Pollard says. He phrases it politely, as if it's an hotel of world renown.

'Months, it seems,' Yvonne has said.

'Seven weeks, I would have thought,' I tell her.

'Months, it seems to me,' Yvonne has said.

She shakes her head.

'There's a woman there who cut her wrists. She follows you about and tells you things.'

Her face, with the Pollards' arrival, has grown quite calm.

'What sort of things, then?' Pollard says.

'About her family.'

Pollard, having asked the question, looks over at his wife.

'How they get on to her,' she adds. 'Her husband tried to kill her once, she says.'

'I suppose some of it's exaggerated,' Pollard says.

'They don't need to exaggerate anything in there,' Yvonne has said.

The waitress reappears; she takes away the empty plates and sets down the two sultana puddings.

'You go ahead. Don't wait for us, then,' Pollard says.

Yvonne, however, has already started.

'One tea one coffee,' the waitress says.

She sets the cups down beside the plates.

'One thing you can say about the service here.'

'It's prompt.'

'It's prompt.'

Mrs Pollard, having loosened her coat, removes her hat.

'It's the only place you can get a meal. That's decently edible. In town, I mean.'

'Some of the food we have you wouldn't touch.' Her spoon raised to her mouth, Yvonne looks up. 'It's often cold before you start. And some of it they serve up,' she adds, 'from the day before.'

'What job did you have, before you went to Westfield?' Pollard says.

'Job?'

'Work. Did you have any work?' He looks at me.

'I used to teach. I was a teacher for a while,' she says.

'I suppose you'll go back to it,' he says.

She shakes her head.

'I don't think I shall,' she says. 'It drives you mad.'

'I get the same feeling too, at times, Mrs Freestone,' Pollard says.

He laughs.

'There's another woman there who screams all night. It took seven nurses once to hold her down. I never thought the human body could have such strength.'

The heads at the surrounding tables turn again.

'It may sound like a lot of old hens to you, but to me it's the music of the stars,' she says.

We finish the meal. I get the bill.

As we get up to leave Yvonne moves over to an adjoining table.

'Have you enjoyed the meal?' she says.

The heads, after an inquiring look, are lowered.

'I've enjoyed mine,' she says. 'The best, in fact, I've had for years.'

She fastens her coat.

'See you on Monday,' Pollard says.

He gets up from the table as Yvonne comes back.

'I hope we'll see you soon,' he adds.

'I shan't be in much longer, I suppose,' she says.

They watch us to the door.

'Did you enjoy the meal?' I ask her when we get outside.

'The best I've ever had,' she says.

'It's time we were getting back,' I say.

'Couldn't we go for a walk?' she says. 'I need some cigarettes in any case, you see.'

As we approach the shop, however, she says, 'I don't like shops. I shan't come in.'

She stands looking at the window as I go inside.

When I come out a few minutes later she's disappeared.

I look for her figure along the street.

I walk back for a while the way we've come: the restaurant in sight, I turn towards the shop. I examine the shop windows the opposite side; I gaze, from the kerbstone, at the figures moving along the road itself. I walk on, in the direction we were going before she disappeared.

I see her, some distance away, briefly, beyond a frieze of heads. She's standing by a shop, almost as I left her, gazing at the window.

When I take her arm she scarcely stirs.

'Why did you wander off? I thought you'd stay by the shop,' I say.

'I haven't wandered off.' She shakes her head.

'You're miles,' I tell her, 'from where you were.'

'Shall we go somewhere else?' she says.

An alleyway, opening from the street, takes us through to the cathedral close. The porch is empty, the doors unlocked.

We go inside. A beam of reddish light crosses the nave diagonally, from left to right.

Workmen are ascending in a lift at the opposite end; men in white overalls, with helmets that glisten in the light.

Their voices echo, faintly, from scaffolding above our heads.

I hold her hand; we sit in the shadows at the back of the nave: a single figure, kneeling, its head in its hands, is visible in one of the pews of a chapel to our right.

'Do you think I'll ever get out?' she says. 'I feel, at times, I'm getting worse.'

Her hand holds mine like it might a piece of wood; there's no engagement of any sort: a kind of anguish, almost communal, that cancels individual feeling out.

'I met a woman the other day. She said she'd been inside for twenty years.'

'You're only in the admission wing,' I tell her. 'The average turn-over there's six weeks.'

'I've been there longer than that,' she says.

'So there's no need to worry. It can't be long.'

There's the faint whirring of an electric motor: a white-clad figure descends from the shadows above. There's the faint tapping of a hammer above our heads.

'I feel I'll never be free again.'

'If you feel as much as that you must be well.'

Her hand squeezes mine with a strange, irregular rhythm.

'I saw your mother the other day. She sends you all her love,' I say.

'It must be hard. For her. To see me as I am,' she says.

'She just wants you out, that's all,' I tell her.

'It's what we all want, but it doesn't get any nearer, love,' she says.

She begins to weep.

I rest her head against my arm.

The head in the pew to our right has turned: a face looks up from the outstretched hands.

'Those people that we met today.'

'Why should you mind about them?' I say.

'I saw the way they looked. I can't help myself at times,' she says.

'I was proud to be with you at that lunch today.' I stroke her hair.

'I can't communicate the things I feel.'

'I feel them, too.'

'There seems no point.'

'There isn't any point. That's why we're here.'

A second figure, a light glistening from his helmet, descends in the lift from the shadows above. There's the sound, somewhere, of an electric drill.

I feel the dampness of her tears against my hand; her grief's been with her all her life: it reminds me of her home, her house, the disintegration that goes on against her will: she's like a plant, harried by its own decay: the bloom itself is a kind of death.

'You seem so calm.'

'I always am.'

'You always were.'

'With you I'm calm. I don't think,' I say, 'with anyone else.'

'I don't like this church.'

'We can go outside.'

'It's time to go back, I suppose,' she says.

Three figures, their white overalls glowing in the light, ascend slowly to the blackness overhead.

She glances up.

She sees, for the first time perhaps, the scaffolding above our heads.

'The ceiling's being repaired.'

'It stands for nothing, I suppose,' she says.

She waves her hand.

'It's so cold in here.'

The figure from the chapel to our right walks past; at the door, to our left, it kneels, crosses itself, then passes through to the porch outside.

She wipes her eyes.

'How are you managing on your own?' she says.

'I'm a great one for living on my own,' I say.

'I suppose you're seeing lots of girls.'

'One almost every night,' I say.

'Are any like me? I suppose they're better, on the whole,' she says.

Yet the inquiry, it seems, is directed at some other person.

'Could we go back on the bus?' she says.

'Don't you want to walk?'

'I'm feeling tired. I'll be glad to get back. I usually sleep in the afternoons,' she says.

4

Buildings, like tall black rocks, surround the village green. The house itself stands on a kind of knoll: a drive sweeps up across a terraced slope. Trees, at the back of the house, release a shower of leaves: rooks rise up as I approach the gates. The wind has caught the smoke from a garden fire: it sweeps around the house in a bluish wreath.

Half way up the drive a dog has barked: a face shows at one of the lower windows. From the back of the house comes the shouting of a child: on the green below a row of mounted figures moves off towards the heath the other side.

As I reach the porch the door's drawn back.

A tall, disjointed-looking man appears. He has long fair hair; he smooths it back, looking up, vaguely, towards the sky.

'Not such a good day.' He gestures to the heath below. 'My name's Pettrie.' He puts out his hand. 'Did you have a car?'

'I came on foot.'

He looks out, beyond the heath, towards the town. 'That's quite a walk.'

'About four miles.'

'Four miles,' he says and gives a sigh.

He glances down to the heath again; other figures, mostly on foot, but some on horseback, can be seen moving along its various tracks.

From inside the house, sharply, comes the barking of a dog.

'Elizabeth isn't down at present. She told us you'd be arriving, though.'

The hall seems larger than it did before, the bowl of flowers, if anything, stronger in its scent. The door to the lounge is already open: a man with red hair is reclining in a chair: beside him, one arm round him, is sprawled the figure of a blonde.

A man in a corduroy jacket is standing by the fire, his hands behind his back, gazing up at the 'View of Delft'. A second woman, dark-haired, dressed in a long gown, is standing at the window, gazing out.

'This is Leyland,' the tall man says, indicating the red-haired figure who, as we enter, has lifted one foot across his knee and removed his shoe.

'Look at that,' he says. 'Straight through.'

He indicates a hole in the sole of the shoe which the blonde girl beside him examines for a while, pushing her finger through and adding, 'Fancy, you see. You never said.'

The man by the fireplace, as if disturbed, has wandered over to the long-gowned figure standing at the window.

'I didn't catch your name,' the tall man says.

'Elsie,' the girl has said. Unlike the red-haired man she offers me her hand.

'This is Colin Freestone,' the tall man says.

'Pleased to meet you,' the blonde girl says.

I shake her hand.

'What do you do for a living?' the red-haired man has said.

'Colin teaches at the local art school,' the tall man says.

'I teach at the local art school, I'm afraid,' I tell him.

'Where's that?'

'Next to the technical school,' I say.

'Where's that?'

'Somewhere in the town,' I tell him.

'My name's Eddie, by the way,' the tall man says. 'And Leyland,' he adds, 'is referred to, amongst his friends, as Johnny.'

'I don't go in for art much,' Leyland says.

'I don't go in for it at all,' I tell him.

'Why do you teach it, then?'

'I don't.'

His head comes up. He has long, thin features, pale, with light blue eyes: there's something fish-like about his appearance, brittle, hard.

'If you don't teach art, what're you doing at the place?' he says.

'I supervise. Attend to the students' moral needs; or, to put it another way, the students' individual spiritual requirements.'

He gazes up for a moment at the other man. His foot, shoeless, is still cocked against his knee.

'Elizabeth invited Mr Freestone,' the tall man says.

'Thank God,' he says, 'it wasn't me.'

I reach down to the shoeless foot: I remove it from the knee; with my other hand, as Leyland's head comes up, I punch him on the nose.

A stream of blood falls, unattended for a moment, across his lips; it falls, in an irregular fashion, onto the lapels of his coat below. The two figures standing by the window turn.

'I don't like rudeness, on the whole,' I tell him. 'And invariably, when I encounter it, I hit people on the nose.'

His handkerchief comes out: the girl beside him gives a scream. His eyes, as he tenses to the pain, are closed.

'Good God,' the tall man says. He stretches down; another handkerchief appears. 'Are you all right?'

'What's going on in here?' a voice has said.

A figure attired in white has appeared inside the door. Mrs Newman is wearing, I decide, at that first glimpse, some sort of suit.

'Johnny's had a fight,' one of the figures across the room has said.

'Oh, my God,' she says as she sees the blood.

'With Mr Freestone, I'm afraid,' the tall man says.

The undersides of her brows are painted blue: grey eyes peer out from beneath mascara-ed lids.

'You know who Johnny is?'

'I've no idea.'

'Hasn't Colin been introduced?' she says.

'We were introduced,' I say, and add, as if this might impress her, 'He didn't stand up.'

'Keep it off the chairs,' she says. 'The blood: for God's sake, keep it off the covers, Ed.'

Leyland now is standing up: initially, he has bowed his head, found no relief, and allowed the girl to tilt it back. Now, one shoe off, he's standing by the chair.

'This is one of my husband's friends, one of his colleagues,' Mrs Newman says. She adds, 'I should take him to the bathroom, Ed.'

Leyland, with the tall man and the blonde girl, starts over to the door.

'I'll see you when I come down,' he says, his voice muffled by the handkerchief around his nose.

'Keep it off the carpet,' Mrs Newman says. She's examining the chair and the floor as Leyland goes.

'My name's Proctor,' the man with the corduroy coat has said. He has a dark moustache, large eyes and sallow cheeks. 'And this,' he adds, indicating the long-gowned girl, 'is Jean.'

She too is dark, with a pallid skin.

'I didn't see it start, I'm afraid,' he says.

'Now the introductions are over,' Mrs Newman says, 'let's have a drink.'

Proctor and the dark-haired Jean move back once more across the room. A moment later I can hear the woman's voice: 'I won't, I won't, I won't,' and then, with her laughter, the laughter of the man.

'There are usually more people here than this.'

She hands me the glass: she gestures with her own.

'Here's to it, then.'

I drink it down.

'Would you like another?'

'I wouldn't say no.'

'Do you often hit people on the nose?'

She takes the glass.

'As often as I can.'

She laughs.

'I'm sorry,' she says, 'it began like this.'

'Isn't your daughter in?' I ask.

She gestures to the heath below. 'Riding. And my husband's still abroad,' she says.

'What sort of work does he do?' I ask.

'All sorts,' she says and gestures to a chair. 'Sit down. Unless you've more fighting still to do,' she adds.

I take the glass.

We sit across the room.

'You'd better tell me,' I say, 'who Pettrie is.'

'Eddie's a sort of owner, I suppose,' she says.

'Of what?'

'Of factories, I suppose,' she says. 'He makes all sorts of things. Like belts.'

'For what?'

'For coal-mines, I believe,' she says. She adds, 'Conveyors, to carry things along.'

'Does your husband do the same?'

She shakes her head.

'You've drunk that quickly too,' she says. 'If you'd like another just help yourself.'

She watches me from across the room; I fill the glass, top it up, look round the room, then, more slowly, move back towards the chair.

'If you like,' she says, 'I'll show you round.'

'How many children have you got?'

'Just one.'

She sips her drink.

A dog barks, briskly, from the back of the house.

'Did you come by car?' she says.

'I walked.'

'I could have had someone fetch you, if you'd only asked.'

'Maybe next time,' I say, and add, 'I'll let you know.'

'What kind of paintings do you do?'

'I don't.'

'That was one of the reasons I asked you here. I intend to buy some pictures over the next few months.'

I begin to smile.

'Do you find that funny?'

'I suppose I do.'

'Why's that?' she says. She closes her eyes.

The gesture comes, I see, when she feels unsure.

'Why not buy something useful, then?'

'Paintings can be useful. If they're attractive. And they can appreciate in value, I suppose,' she says.

'So could a house.'

'We've got a house.'

'What about jewellery?'

'I've enough of that.'

'A yacht, I suppose.'

'You can hire a yacht.'

'Apart from people,' I say, 'there's nothing else.'

'Only paintings, and works of art,' she says.

The woman across the room has laughed. She slaps one hand against the other. 'I won't,' the man has said. 'I won't.'

'It's hardly the place for paintings, then.'

'At least,' she says, 'I could make a start. I've got one here, as a matter of fact.'

She puts down her glass, gets up, waits for a moment while I finish mine, then leads the way to the hall outside. She opens a door on the opposite side.

A woman with grey, close-cropped hair, is standing at a desk. She's smoking a cigarette in a yellow holder, talking into a phone which, as we enter, she covers up.

'Will you be long in here?' Mrs Newman says.

'A couple of secs,' she says, and adds, uncovering the phone, 'Mrs Newman, I'm afraid, is out, and his majesty, as you're aware, is overseas.' She covers the phone again and looks across. 'The silly old bitch. Put arsenic in her tea when she comes again.'

A painting, its back to the door, is propped against a chair.

Through a window, beyond the desk, I can see the garden at the back of the house: a tennis court with its net removed; an old stone wall, the roofs of several old stone buildings and a clump of trees.

'We'll take it out,' Mrs Newman says.

Books line one of the walls; a filing cabinet on wheels stands behind the door. Behind the desk is a swivel chair.

'I can't help it if she's out,' the woman says. 'What message shall I give her, then?'

The cigarette in its yellow holder is rested on the desk. Beside the telephone stands a framed photograph of Mrs Newman, anonymous, smiling: a necklace glitters at her throat; some other kind of jewellery glistens in her hair.

Her finger to her lips she tiptoes out; I take the picture as we reach the door.

'We won't go in with those other two,' she says.

She recrosses the hall, opens a door diagonally opposite, and steps inside.

The walls of the room are lined with shelves; none of them,

however, are occupied. A crate, presumably containing books, stands by the door: there are several chairs, a table, and a cabinet with a number of coloured rocks inside. The window, like that of the previous room, looks out to the garden at the back of the house. A child, perhaps seven or eight years old, is playing with a dog on a windswept lawn. 'That's Mrs Brennan's,' Mrs Newman says. 'She's one of the women we have up here.'

There's a smell of dust; the room is cold.

I lean the picture against the crate.

'You can see how awful it is,' she says.

It's composed almost entirely of coloured triangles; where the triangles overlap the colours coalesce.

'My husband bought it, as a matter of fact.'

'Who for?'

'Himself,' she says, then adds, 'And me.'

'It runs in the family, I suppose.'

'What's that?'

I draw the shape.

'Rebecca? She got the idea I think from this.'

She holds her hand against her cheek.

'We're not sure where to hang it, though,' she says. From outside the door comes the sound of Leyland's voice.

'You ought to have it X-rayed,' the girl has said.

'You've upset Leyland,' Mrs Newman says. 'He's a terrible temper when he's been aroused.'

She lifts her head.

'We shouldn't be disturbed in here,' she says.

'No need to hide.'

'It's hardly hiding. I want to know what you think of the picture, then.'

'I've no idea.'

'Don't you have any views on art?' she says.

'None I could put into words,' I say.

'Do you think I should hang it up?' she says.

'Depends how much you paid for it,' I tell her.

'Honestly,' she says. 'You're not much help.'

The cries of the child outside have turned to screams. A figure, wearing a white overall, runs out across the lawn.

'I tell her to leave the dogs alone.'

88

There are three retrievers, like small ponies, dancing on the grass.

The child, transfixed, is sitting in their midst. The overalled woman picks it up: red-faced, she glances back towards the house.

'You haven't been here,' I say, 'for long.'

'Nor likely to be, I suppose,' she says.

I move the picture away from the case; I prop it up against the shelves.

'Aren't abstract pictures like this the thing to buy?'

'They don't paint pictures any more,' I tell her.

'What do they do?'

'Hit Leyland on the nose,' I say.

She laughs.

'Events of that nature,' she says, 'are hard to find.'

'It's the art of being a collector, I suppose,' I say.

She smiles.

'There are no artefacts of any sort,' I tell her. 'They don't make objects any more, you see.'

There's a knock on the door. She lifts her head.

On the lawn outside the child has gone: the dogs bound about amongst themselves.

Footsteps go off the other side.

'You buy the process instead of the product, I suppose,' she says.

'Some events are still objects, I suppose,' I tell her.

'Like you.'

'Like me.'

She laughs again.

'Would you like to see the other rooms?' she says.

We go outside. The door to the lounge is closed.

'The painter by the way is dead.'

'In that case, I suppose, you could hang it up.'

'As a momento.'

'A memorial.'

'I suppose I could. It cost enough, in any case,' she says.

We go upstairs. A dance tune, faintly, is playing from a room above.

'Did Beccie show you round?' she says.

'Your room,' I tell her, 'and not much else.'

'She showed you that?'

We reach the door.

'You won't need to look inside again.'

'It was too dark,' I tell her, 'to see the view.'

'The view?' she says. 'She mentioned that.'

'About the only thing she did,' I say.

The bed, the four-poster, is still the same. The photograph of the blond-haired man still stands beside the bed.

'It looks out towards the town,' she says.

The village, with its ancient, black-stone houses, is spread out around the green below.

Black, mullioned windows look down towards the heath.

The town is scarcely visible beyond, a long, drawn-out ligament of rock, dark, knotted, mounded up against the valley side.

Her hand, I notice, as she holds the curtain aside, is small; the sharp-featured face is set in profile against the whiteness of the cloth behind.

She turns her head.

'Nothing to excite you much,' she says.

A car comes up the drive below: there are several shouts, a cry.

'I'll show you the other rooms,' she adds.

When we go back down two men and two women are sitting in chairs around the fire. The blonde, her head on her knees, is sitting on the floor. Pettrie, his hands in his pockets, is standing at the window, gazing out. The other couple, it seems, have gone.

'Here comes the ape-man,' Leyland says.

He sits, his knee up, his nose inflamed, his lip swollen, on one of the couches across the room.

'I'm thinking of suing him,' he says.

The heads of the newcomers have already turned: Mrs Newman reels off a list of names, then adds, 'No more fighting. For today, at least.'

'I didn't start it,' Leyland says. 'I only asked him where he worked. The next thing I knew he'd knocked me out.'

The four figures across the room have laughed.

'Do you know what Johnny is?' a man with short black hair and dark protruding eyes has asked.

I shake my head.

'Have a guess.'

'I take it we're keeping to professions,' Leyland says.

'Perhaps he has views on other things,' he says.

'In terms of identity as well as job.'

They laugh.

'No,' I tell him. 'I've no idea.'

'Going by his dress: bohemian. You notice the muddied jeans, the collarless shirt.'

'A solicitor.'

They laugh again.

'How did you guess, for God's sake,' someone says.

'Is this something you've arranged, Elizabeth?' the other man has said.

He's built like a wrestler; his arms, it seems, are suspended from his ears; fists the size of melons dangle lamely in the region of his knees.

'I've told him nothing,' Mrs Newman says.

'Eddie?'

'Not a thing,' the tall man says. He shakes his head.

'He's such a rotten egoist, he's surprised when anyone sees through him,' Mrs Newman says. 'He's only tolerated in a place like this. Anywhere else he'd get his teeth pushed in.'

'They very nearly were, Liz,' Leyland says.

The men across the room have laughed.

In the hall outside the girl appears; she looks into the room, sees me, then comes across. She's wearing a jumper and a pair of jeans.

Without looking at anyone else in the room she sits down heavily in the chair beside me; breathless, red-cheeked, she dangles her hands between her knees.

'Have you been here long?' she says.

'Long enough for some,' I tell her.

'I've been out riding.' She looks over to her mother. 'Did you show him the picture, Mum?' she says.

Her mother nods.

'He was full of admiration, Bec.'

'I told you he would be, Mum,' she says.

Pettrie, his hands in his pockets, has come across.

'We ready for off?' he says. He looks at his watch.

'I'm feeling tired.' The girl has shaken her head.

'Don't you want to come?'

'I suppose I ought to, since it's all arranged.'

'Ed's showing her the factory,' Mrs Newman says. 'There might be something there to draw.'

She adds this more coolly, looking at the girl.

'If Ed's arranged it, Bec,' she says.

'I suppose I'd better, then,' she says.

'Don't let me force you, Beccie,' Pettrie says.

'Do you want to come as well?' she asks.

'Maybe another day,' I tell her.

'Mr Freestone's recovering from his fight, Bec,' Pettrie says.

'What fight?'

'He's been fighting Mr Leyland, Bec,' her mother says.

The girl looks over to where Leyland, his shoeless foot in his hand, is showing a hole in his sock to the figures round the fire.

'Did he hit him on the nose?' she says.

'That's right.'

'Johnny's working out at present how to get his own back, Beccie,' Pettrie says.

'I say. How super. I wish I'd been here,' the girl has said.

Pettrie glancing at his watch, has sighed.

'I suppose we better be off,' he says.

'Do you need a coat, Bec?' Mrs Newman says.

'I don't know,' she says. She shakes her head.

'I think you should.'

The girl looks up.

'I shan't be a minute, then,' she says.

Somewhere at the back of the house a door has opened. The dogs come in the room.

Leyland, seeing them, begins to bark; he stoops down, barking; then, shouting, climbs back on his chair.

The blonde girl holds her cheeks and laughs.

The man built like a wrestler begins to laugh as well: his teeth, large, gleaming, are set wide apart inside his mouth. The man with the coal-black eyes is standing by the fire.

'We'd better see you off,' Mrs Newman says. 'Will you come and see Bec off?' she adds.

As we reach the hall she takes my arm.

The small red shooting-brake is drawn up outside the door.

Pettrie, followed by Leyland, comes out from the house. A moment later the girl appears; she's followed by the dogs.

'Bring her back alive, Ed,' Leyland says.

Pettrie, dressed in a suede overcoat, has climbed in behind the wheel. The dogs, barking, leap up at the door.

The girl gets in the other side. She glances out, briefly, towards the porch.

'She's furious at having to go,' Mrs Newman says.

The car moves off: a hand appears on Pettrie's side; it's waved for a moment to and fro.

'Poor old Eddie,' Leyland says.

'Eddie's all right,' Mrs Newman says.

'And poor old Beccie,' Leyland says. He looks at me.

'It's time I was leaving as well,' I say.

'You might have said that sooner,' Leyland says. He steps up, limping, towards the door.

'I'll walk with you. For some of the way,' Mrs Newman says. 'I could do with getting out.'

She steps inside the hall.

'I'll get a coat.'

The woman with the greying, close-cropped hair has appeared at the door of the room opposite the lounge.

'Are you taking calls yet, Liz?' she says.

'I'm out all afternoon,' Mrs Newman says.

'You here again, then, Leyland,' the woman says. 'I thought I heard your inimitable cries.'

The phone has begun to ring in the room behind.

'This is Jacqueline Spencer, my husband's secretary,' Mrs Newman says. 'This is Colin Freestone,' she adds. 'He came up this afternoon to see the picture.'

'What does he think of it?' she says.

She turns to me.

'He likes it on the whole,' she says.

The secretary, nodding, has looked across.

'Where did you put it, in any case?' she says.

'In the library, Mrs Newman says.

'I knocked on the door. There was no reply.'

'That was me, I'm afraid,' Mrs Newman says. 'Not to be disturbed.' She smiles.

'I'd better see to the phone,' the secretary says.

She closes the door. The ringing stops.

'I shan't be a second,' Mrs Newman says.

Leyland reappears at the door of the lounge. He runs his tongue across his lips.

'You're going now?'

'That's right.'

'All being well,' he says, 'we'll meet again.'

His eyes, for a moment, examine mine.

The man built like a wrestler is standing on his head in the room behind. His face, reddened, inverted, is turned towards the door.

The man with the coal-black eyes is visible between his outstretched legs.

'The odds'll be more even then.'

'A dozen of you,' I tell him, 'to one of us.'

'Something of a joker, then.'

'That's right.'

'I should watch out for Mrs Newman, too.'

He glances back, idly, towards the stairs.

'The odds are mounting up.' I smile.

'There've been people like you before,' he says.

'Here?' I ask him. 'Or somewhere else.'

'Wherever the Newmans settle, friend.'

He tries to grimace now himself.

'I should see a doctor about your nose.'

'I shall.'

Mrs Newman appears at the end of the hall. Leyland, seeing her, moves over to the door of the adjoining room.

'I know you're in there,' he says, knocking. 'Sending coded messages to the gestapo bloody chief.'

A dull thumping and a muffled voice answers from the other side.

'I won't go far,' Mrs Newman says.

She's dressed in slacks now, and a fawn coat, with a scarf around her head.

'Tell him everything's under control, then,' Leyland says. He bangs against the door again. 'Do you hear that now?' waiting for this to be confirmed. 'I should be careful what you say,' he adds to me, genially, as if no word of any sort had passed between us. 'I won't tell you where the mike is in the loo, but when you grab hold of it it flushes.'

He goes back in the lounge. The man who was standing on his head is now kneeling on the floor: he's trying to pick up some object between his teeth.

'This is how we spend our week-ends,' Mrs Newman says. 'When Neville's back it's even worse.' She takes my arm.

The dogs, barking, follow us to the porch.

'In. In,' she says. She drives them back. 'Leyland, you see,' she adds, 'has made them worse.'

She closes the door.

'What do you think of that?'

She points to a coat-of-arms above the door.

In the form of a plaque, the design represents three sheaves of wheat surmounted by a stork.

' "Nunc mea, mox hujus, sed postea nescio cujus",' she says reading the inscription. 'Now mine, soon thine, but afterwards I know not whose.' She gestures round. 'When the village was built it stood at the edge of Sherwood Forest. Robin Hood and the bad King John. At least, that's what they told us when we first moved in.'

She takes my arm.

'Latin's not one of your other subjects, then.'

'That's right.'

She laughs. 'Leyland translated it for us when we first arrived.'

'He's been with you, then, some time?' I ask.

'Years,' she says. 'I couldn't count.'

We reach the green.

'And the other two?'

'The one with the staring eyes?' She laughs again. 'That's Groves.'

'And the one built like a tank?'

'That's Fraser.'

'And what do Groves and Fraser do?'

'They work with Nev.' She shakes her head. 'Do you want to see the Hall?' she says.

The village consists, in fact, of several large stone mansions, the most recent at least a century old, the remaining five or six so ancient that the largest, it seems, is falling down: its remaining balustrade is silhouetted against the sky like a set of broken teeth.

The second largest house, with steps leading up to its massive portico, has been converted into offices: a number of cars are parked outside; figures can be seen moving to and fro in several of its windows. The remaining houses have been converted into flats: the driveways and gardens are overgrown; a row of bells shines from a plastic surround by each of the ancient doors.

It's the largest of the houses, it seems, that Mrs Newman is making for. We cross the road beyond the green and enter a narrow lane at the end of which, beside a gate-house, stands a pair of metal gates. On top of one of the gate-posts stands a metal stork, on the other merely a pair of long thin legs and the lower half of a stork's thin body.

The driveway, overgrown, and overhung by trees, bends slowly to our left.

Immediately to our right the house appears, a curving flight of steps running up to its central door which is heavily barred and bolted.

'Too dangerous to go inside,' she says.

The same coat-of-arms of the stork and the sheaves of wheat is carved above the door. Mullioned windows above and on either side run up to the crumbling, soot-encrusted balustrade. Tower-like structures with battlemented crests are set at either end of the black façade.

'The gardens ran down there,' she says.

A series of low mounds and overgrown terraces stretch down towards the heath below. A stone wall separates the gardens from the heath itself.

'If you stand on the steps you can see inside the rooms. The floors have rotted and the ceilings are coming through. They've got panelled walls, you see, like ours.'

We climb the steps; the wind, still fresh, has caught the scarf: she stands on tiptoe, gazing in.

'I'll walk with you to the heath,' she says, finally, when we climb back down.

A path winds down between the mounds. As we reach the wall a man appears from behind the house. He wears a belted raincoat and a trilby hat. He gazes up, in much the same fashion as Mrs Newman had, first at the door and then at the windows. Finally, his hands behind his back, he glances down towards the wall itself.

'If you'll hold my hand,' she says, 'I can climb across.'

At the other side I help her down.

The man, briefly, has removed his hat.

'You sound,' I tell her, 'as though you've walked here quite a lot.'

'Once or twice. I bring the dogs. Sometimes Beccie comes as well.' She says, 'I'm the only one, you see, who likes to walk.'

The path beyond the wall leads down to the road which runs up, circuitously, towards the village. Below us, a group of men in coloured jerseys are playing football on a pitch marked out between the clumps of heather.

'Perhaps one night you could come to dinner.' She glances back. 'I'm sure *some* of the people we have you'd like to meet.'

'I don't mind anyone,' I tell her.

The man in the raincoat has disappeared.

'Not even Leyland?'

'Him least of all,' I say and laugh.

She laughs herself. By the football pitch, for a moment, we watch the game.

'But then you have an advantage, I suppose,' she says.

'In what?'

'In fisticuffs,' she says. She shakes her head.

'I have an advantage,' I tell her, 'in lots of things.'

'It just takes people time to recognize it, I suppose,' she says.

'That's right.'

'You're very cocky.'

'I believe I am.'

She laughs.

There's a shout from the pitch. The ball appears. A figure leaps up. There's a shout of, 'Goal!'

The people standing at the side have clapped.

Across the pitch the man in the trilby hat has reappeared.

'I'd better be getting back,' she says.

A string of riders gallop past.

'Will you come up to the house again?'

'I suppose I shall.'

'One evening, then?' She glances back.

'I'll do my best.'

'I know some days, of course, you're free as well.'

'I'm free nearly all the time,' I say.

She begins to laugh.

'If you walk up to the house I could drive you back.'

'I think I'll take the bus,' I add.

'In that case,' she says, 'we should say good-bye.'

She holds out her hand as we reach the road.

'Our ways divide.'

She shakes my hand.

'Until our next encounter, then.'

There's a sort of arrogance in the way she moves, her hands thrust down in the pockets of her coat, aware of being watched, it seems. Having set off up the heath she doesn't look back.

Her scarf, loose around her shoulders, flutters in the wind.

I sit on the wall at the foot of the heath and wait for the bus. I'm joined a little later by the spectators and some of the players from the football match. At the back of the queue stands the man in the belted raincoat and the trilby hat. He lights a cigarette, his hands cupped to his mouth; then, almost slily, his face still shielded by his hands, he looks at me.

Part Three

I

A yellow beam of light, from one side of the apparatus, meets a blue beam of light projected from the other; the colours coalesce to form an electric green. As the green dissolves the blue beam of light has been changed to red: the colour in the centre of the apparatus, beneath an inverted reflector, changes to a vibrant orange.

'No colour's ever constant,' Kendal says.

Coloured discs revolve on either side, and from a third aperture below is projected an amorphous shadowed mass that changes its shape rhythmically in the centre of the coloured beams.

Kendal is a small man, slight; he has dark, almost melancholic features, thin and sharp, the eyes large and full of liquid, glistening: hands like tiny claws manipulate the knobs and switches.

'When the thing's complete there'll be a dozen beams, each projected through a multicoloured disc, each disc revolving,' he he tells me, 'at a different speed. You can do the same thing, too, with the revolving form. The thing's invisible, you see.' He switches it off.

The beams disappear.

We're standing in the dark.

He feels behind him, against the wall.

'You can even switch it off,' he adds, 'in cycles. So the form dematerializes slowly; or, conversely, you can let it come on as quickly as you like.'

The room, suddenly, is full of light.

The apparatus, with its switchboard, stands on a table in the centre of the room.

Other shapes, in metal and plastic, in wood and hardboard,

partly dismantled or in the process of erection, stand on the other tables, or on the floor. The walls are festooned with wires, metal strips, and with racks containing welding, soldering and metal cutting tools.

'Is this the students' work, or yours?'

'Theirs. My own,' he says, 'is over there.'

On a box, in the corner of the room, stands what appears to be an Easter egg; it's made of glass, its surface pitted with tiny scratches. Inside, distorted by the glass, is an assemblage of glistening rods and plates. A cable runs from the box to a plug on the wall.

'If you turn off the light I'll switch it on.'

He pulls the box out to the centre of the room.

'Hold onto your hat,' he says, and laughs.

I turn off the light.

For a moment the room is dark.

Then, faintly, a reddish glow appears. A low humming tone emerges from the bowl: the light, as if fractured, moves in odd patterns across the walls; alternating electronic notes, long, then short, oscillating, then abrupt, accompany the movement of the light itself. The colours change; the original red disintegrates; a kaleidoscopic frieze of colours blends slowly in the air around my head; a second, contrasting rhythm of electronic notes begins. The colours darken. In the bowl itself, with a sharper intensity of light, the assemblage of metal rods and plates revolves slowly, first one way then the other.

The other objects in the room appear to move; it's as if, suddenly, they've acquired their own momentum. The oscillation of light and shadow corresponds, it seems, with the rhythm of the electronic tones.

The sounds grow more complex; the colours disintegrate; one side of the room has turned bright blue; the centre of the room is yellow. The air around my head turns green.

Kendal, too, like some strange component of the machine, is moving round the room himself; at odd moments he disappears in shadow; at others, only his features are alight, the sharp nose and cheekbones, the gloomy, melancholic eyes. Then, like a block of wood, he fuses with the tables, the other assemblages, the tools, the walls.

'What do you think of it?' he says.

'I don't know where I am,' I tell him.

'Still here, I hope,' he says. 'I'll switch it off.'

He crosses to the plug.

The light, abruptly, disappears.

The sound has stopped.

I turn on the light beside the door. The room seems smaller, more compact, lifeless; some debris of the light itself.

'The idea is to get three or four of these.' He indicates the glittering bowl. 'The variables, at the moment, are limited. And limitation in a thing like this is definitely a sign of impotence,' he adds.

'If the movements are definable, however many variables you have, the limitations,' I tell him, 'will be always there.'

'That's the trouble with this kind of art.' He shakes his head. 'Like the impressionists with that tedious, repetitious brush-stroke: the texture of the thing, in a way, can never change.'

'What does Wilcox think?'

He looks across. 'He's threatened to close us down.' He begins to smile. 'What's an artist need with an electric wire?'

He picks up one of the soldering tools.

'"What's this, then? For mending somebody's fuse?"' He runs his small, mouse-like hands across the bench. 'When I tell him we're in the post-art age he goes a sort of red. "What're thee, then, Kendal? A bloody mechanic? While there's a tube o' paint, a canvas and a brush you'll not say art's dead in my bloody college."'

Kendal has a small moustache; he might, quite easily, I imagine, have been a dentist, a locksmith, the inventor of some improbable toy. The bench we're standing at is littered with metal tubes, with wire, with electronic circuits, with alternators, electric motors, bulbs, plugs, reflectors, pliers; a welder's visor, a metal grinder and a machine for moulding plastic sheets stand on an adjoining bench against the wall.

'Wilcox,' he says, 'is a kind of fossil. Preserved by the remoteness of the air up here. Provincial life.' He waves his hand. 'He comes in of an evening with a dustpan and a brush. An hour, sometimes, before the cleaner's due. If I don't lock everything away I'm sure, next morning, I'd find it gone.'

'He's invited me to dinner.'

'He never has.'

'Tonight.'

'He's coming here?'

'To pick me up.'

He begins to pick up pieces from the benches, putting them hastily in cupboards by the wall.

'I couldn't find the house, he says, alone.'

'I better get these away before he comes. He's usually at home on Monday nights.' He adds. 'That's why I'm here. They'd be in the dustbin if I left them out.'

I go out to the hall. The door to Wilcox's office is standing open: it's half-past six. Two cleaners, with mops and buckets, are working round the desk. On the wall, beyond the desk, is a rack of bottles, small, frosted, like the ones for holding acids in a chemistry lab.

'*You've got here, then?*'

Wilcox is standing in the passage that leads out from the hall to the back of the college.

'I've just parked it in the yard.'

He looks over to the office. At the same time as he sees the cleaners he sees the light in Kendal's sculpture room.

'By God: what's happening there?' He strides across.

Kendal, it seems, has reconnected one of his machines; there's a whirring sound from inside the room and a familiar purplish glow appears within the open door itself.

'That's not Kendal running up current, then?'

He steps inside the room.

'What's going on in here, then? A mothers' meeting, is it, or can anybody join?'

The two women cleaners in the office have doused their cigarettes. Mops in hand, they saunter to the hall.

'Do you know how much we pay in electric bills?'

A fainter, less challenging voice has answered from inside.

'There's not just this, you know.'

The purplish light goes out.

'There's the heaters in the life room. There's the lighting for every evening class. There's the electricity for the kiln. There's money pouring out of here like water.'

Some object, it seems, has fallen over.

The Principal's figure reappears. He rubs his arm. There's a slight cut above his brow.

He limps across. The light in Kendal's room goes on; the cleaners, relighting their cigarettes, turn back towards the Principal's office.

'Just pouring out,' he says. 'The electric here.'

He gestures to the yard.

'If you wait by the car, I shan't be long.' He goes to the stairs. 'They're not expecting me tonight, you know.'

His voice, a moment later, echoes from the rooms above.

'*And what's going on in here? A mothers' meeting, is it, or can anybody join?*'

'I thought once,' Kendal says, emerging from his room, 'of electrifying the handle to the door. I could always have found an excuse, afterwards. Not to mention being able to justify the expense,' he adds.

He looks to the stairs.

'As it is, the sod's too devious by half.'

He locks the door.

'That, at least, I've changed. Once locked there's nobody else but me can go inside.' He calls to the cleaners. 'You can give me a miss tonight, my dears.'

'Won't Mr Wilcox notice, then?' Their cigarettes alight they sidle to the door.

'He's taking Mr Freestone to dinner, then.'

'Ooh,' they say. They look across.

'I'm not saying who's paying, though,' he says.

He goes to the glass doors that open to the street. He waves goodnight.

'I'll go while the going's good.'

He disappears.

'Is he taking you out, or going to his home?' the cleaners say.

'His home.'

'Tell us what it's like.'

'I will.'

'Nobody's ever been inside.'

I go out to the yard. The Armstrong Siddeley is parked at the foot of the steps. Hendrick's sports car has already gone. The lights are out in the modelling shed.

I try the boot, find it locked; try the doors: they're locked as well.

I light a cigarette: he appears in the doorway after a little while, silhouetted briefly against the light inside.

'Not smoking are you?'

'I've stubbed it out.'

'I don't like smoke, you know, inside the car.'

He produces from his pocket a bunch of keys.

'By God, the money that's wasted in a place like this.'

He gets inside; the lights come on.

'Jump in,' he says. 'It won't take long.'

The car smells like his office; a stale smell of senna pods and weakened tea.

'They don't make them any more.' He taps the car. 'Not like the ones, you know, they have today.'

The engine starts. The car moves off.

We turn into the street.

I lose track of the route after a little while: the road dips down towards the valley, then turns off, it seems, towards the west.

Buildings loom up on either side; after a while it appears we're driving through a tunnel. Trees enclose the road; an occasional light flies past.

'Look at that, then,' Wilcox says.

He taps his finger at the petrol gauge.

'There's a garage on the road up here.'

His voice is quieter now, his face lit up by the reflected glow from the lights outside.

An illuminated garage sign appears some time later in the road ahead; the car turns in towards the pumps; the window's lowered. Wilcox, with a strangled ejaculation, puts out his head. He calls to the attendant: the petrol, after a moment, flows into the tank behind.

I can hear it gurgling inside the car.

'That's a nuisance.'

Wilcox, stooping forward, is tapping at his chest.

'I've come without my purse.'

'You better tell him before he puts it in.'

'It's already in. God damn and blast.'

He taps his pockets once again.

'It's not in that. Nor that. I could have sworn . . .' He brings out a handkerchief, a pair of gloves: having looked at them briefly, shaking the latter out, he puts them back. He brings out a wallet. 'Not in that.'

The attendant, his face perspiring, appears at Wilcox's side.

'That's two pounds, twenty pence,' he says. 'If you count the oil as well.'

He passes inside a can of oil.

'I got that to put in when I got back home.' Wilcox holds the can out for my inspection. 'It's not worth looking at the dipstick here.' He lowers his voice. 'These attendants, you know, can never tell. Say you need a thing when it's really full. I look in the garage, you know, when I'm by myself.' His voice is harsh, almost inaudible, confiding. 'You haven't got a couple of pounds or so yourself?'

I reach inside my pocket.

Something tells me to shake my head.

I bring the money out.

'That's very good of you,' he says. He adds, 'If you've got a tip, you know, it goes down well.'

I pass another coin across.

'I usually call in here,' he says. 'They give you good service, if you treat them well.'

The attendant's face has disappeared; the car moves off.

'Cold tonight.' He winds the window.

The darkness of the road returns; I'm reminded, briefly, of Kendal's oscillating glow: a pair of white, wooden gates, however, materialize after a while where the headlights of the car converge.

'Be a chap. There's a catch at the top. Just push them back.'

I get out, step round the front of the car, find the catch: the gates slide into gravel the other side.

'You need to push.'

His head sticks out from the side of the car.

'A bit harder,' he says. 'But mind the wood.'

I can feel it splinter beneath my hand; I wonder whether to uproot it from its hinge: one side of the gate is stuck.

'The knack's to lift it,' Wilcox says.

I hoist it up: it slides across the gravel; the car comes past.

'If you could just close them now, old man.' His head leans out. 'There're not many people come past at night. But it's best, you see, to have them shut.'

I lift them back.

'And set the catch.'

I set the catch.

As I climb back in he says, 'It's a longish drive. The house, you see's, in a kind of wood.'

The trunks of trees, like sentinels, glide slowly past.

A house appears, low down, made up of white plaster-work and wood. A light, fainter than the beams of the car, glows inside a lattice window. The roof, it appears, is made of thatch.

'Not many people know we're here.'

The engine stops.

'The house, I mean. But for the gates, you'd never tell.'

He gets out from the car.

'We don't often have a fire, in any case. A cold shower on a morning's a damn good thing. A walk in the woods. There's nothing wrong,' he says, 'with God's good gifts.' He swings his hand. 'All the tools of existence you'll find round here.'

The inside of the house is colder than the air outside. Even Wilcox, after opening the door, has clapped his hands.

'We're here, my dear,' he shouts, and adds, 'Thatch keeps you warmer in the winter, cool in summer, and lasts, in my view, a damn sight longer than any stone.'

Beams loom blackly above our heads: whitewashed walls, stained by soot, enclose the hall on either side. From the door at the end of the hall appears a light. It's held by a woman with whitish hair.

'Here's young Freestone,' Wilcox says. 'Not too late for the food, I hope?'

'No,' the woman says. 'Just right.'

No sooner has she appeared, however, than the woman turns and, with the light, vanishes into the room beyond.

'Straight ahead: no dithering,' Wilcox says as if, by the warmth of this encounter, I might, quite easily, be over-whelmed. 'The food awaits us, lad. Anon. Anon.'

Three places have been set at a bare, rectangular table, one at its centre, halfway along one side, and the two others, some considerable distance away from it, at either end.

'Food. Food. That's what a man craves for in the evening,' Wilcox says.

The woman, as if her mission has been completed, has disappeared. There's a faint tapping then a kind of groan from a room at the back of the house.

'Take a seat,' Wilcox says. He's already found his own place at one end of the table.

He tucks a napkin in the collar of his shirt.

'I should sit in the middle, old man. Half-way between the two. I think that's best.'

He hums to himself a moment. There's a further faint tapping from the back of the house.

'Don't want to wash your hands?'

'No thanks.'

He gestures round. 'You won't find a modern house like this. Dedication. Art. Nowadays it's nothing but bricks and regulations; trade unions,' he adds, 'and how much they can get. In the old days they built a place for living in, not for seeing how much they could squeeze you for. Just look at this.'

He knocks his fist, sharply, against the table. It too, like the beams, is black with age. Apart from a spoon set in each place, a salt cellar and two glasses, one in front of Wilcox's place and one in front of mine, the table itself is completely bare. The light immediately above it comes from a yellowish shade. I can barely, in the shadows, make out the shape of Wilcox's face.

'Fancy water?'

I shake my head.

'The wife doesn't drink. Liquids. At night. They're not much good.'

The door has opened. A tray appears. Standing on it are a metal jug, three plates, and a metal scoop. The woman's head, white-haired, manifests itself beyond.

'Here we are. Worth waiting for is that.'

A faint cloud of steam, almost incandescent despite its faintness, rises from the jug.

'Stew.'

'Soup.'

The two words collide, it seems, above my head. I can imagine the looks which, in the shadows, converge from either end of the blackened table.

'The grocers were closed,' the woman says.

'Closed?'

'By the time I got there.'

'No idea of service. Not nowadays,' Wilcox says. 'Open a couple of hours they think they've done enough.'

The metal scoop, after some further hesitation, is inserted in the jug.

A thin, watery liquid is lifted out.

'No finer sustenance came from God's good elements,' Wilcox says.

The woman's bowl is filled, then his.

Finally, scraping the scoop in the bottom of the jug, she turns to mine.

The liquid filters in.

'Potato. Grown in the ground outside that window there.' Wilcox, it appears, is drinking his. There's the slurping of liquid against his lip, a smacking of the lip against the spoon; then comes a kind of gulp and a rasping sigh. 'What better sustenance could you find than that.'

The woman, in shadow till now, stoops, briefly, towards the light; dark, cavernous eyes look out, sharply, first at Wilcox and, then, less feverishly, at me.

'Could you pass the salt?'

'Salt?'

'In front of you.'

She's already taken her place at the end opposite to Wilcox. Apart from sliding the salt along the blackened wood there's no means of conveying it to her other than by getting up.

I push back the chair, pick the cellar up and take it down the table.

I wonder, for a moment, whether I might take it back.

The white grains settle on her soup. Without waiting for the cellar I go back to my chair.

No sooner have I sat down than Wilcox smacks his lips again.

'It could do with a bit of salt. You're right.'

He looks at me: I can see the two shadows where his eyes belong and the bold protuberance of his nose between.

'Be a chap.'

I get up from the chair again.

I reclaim the cellar, take it down the table, wait for Wilcox to use it then take it back. Passing my own bowl I shower it with several grains: I replace it in front of the woman's plate.

There's a kind of groan. I wait. No other sound, however, follows it. I go back to the chair.

'Minerals; carbohydrates: the potato's got almost everything,' Wilcox says. 'With that and milk you could live a long and exceedingly healthy life,' he adds.

The woman herself, apart from an identical smacking of the lips, makes no comment of any sort at all.

Only now, accustomed to the gloom, do I see the pictures hanging on the wall, their subject-matter indistinguishable in the feeble light. A fireplace is overhung by a wooden beam; in a metal grate stand several blocks of wood, unlit, above them a metal cauldron attached to a chain which disappears into the shadows of the chimney overhead.

Apart from two chairs, half-upholstered, set either side of the unlit fire, there's no other furniture in the room at all.

'Damn cold.'

I nod my head.

'Outside.' He gestures round. 'Appreciate it,' he says, 'when you get in here. It's the straw, you know. Not like your modern tiles.'

A spoon is scraped round the bottom of a bowl: from the opposite end of the table comes a kind of groan; lips are smacked. A chair scrapes back.

'Finished, Freestone?' Wilcox says. His own spoon, as if in illustration, he rattles in the bowl. 'One large potato, per person, per day, fresh from the garden: this nation wouldn't be what it is today. You'd see some difference, then. You would.'

The woman reappears, her bowl in her hand, moving down to the opposite end; she picks up Wilcox's plate, takes mine, sets them on the tray with the ladle and the empty jug and then, like some manifestation of Kendal's light-machine, vanishes abruptly.

'Heavy meals late at night.' The Principal shakes his head. 'No good. Digestive juices: they never get a chance. They need to recuperate, you know, themselves. Need the rest. What sort of stomach do you have if the juices are champing up food all night as well?' He smacks his lips. 'Treat your stomach right, the rest will follow. Good digestion, Freestone, is the key to a well-directed life. If you don't digest things well everything else, you'll find, will go astray: work, concentration, application, anything you care to mention.'

My hands, it seems, have begun to tremble.

My teeth, a moment later, begin to chatter.

'Take Kendal, for example. These weird ideas he has. They come, primarily, from an unbalanced diet. His juices, as a consequence, get out of hand; they send garbled, or over-sensationalized messages to the brain: the brain reacts: instead of an artist, modelling with his clay, or painting at his canvas, you get a man who ends up making electric bells. And he's not aware. He's not aware. When I talk to him he thinks I'm mad: you can see his stomach inwardly revolting. What it sends to the brain the brain can't understand. It obeys whatever directions the stomach gives, but in essence the brain is as confused as Kendal is himself: after all, we are, first and foremost, a living body: and the reason that we live is because we eat. Only by consuming certain elements of our environment do we survive: if those elements are in any way unbalanced then our existence itself becomes unbalanced. We can only put things right by a conscious act of will.'

The door once again has opened: the tray appears, the whitened head beyond.

'Kendal comes from the new brigade: the let-it-happen boys. They think life's made up of all sorts of instincts: sit back and let it happen. You can see it in his face.'

The tray, clutched in a pair of claw-like hands, is set down once more at the end of the table. It contains three apples, three plates, two knives and a piece of cheese.

'He doesn't realize that art, like life, is a conscious act of will. It comes from the stomach: it needs direction. Direction implies discipline: discipline implies skill, skill implies tradition, taste, tuition. In other words, in a nutshell, it demands a school of art.'

One plate, one apple, one knife are carried down to the end of the table. A second plate and an apple are brought to me. The third apple remains with the woman at the opposite end.

'Like potato, cheese is one of life's organic foods. One of the mind's ingredients,' Wilcox says. His knife, in anticipation, is already raised.

I get up, pick up the cheese, and carry it down to the opposite end; the woman herself, for a moment, appears surprised. She gives a groan; there's a rasping in her throat: she moans.

Wilcox, as if alarmed, has coughed the other end.

'No. No. Go ahead. Ladies first. Even if they haven't put in a day's hard work,' he says.

The woman cuts a piece. She lays it on her plate, beside the apple. Having put down the knife beside her plate she makes no other kind of move at all.

I carry the cheese to the other end.

'Here it comes: life's providence,' Wilcox says.

He takes over half of the remaining lump.

The remnant I carry back to where my apple stands, knife-less, beneath the light.

I rub my hands.

'No need to peel the skin. Half the goodness lies beneath the skin. People don't realize that, you know. The same with potatoes: a good wash, that's all they need. And often,' Wilcox adds, 'not even that.'

The cheese is hard.

'Fresh cheese,' he says, 'of course, has not had time to conglomerate.' He chews his apple. 'By conglomerate I mean, not had time to synthesize. The elements are not, as it were, in equilibrium. They need time, like all things, to settle down. To achieve harmony. To acquaint themselves with one another.'

A soft, hesitant munching comes from the opposite end.

'That's why we're here. A new element in the college. It demands acquaintance of all the rest. It needs time, as it were, to conglomerate.'

I feel now he's speaking, not so much for my benefit, as for that of the woman at the other end; it might, for all I know, be a nightly homily which passes one way along that blackened table whenever Wilcox comes home from work.

'The same principle applies to a work of art; each part is separate yet an integral part of all the rest.'

'All for one, and one for all.'

The room, the sound of munching apart, grows quiet.

I'm aware of the silence, too, outside the house.

'Reality disintegrates,' Wilcox says, 'in direct proportion to the amount of synthetic foods that people nowadays are encouraged to consume. The last war, for instance, the greatest catastrophe the world has ever known, was a direct consequence of certain elements on the continent eating too much bread.'

I look across: the eyes, faintly, have glistened in the light. The familiar image of Wilcox fades away: it might, quite easily, be another man who's sitting there. I'm reminded again of the strange distortion of objects effected by Kendal's eccentric lights.

'Too much carbohydrate, for instance, can affect the brain in any number of ways. Not only,' Wilcox says, 'does the body grow fat, but it uses up energy in a way which nature never intended. The history of bread-eating peoples, for instance, would indicate that strife, particularly inter-denominational strife, is a natural consequence of the consumption of too much bread.'

'What about the Chinese?'

'The Chinese have rice, which is just as bad.'

My feet, in reaction to the cold, have banged against the floor; even the chair has begun to tremble.

'Should we light the fire?'

'The fire?'

I indicate the grate.

'We don't have a fire in there.' He smiles; his teeth, discoloured, glitter in the light. 'Except at Christmas, mind. We sometimes light it then.' He rubs his hands. 'There's a fire in the other room, in any case,' he says.

He clears his throat. His cheese has gone; he clatters his knife against his plate.

The woman rises.

As she passes round the table she collects the knives; she piles the plates, puts the apple cores on the tray and with the empty cheese plate carries them out.

'We can go in the other room for toddy. The good lady,' Wilcox says, 'will bring it in.'

He pushes back his chair; we rise. I cross over to the door.

Wilcox, with a grunt, has followed me through. His shoulder catches mine as he pushes past.

'Straight ahead.'

The door directly opposite is closed.

'I shan't be a second, old man.'

He disappears; his footsteps fade away to the back of the house.

I try the door handle.

I turn the handle, press my weight against it and feel it give.

Somewhere at the back of the house a chain is pulled.

Wilcox, his head bowed, has reappeared.

'Anything the matter?'

I press against the door.

'It's stuck.'

'Probably locked.'

He rattles a bunch of keys inside his pocket. He makes no attempt to try the door himself.

He fits a key: the door swings back.

'Of course, a night like this, you don't need a fire. The air being fresh,' he says, 'it's more in the way of a stimulant than anything else.'

A faint glow erupts; a yellowish shade is mounted on a plastic bowl.

'Heat, I always think, discourages circulation. I'm sure there must be a connexion between the incidence of heart disease and the prevalence of central-heating and open fires. In the old days, the fire was used primarily for cooking, little else. Vigorous exercise was the answer to people who felt the cold, you know. That,' he says, 'and work itself.'

The fireplace, in confirmation of these remarks, is standing empty. Made of brick it contains a rusted grate that appears never to have seen either coal or wood. Two chairs, identical to the ones in the other room, are set on either side. On a sideboard stands a photograph and, beneath a casement window, a narrow desk.

On the wall are hung a number of pictures in the style of the English post-impressionists, the simplified shapes reduced to an almost illustrative flatness: a nude, a landscape, the interior of a room.

The photograph on the sideboard is that of a young woman, her hair brushed back, her eyes starting, dark, piercing, with an almost maniacal intentness.

'Daughter. Married,' Wilcox says.

He sits down in one of the chairs and slaps his legs.

'It's good to get home of an evening. What d'you think?'

Expecting no answer, he doesn't look up.

'Home, too, is related to digestion in a way that people, on the whole, don't understand. Family life, that of husband, wife and child, depends almost entirely, if it's to achieve any kind of harmony, on the balance of nutrients that each member of the household gets. Once an imbalance in the intake of nutrients occurs – one member of the family eating out of tune, as it were, with all the rest – it's like an orchestra with a discordant member: the emotional harmony of the whole of the family is, quite markedly, disturbed.'

The door has opened; the tray, clutched between two claw-like hands, manifests itself again.

The whitened head appears. The tray's set down, cautiously, beside the empty hearth.

'Sugar, too, is another enemy. Tooth decay, in certain native tribes, for instance, is virtually unknown. So is heart-disease,' he says.

Having released the tray and straightened, the woman glances anxiously at Wilcox, sees there, evidently, no further desire maturing, and turns quietly to the door.

'Would you like a chair?' I ask.

She pauses for a moment, confirms from my expression that it's her and not Wilcox who's been spoken to, and, after a further moment's indecision, glances over at Wilcox then slowly shakes her head.

'I've one or two things to do,' she says.

The door, after a moment's hesitation, is quietly closed.

A jug and two glasses are standing on the tray.

'Fruit-juice toddy,' Wilcox says.

He half-fills one of the glasses, sips it, then pours a slightly smaller quantity into the other.

He leans across, holds the glass out, motions for me to taste it, then, nodding, waits for my remark.

'What kind of fruit?'

'Citrus.'

He sips his own.

'Unsweetened. Natural juices only, mind. With citrus,' he adds, 'you get the sun.'

He leans back in his chair.

He sighs.

'I thought of inviting Kendal once. He's been at the college, you know, two years. Studied in London. I don't think, unless you feel someone's sympathetic, you should invite them to your home. After all, invitations, like disagreeable food, can be a matter of digestion.'

He sips his drink again.

'One of the reasons you got the job.'

'The food.'

'No, no. Well-built. Thick-set. Can knock them into shape. It's what they understand round here.' He waves his arm. 'All art's related, you know, to a particular place. You wouldn't get Siennese painting, for example, going on in Florence. Nor would you find Constable painting his great landscapes in the middle of Madrid. It's what these let-it-happen boys can never understand. Full of abstractions because they're easy to transmit. Real art comes from particular places, from particular people doing particular things.'

He presses the glass against his lips.

'That's one of the reasons I asked you here.' He takes a sip. 'It's a question of morality, you see, as much as anything else.'

I look across.

'Of deciding what you want from life, determining its value, then pursuing it. The same principle,' he says, 'that you apply to painting. Or to any of the arts, if it comes to that.'

He finishes the glass, leans to the jug, half-fills it again and takes a sip.

'You've been to the Newmans', I understand.'

He looks across.

'Mr Newman's been a great benefactor since his daughter came to the college. He's agreed to put money into one or two schemes I have.' He says, 'I can't mention them, of course. As yet. When they come to fruition you'll be the first to hear. The rest of the staff, that is, as well.'

He clears his throat.

'I wouldn't want to jeopardize these plans.' He shows his teeth. 'By a too intimate relationship with the family. I mean, by communicating to them ideas about art which might, as it were, contradict certain attitudes they may have formed themselves.'

'Has he offered,' I ask him, 'to buy your work?'

'No, no. It's the college I'm talking about,' he says. 'If we want to attract a better kind of student, and recruit, as a consequence, a better kind of staff, we require facilities to do it with. What we have to offer at present isn't adequate by any standards. For instance, in the study of the Old Masters we have scarcely anything at all to offer the aspiring student. Verrocchio and Donatello worked essentially from studios, you understand, where every facility for the student was provided by the master; in this age of diminishing public patronage it's encouraging to find, as it were, a private patron; someone who's prepared to accept the master's insight into things and provide the material wherewithal with which, given good fortune, he can put his particular disciplines into practice.'

The jug is empty. He gazes at his glass.

'It's not often the opportunity provided by Mr Newman arises in the Arts. Usually assistance of this kind is given to the Sciences; it would be unfortunate if someone were to persuade him that the Fine Arts aren't Fine, for instance, any longer, but responsible for turning out devices not unlike the ones that Kendal has. Mr Newman agrees with me that art is to do with the observation of real, verifiably present life. He doesn't go in at all for these fashionable abstractions.'

He looks across.

'I only thought I'd mention it. Not in the way of a warning, you understand. More in the nature of an invitation. A plea for help. The beneficiaries, after all, will be the college's future students.'

He gestures round.

'What do you think of the paintings, then?'

I get up from the chair. I stamp my feet. I bang one hand against the other.

'You haven't got a drop of Scotch?'

'Scotch?'

'Anything to warm you up.'

'My dear Freestone,' he says, 'I'm warm already.'

I bang my arms against my chest.

'Central heating: it's what I've been saying about circulation. A night like this, a meal inside you.' He waves one arm above his head. 'You see how that college undermines you. I suppose you've got the same sort of thing at home as well.'

He gets up quickly, crosses the room, and pulls open a door which, until now, I haven't noticed. From the shadows he hauls out what, at first sight, appears to be an electric fire. He sets it down beside the hearth.

It's a metal box. A large red cross is painted on the lid.

'We keep our medical concoctions, you know, in here.'

Stooping to the light he rummages about.

'Here it is.' He holds up a bottle. 'A drop of this'll set you right.' He reads the label. ' "*For all colds, flu, or disturbances caused by inclement weather.*" '

He takes my glass.

A stream of yellowish-looking liquid is poured inside.

'Drink that, and you won't complain about the cold again.'

He watches me avidly as I take it from his hand.

'Don't gulp it. You can savour the taste as well as enjoy the benefit,' he says.

I swallow it down. There's a bitter, acrid taste against my tongue, then a burning sensation somewhere in the throat. A moment later it's as if my stomach's being removed: there's a tearing, convulsive sensation somewhere in my chest.

'I can almost taste it now myself.'

He replaces the bottle inside the box.

I begin to gasp.

'We brew it up from fungi, and from toadstools you can find in almost any wood. You've got to know which ones to pick. Some native toadstools, of course, are toxic. One bite, you know, and you can drop down dead.'

He carries the box back to the cupboard in the wall.

'Nature provides its remedy for almost anything,' he says.

He comes back to his chair; there's a burning sensation now around my neck; it spreads out to my arms and then, more certainly, with a sudden rush, towards my legs.

'Brandy, you see, which has the same effect, is an intoxicant. You could say, in the end, it does more harm than good. But that,' he gestures to the cupboard door, 'you could drink as often as you like. You could enjoy it as a beverage, as well as a remedy for feeling cold. You've probably caught it in the modelling room. If the models didn't demand those ridiculous fires they'd all feel the benefit, I'm sure of that.'

I sink down in the chair. Movement now, except from a horizontal position, seems virtually impossible. I can only see Wilcox through a kind of a haze.

'What I might have checked was how long we've had that remedy in stock. You're supposed to renew it every year. It must be three or four years old, at least. On the other hand,' he says, and looks across, 'it's had more time to mature than most. It's always a benefit, with these medicines, if they're never rushed. Life nowadays,' he adds, 'prohibits remedies, of course, like that. It's got to be a needle, or a pill, or rushing off to some hospital bed. In the old days nature made the pace; now we're governed, like Kendal's devices, by electric current and little else.'

I'm aware of some further conversation from the other side of the empty fireplace; then, some time later, I find I'm standing in a studio. Its walls are white, a white curtain is drawn across a skylight immediately above my head; to one side a flight of steps leads up to a wooden gallery on which are stacked a number of canvases, their sides lettered and numbered like the spines of books.

Wilcox has evidently gone to some trouble to bring me here; I have a vague recollection of keys being turned, bolts being drawn and chains removed; of lights being switched on brighter than those inside the house; we've crossed, to get here, a stretch of garden: the night air alone, as if fulfilling Wilcox's claims for it, has – relatively – brought me to my senses.

'It's really why I asked you back. It's not everybody, you know, I let in here.'

An old type of studio easel on castors occupies the centre of the floor. A rectangular-shaped canvas, set vertically, and almost as tall as Wilcox himself, is covered by a paint-flecked sheet.

'Most of my compositions I keep up here.' He gestures to the gallery overhead. 'This is the one I'm working on at present.'

He removes the sheet.

Several overalled figures are standing round a hole: there's a pile of sand, a cement-machine, a lorry loaded with bricks, a telephone pole, a road, made up of cobbles, a house, with a man standing at a door and a woman at the gate, stooping to a pram, and, in the sky, an aeroplane is passing by, leaving behind it a streak of vapour. On the branch of a tree which frames the picture a bird is standing with its beak wide open; on closer inspection, amongst the leaves, I can make out a nest containing three as yet unfinished eggs.

'I'm just doing those,' he says. 'Blackbird's. The blue matches the blue of the mother's dress.'

Faint lines on the barer patches of the canvas indicate that the picture itself has been squared off; each workman is carefully posed against the hole, the stitches on each overall drawn in, the wedges of clay beneath each boot, the rime of dirt beneath each nail. One of the workmen smokes a cigarette: '*Fight Cancer*', the lettering on a poster, is outlined on a wall beyond his head.

'It's a scene from contemporary life,' he says. 'Nothing you could get in a photograph, or on a film. The composition, as you can see, is a conception in itself: it's all determined, nothing arbitrary, or accidental. There's nothing *electric*, you know, in that.'

A pool of water has collected amongst the cobbles: it reflects not only the leaves of the tree, the bird, the face of one of the workmen, but the aeroplane itself.

'A symbol of life and death.'

He gestures to the canvas.

'The puddle?'

He shakes his head.

He points irritably to the workman with the cigarette: his head, I realize, is reflected in the puddle.

'The bird gives out a warning.'

His finger, short, square-ended, hovers above the open beak.

'The messenger.'

His finger moves up towards the plane.

'Between heaven and earth. While up above.' He looks across. 'The harbinger of death.'

'The plane.'

'The bringer of catastrophe.' He nods his head.

'It looks like a passenger plane to me.'

'It's a symbol, merely, of domination from the air,' he says.

Perhaps the distillation of toadstools and fungi moves into a second cycle of effect.

I begin to smile. I can see Wilcox's face begin to redden.

'A picture within a picture. You can't get that, except with art. There's not any fortuitous effect anywhere in that picture. It's all measured out. The product of the will.'

He staggers back, his foot caught in the sheet; he drags it out from between his legs.

'You'll find it coming back. When these let-it-happen boys have had their day. You'll find the old values coming through. You'll find the public growing disheartened by these ephemeral, fortuitous effects that people like Kendal, for instance, try to produce. They'll come back to pictures by people who put down exactly what they see, but in compositions created by good taste, tradition, by the instinct of the eye and hand, and by the intelligence which is the natural and inevitable outcome of a good digestion.'

Only seconds later, it seems, we're standing in the yard outside; I can see the house several feet away, the casement windows, the plaster and timber-work, the edge of the thatch and have a vague recollection, before we finally emerge, of Wilcox, panting slightly, climbing to the gallery and bringing down several of the canvases stacked up there. I have an impression of other workmen gathered round a hole; of fishermen at a quay unloading fish; of a male figure with an arm upraised, one leg forward, one leg back; of soldiers, with tears in their eyes, gathered round a grave: now, however, Wilcox is looking at his watch. A barn-like structure behind us has just been locked.

'You'll have to be going,' he says. 'It's getting late. The last bus goes, I should think, in twenty minutes. You'll just have time to walk to the stop.'

'Aren't you going to drive me back?'

'I've just put the car away, old man,' he says.

I've no recollection of this at all; certainly the car has vanished from the front of the house.

'The bus gets you there in half an hour. It's a damn good service, I'll grant you that.'

He turns to the drive.

'I'd better say goodnight. To your wife,' I tell him.

'Oh, I'll say it for you,' he says. 'She'll be in bed.'

I splash through several puddles as we walk to the gate.

'I'll leave you here,' he says. 'You can see the road. Straight ahead, then over to your right.'

'How far's the stop?'

'About a mile.'

He slaps my back.

'It was good of you to come.'

As I turn to the gate he suddenly calls, 'Is it true, by the way, about your wife?'

His figure's several feet away, scarcely visible beneath the trees.

'This hospital she's in: it's not one of these for mental cases, then?'

'That's right.'

'You mean she's mad.'

'More sane,' I tell him, 'than you or I.'

'She's not been certified, then?'

'She volunteered.'

'We should have been informed.' He rubs his face. He comes no closer in the dark. 'A thing like that: you can never tell.'

'She's well looked after, on the whole,' I say.

'I mean the staff we employ at the college,' he says. 'It reflects on us, a thing like that. We've a responsibility to the students, after all,' he adds.

'I'll see,' I tell him, 'what the hospital says.'

'I'd have a word with them, if I were you.'

'I will.'

'And explain the situation. They'll understand. They've dealt with cases like this before.'

'I'll get onto them,' I tell him, 'right away.'

'Mention my name,' he says, 'it could do the trick.'

His feet crunch off along the drive.

I turn to the road.

I find no stop at all that night. I pass occasional trees, animals in fields, an empty house. Finally, I reach the garage. The lights are out, the doors are closed.

I hitch a lift on a passing lorry. Dawn is breaking by the

time I reach the town; perhaps the toadstool and fungi distillation moves on into some third and more devastating cycle of effect: as soon as I reach my room I fall asleep and a day and another night have passed before I wake again.

2

'I thought I might drop by.'

She's wearing a black fur hat and a black wool coat, standing at the door, a parcel in her hand.

'A man with a red moustache let me in downstairs.'

She holds up the parcel.

'I've just been shopping.'

'Come in,' I say. I step aside.

In her other hand is a leather bag; it's like a pouch, with a metal clasp.

'It's hard to find.' She looks around. 'But you've something of a view,' she says.

She crosses to the window.

'Isn't that the village you can see from here?'

'That's right.'

'With a pair of binoculars you could see the house.'

'I've never tried.'

'I'm sure you haven't.'

She turns to smile.

'I got your address, you know, from Bec.'

'Does she know you're here?'

She shakes her head.

'Would you like a drink?'

'I'd like some tea.'

I go through to the kitchen: I can see her through the door examining the furniture, the chairs, the table.

'Is the furniture yours?'

'It was already here.'

'Have you been here long?'

'About two months.'

'Do you like it here?'

'Not really. No.'

She comes to the door.

'Could I take this off?'

She unbuttons the coat.

She disappears, as she takes it off, around the door.

When she reappears the coat has gone. Her dress is dark, buttoned at the throat and wrists.

'Can I help you with the tea?'

'It'll be all right.'

'Has Leyland been in touch?'

'Not yet.'

'He talks of nothing else.'

'I bet.'

She comes through to the kitchen.

The window looks down to the back of the house, to the tiny yard and, beyond that, the backs of the houses in the adjoining street. Above the roofs rears the blackened edifice of the cathedral spire, its tall, dog-toothed cone surmounted by a golden cockerel.

In the yard below a man in a white string vest and white shorts is exercising himself with a metal bar.

'Was the man who let you in dressed like an athlete?' I ask.

'He was, now you mention it,' she says.

'With bright red hair.'

'That's right.'

'You can see him here.'

She goes to the window, looking down.

'That's him,' she says. She begins to smile. 'Do you know who he is?'

'I've no idea.'

'Haven't you seen him before?'

'Not dressed like that.'

She presses her head to the pane. She laughs.

'Who else stays here, in any case?' she says.

'There's a couple above. A couple below.'

'They used to be family houses, I suppose,' she says.

'Though what they do,' I tell her. 'I've no idea.'

She goes back to the room; I follow her through.

'Won't you have some too?'

'I'm recovering from a concoction I had at Wilcox's,' I tell her, 'the other night.'

'The Principal,' she says. She laughs again.

'He warned me off.'

She takes the cup as I lean across.

'He thinks I might jeopardize the plans he has.'

'For what?'

'For improving the college with your husband's cash.'

'I didn't know he'd had any money, then.'

'He probably hasn't.'

'Sounds like another of Neville's ideas,' she says.

'I shouldn't tell Wilcox that,' I say. 'He's built up a brand new school already.'

'It must be something he said when he first took Bec.'

'There's nothing in it, I suppose,' I ask.

'With Neville,' she says, 'you can never tell.'

She crosses her legs.

'Do you want a fag?'

'That's nice,' she says. 'I've come without.'

'I've almost given it up,' I say. 'I have instant recoil, with Wilcox, whenever I get one out.'

'Does he disapprove of smoking, too?'

'Of almost everything,' I say.

I hold the light.

'So Wilcox invited you out,' she says.

'I paid for his petrol when his car ran dry; we shared a potato, a piece of cheese, of which he and his wife had the larger part, three apples and, between Wilcox and myself, a jug of toddy – comprised primarily of unsweetened lemon – and finally, to ward off the rigours of his unheated house, a distillation of fungi and the common woodland toadstool which I alone was privileged to imbibe . . .'

She begins to laugh: she holds her hands against her cheeks.

'On top of which he showed me all his pictures. If you want an investment you've got a starter there. The latest looks about a century old.'

She shakes her head.

'He's quite worried about you, in any case,' I tell her. 'He thinks I might undermine his position vis-à-vis the college, not to mention your taste in pictures.'

'I better be on my guard,' she says.

She gets up from the chair.

'It's quite cosy up here. High above the world.'

'And cold.'

She looks across.

'Doesn't the fire work?'

'It's supposed to be gas. The pressure's so low it'll hardly light.'

'Have you told the landlord?'

'It's to do with the house. In a year or so they'll pull it down.'

'And all those concrete towers go up,' she says.

She gazes out to the view below.

'You can see the road across the heath. I'm sure those are the trees behind the house.'

She turns her head.

'Do you mind me coming?' She begins to laugh.

'I don't mind you coming at all,' I say.

'Do you have a bed?'

I gesture through.

'Would you mind if I look?'

'You can try it out, if you like,' I say.

'That I'm not sure of,' she says and laughs.

'The chance might not come again,' I say.

'Oh, it always comes. It's just a question of convenience,' she says.

'It's convenient to me: but then, I'm familiar with it, I suppose,' I tell her.

She sits on the edge. She crosses her legs.

'Well? Do I have to beg for encouragement?' she says.

'What I don't like are the headaches,' Lennox says. He leans back in the chair behind his desk. 'They haven't diminished during the last few weeks.'

'Has she been X-rayed?'

'It's nothing organic,' he says. 'I'm sure of that.'

He fingers his nose. His hair is grey. His eyes are blue, his cheeks bright pink, thin-veined, half-bloated, red. By all accounts, at Christmas, he plays the part of Santa Claus, visiting the wards, giving out presents, singing carols with a choir of nurses, receiving visitors personally behind the snack-bar in the reception wing.

'It's more a symptom of stress,' he says.

'What sort of stress?'

'She's such a sensitive girl,' he says.

It's as if sensitivity, like diabetes, is invariably a nuisance in a case like this.

'She takes so many things to heart. These wars she's always on about. And famine. And as for women's rights.' He shakes his head.

I wait.

'What's the solution, then?' I ask.

'I thought a week-end at home, with you.' He looks across. 'We've changed her pills. The ones I can give you she shouldn't keep herself. You could have them in your pocket or somewhere, normally, where she wouldn't look.'

'Isn't it better to tell her where they are?'

'I'll leave that up to you.'

He picks his nose; his head, as a consequence of this action, turns slowly to one side.

His eyes, however, are gazing at the desk, at a set of papers across which is written not Yvonne's name but that of some-one else.

He looks across. 'You could have her report back on Monday morning. If you have any trouble just give a ring; or if you get into difficulties,' he says, 'you could bring her back. The change, in any case, will do her good. What sort of house have you got?'

'A flat.'

'It's where you were living before?'

I shake my head.

'As long as there's room to sleep,' he says.

'I'll pick her up on Friday, then.'

'I'll tell them about the pills,' he says.

As I go to the door he calls across.

'It might be better if she didn't go home. To her mother's home, that is,' he says.

I stand by the door and gaze across.

'I'll try and bear it in mind,' I say.

'And maybe next week we can see how she is.'

He doesn't look up as I close the door.

There's a row of other figures on the chairs outside. The nurse calls a name: a woman rises. Small, grey-haired, her head on her chest, she shuffles over towards the door.

'If Doctor Lennox wants to see you again,' she says, 'he'll let you know. Otherwise, for any information about a patient, you can ask downstairs.'

I go through the door to the corridor outside.

Steps lead down to the gleaming, glass-covered hall. There's a man sitting there with his back to the wall. He doesn't look up.

I go to the ward.

Yvonne is sitting in the dining-room, her hands in her lap, her head bowed. On the table beside her is a glass of milk.

She must have heard me in the corridor: as the door swings back she's looking up, her cheeks flushed, her eyes bright. Evidently it's the news of her release she's been waiting for.

'Did you see him, then?'

Her hands are clenched; the eyes, like those of a child, have opened wide.

'He says you could come home for a week-end, then.'

'Home?'

'To the place I've got.'

'For only two days.'

'Three nights. There's Friday, you see, as well.'

She lowers her head.

'Don't you fancy coming out?'

'For only two days? It's a sort of test.'

'You could always walk out and never come back.'

'They'd only have me certified,' she says. 'What's the point if I haven't been cured?'

A nurse in the kitchen is washing cups. Behind her head is a wooden rack: plates and pans are arranged in rows. A cloud of steam obscures her head.

'Shall we go for a walk?'

'I'm fed up of walking here,' she says.

'We could go in the lounge.'

'They're watching television there,' she says.

She seems much better; clearer in her mind, depressed.

A small, white-haired woman, wearing what appears to be a

sailor's hat, has come into the room. She smiles at Yvonne then looks at me.

'This is Peggy,' Yvonne has said.

I shake her hand.

The woman's face is round and red, the eyes light blue, and narrowed, shielded above and below by thick white lashes.

'And how's Yvonne today?' she says.

'I'm out for the week-end,' Yvonne has said.

'What did I tell you?' the woman says. 'If you're good to them they're good to you.'

'Peggy's been in six times,' Yvonne has said.

'Seven,' the woman says. 'This is my seventh,' she adds to me.

'She only lives across the road.'

'My daughter lives across the road,' the woman says. She looks at me. 'They have such busy lives,' she adds. 'Her husband's a greengrocer. They've to be up at five.'

The hat she wears has a shiny neb, with the crest of an anchor and a piece of rope embroidered in yellow and white above. Her dress is blue and patterned with flowers.

'She's always getting me into trouble,' Yvonne has said.

'Not me,' the woman says. She turns aside.

'She's always tearing up notices,' Yvonne has said. 'And bits of paper.'

'I don't tear anything up,' the woman says.

'And puts them in my locker.'

'Now, my dear, don't exaggerate.' The woman smiles.

'Notices like, "No Entry", "Don't smoke in here".'

'They don't allow smoking in some of the wards,' the woman says. She looks at me. 'I've seen them. They're very good to us in here.'

'And when she's had her lunch she sometimes puts her plate inside my locker.'

'Honestly, how you exaggerate.' The woman smiles.

'But she gives me cigarettes, as well.'

'Oh, I don't smoke much,' the woman says.

'And buys me cups of tea.'

'I like to see people happy,' the woman says.

'She's been in here six months.'

'It's nearer five.'

'I thought it was six.'

'By Christmas-time, I suppose it will. Be six months here, I mean,' she says.

'We're just going for a walk,' Yvonne has said.

'Oh, I like going walks,' the woman says.

'I'm going with my husband,' Yvonne has said.

She puts her arm in mine.

The nurse in the kitchen has raised her head: she lifts the window, smiling, then calls, 'Mrs Kennedy: it's time for your pill.'

'I've had enough pills today,' the woman says.

'We'll find something nice to go with it,' the nurse has said.

'It's always something nice.' She smiles. 'They look after you here,' she adds, 'so well.'

We go out to the drive.

It's cold. A wind blows the few surviving leaves along the ground. At one side of the drive a gardener clips a hedge; a man with a large head and protruding eyes is picking up the twigs.

'My mother's coming today.'

'I know.'

'She usually comes in time for tea.'

'I rang up Lennox: it was the only time he had.'

'He's very busy.'

'So I've heard.'

'He works sixteen hours a day.'

'He told you that?'

'He told me it,' she says, 'the other day.'

'He picks his nose.'

'I've never noticed that.'

We've turned from the empty gates and are walking down the drive to the opposite end.

'Aren't you teaching today?'

I shake my head.

After some hesitation she takes my hand. Her beret, pulled down, obscures her eyes.

With her other hand, stooping, she pulls up the collar of her coat.

'What made you ring him?'

'I was tired of waiting.'

'Was he mad that you came?'

'I've no idea.'

Other figures, like ghosts, move off beneath the trees.

'I bet he was angry.'

'I hope he was.'

She glances across.

'Better some feeling,' I say, 'than none at all.'

'He's very concerned.'

'I'm sure he is.'

'It's a rotten job.' She gestures round. 'This all day.'

'For sixteen hours.'

'He's very kind.'

'They always are.'

'Don't you believe he helps?'

'I believe he tries.'

'Peggy's family, you know, have let her down.'

'How's that?'

'They live down the road, but they never come. If she'd somewhere to go they'd let her out.'

'Do you want her to live with you?'

Her hand, momentarily, has tightened in mine.

'I thought that she might. She's ever so good.'

'Another lost cause.'

'When they let me out.'

'She's seventy, or over.'

'She's sixty-four.'

'Your mother won't like it.'

'I can't see why not.'

'She lives on her own.'

'We could have them both.'

The trees to our right have been replaced by a shrubbery; to our left, beyond a hedge, the playing-field ends abruptly against the back-yards of a row of houses. Immediately ahead, the tarmac surface of the drive fades out into a clayey track. One side turns off towards a compost-heap. A man is standing there, with a fork, gazing back, abstractly, the way we've come.

'I've to live with two old ladies, as well as support them both,' I say.

'They have a pension.'

'Two weeks with them and you'll be back inside.'

'You think I would?'

She releases my hand.

'If I don't care for them,' she says, 'who would?'

'They can care for themselves,' I tell her.

'They're both too old.'

I wonder, in fact, if it isn't her mother's idea; though typical at one time of Yvonne, after her experience here she'd hardly think of it herself. It would be like taking a piece of the place back home.

'Lennox isn't keen on your mother,' I say.

'Why not?' she says.

She seems alarmed.

'He puts her in the same class,' I tell her, 'as Vietnam, China, the poor in India. And women who've been displaced throughout their lives by men.'

'If no one dealt with the world's suffering what point would there be in living?' she says.

We've had this argument, it seems, before; on the night before she was admitted she'd lain in a chair, weeping, before her the photograph of a child half-starved to death in some West African village.

'I deal with it,' she says, 'in the only way I can.'

'You're crazy.'

'With the individuals, Colin,' she adds, 'I can see around me.'

She's begun to cry. There's something frightening about her grief. It's like someone looking in a mirror. 'If *I* can weep: I *must* be real.'

The clayey track has petered out. It runs off to a grass embankment on either side. On top of the embankment is a wooden seat.

She climbs towards it, her legs thrust out, her hands pushed down, fiercely, into the pockets of her coat.

By the time I reach her the crying's stopped.

'What else did Lennox say?'

'He thinks your concern is too abstracted.'

'I can't see anything abstract about my mother. Nor about Peggy, either,' she says.

She sits on the bench.

'They're all lost causes. To do with things, in the end, you can't affect.'

'I can affect my mother. And Peggy too, if I had the chance.'

'They're things that are finished. You need something new.'

'I had a new life. It never got born.'

'You've a life of your own. You could start that as well.'

'Why start a new life, when the old life's as bad as it is?'

She holds her head.

'I've a terrible headache,' she says. 'And I've just had a pill.'

We say nothing further. I sit by her side.

Below us the embankment runs down to a tall brick wall, old, buckled, streaked with salt. Beyond, a ploughed field runs off towards the river. The land's been flooded the other side; stretches of water reflect the lightness of the sky. On a low knoll, across the river, the first buildings of the town begin.

'I'm surprised he agreed to me going out.'

Her hands, clenched, she rests them in her lap.

'It's to get you away from Peggy. You feed off her, you know, not the other way about.'

'I don't feed off anyone,' she says. 'And she, I know, doesn't feed off me.'

A train, on a low embankment across the river, lets out a two-tone wail.

I can see the carriages winding away across the valley; moments later comes their dull rumble as they cross a metal bridge.

'You take refuge in these people,' I tell her, 'not they in you.'

'I don't take refuge in anyone,' she says. She moves her hand. 'What refuge have I ever had?'

'You take refuge in ideas. In service, in selfishness; you take refuge, at times, in a place like this: abstract yourself from it, then feed yourself back into it, bit by bit.'

She holds her head.

'My mother should be here quite soon.'

'There's another hour.'

'She's sometimes early. You can never tell.'

'Do you want to come out at the week-end, then?'

'If we're going to quarrel, there's not much point.'

'I've said all I want to say,' I tell her.

'Peggy knows my mother, in any case,' she says.

'Forget her.'

'How do you forget people's loneliness?' she says.

She looks across.

'If I lived for myself I suppose I would.'

'If you lived for yourself you wouldn't be here.'

The wind, blowing freshly across the fields, tugs her coat. She holds up her head so that it blows across her face. There's a degree of consciousness I've begun to like; she doesn't mind feeling things, it seems.

'I'll come at seven.'

'Seven?'

'To take you home. I've to be at the college, you see, till then.'

I get up from the seat.

A man comes out at the end of the path; he pauses below us, rubs his hands, stares at his feet, then, bright-eyed, sets off back the way he's come.

'A woman got over the wall one night.'

She gestures off to the fields below.

'She jumped in the river.'

'Did they get her out?'

'They found her next morning.'

She adds nothing else. Something of her earlier mood returns; a kind of aloofness, uncertain, discomposed.

'Lennox doesn't want you better.'

'What does he want?' she says.

'To see you out. The symptoms gone, if nothing else.'

'I suppose that's as good as anything else.'

'It's what I'm counting on,' I tell her.

'If he says I can go, I'll be content.'

'You seem calmer today.'

'I suppose I am.'

A flock of sea-gulls has risen from the flooded fields. They wheel in the wind, flung up, like bits of paper, drifting out across the river.

'They let me in the kitchens the other day. Not the one in the ward; the one where they cook for the men,' she says.

She strokes her thumb.

'I baked a cake. You should see the ovens. There was room for ten.'

'Have you been down again?'

She shakes her head.

'They were busy the next time. I got in the way.'

It's like waiting for a storm; beforehand, there's the thrashing of trees, the crashing of branches, the groaning of timber: but the final holocaust you can't imagine.

'If I'd been a man I wouldn't be like this.'

'Like what?'

'I wouldn't care about anything,' she says. 'You can see them here. They're different from the women. The men don't care; they're wrapped up in themselves. It's their grief, it seems, or nothing. With the women, they're always looking out. They care what some of the others feel.'

'It can't be true.'

'But look at you. Whenever you're threatened there's no one else.'

'You're feeling better.'

'I suppose I am.'

'You know I'm right.'

'You don't know how to care.'

'I care about you.'

'But it's caring about people you don't *have* to care about that counts. Caring about me doesn't cost you anything,' she adds.

'It costs me more than you imagine.'

'Such as?'

'I wouldn't be where I am right now if it wasn't for you.'

'Here?'

'At the college.'

'What sort of freedom do you want?'

She holds her head.

'You don't have to sacrifice yourself,' she says.

'That's what I'm trying to tell you, love,' I add.

She's silent for a while. Across the valley, where the houses begin, a cloud of smoke has risen from a factory chimney. Black, bulbous, it's slowly torn to pieces by the wind, the thin, fraying fragments sweeping out across the river.

The sea-gulls, as if in answer, have drifted down, gliding back to the other side then re-alighting on the flooded fields.

'Do you think Lennox picks his nose quite consciously, as an indication that he's busy?'

'What?'

'You've never seen him do it, then?'

'He's always been very kind to me,' she says.

'In that sense, I suppose, I could be right. He didn't want to see me, I suspect, at all. This week-end, I suppose, is to fob me off.'

'We better get back.'

'For what?'

'My mother's coming.'

She gets up from the seat.

'I can't see at times,' she adds, 'what we have in common. You want to break things all the time; I only want to put the bits together.'

'Single-handed.'

'I'd do it with other people, if they'd only let me.'

'You'll feel different if you have a child.'

'I don't want a child.'

The man who appeared at the end of the path a few moments before is pacing up and down at the side of the drive: he walks several steps in one direction, his head bowed, rubbing his hands, then, with something of a quicker momentum, still rubbing, hurries back the other way.

'It's a mockery.'

'That's right.'

'Without charity,' she says, 'a life like this means nothing at all.'

'Even with it,' I say, 'it doesn't add up to much.'

'It adds up to something.'

'Solar oblivion, I suppose,' I tell her.

She walks ahead; it's as if, given this sudden incentive, she's going to walk on to the open gates. Only, as we reach the turning to the house, I see her mother's figure, tall, round-shouldered, standing in the porch.

'There you are. They said you'd gone for a walk.'

Yvonne, seeing her, has given a kind of jerk: her head comes up sharply; almost involuntarily, it seems, she puts out her arms.

Her mother, her arms already out, comes down the steps.

'I came up early, love. They told me you were out.'

Red-eyed, her face comes down, her lips pouting. Their two figures, for a moment, are held together, Yvonne's head crouched against her mother's arm.

'I didn't know Colin would be here.'

'I just dropped by.'

'It's so good of you. I'd have come sooner, you know, if you'd only asked.'

'Colin's been to see Doctor Lennox,' Yvonne has said.

'Are you coming out?'

She shakes her head.

'I can go for the week-end,' she says. 'That's all.'

'But that's something, love. They must be confident if they'll give you that.'

She takes her arm.

'I've brought you some cakes and some chocolate, love.'

'I've baked you a cake,' Yvonne has said.

'For me?'

'I did it in the ovens here.'

'You shouldn't have bothered, love,' she says.

'Who else would have bothered?' Yvonne has asked.

The glass doors, released, crash to behind.

'You can come and have some of it at the week-end, then.'

'I'll look forward to that.'

'You can stay at the house if you want, you know.'

'We thought,' I tell her, 'we'd stay at the flat.'

'The door's always open,' her mother says. 'I keep the beds aired, in any case,' she adds.

'Then again,' I tell her, 'we could book in, I suppose, at some hotel.'

'You don't want to go to that expense,' her mother says.

'I'll see you on Friday,' I tell Yvonne.

'Are you going, then?'

We've reached the hall; she's looking back, her beret pushed up from her mother's embrace.

'I have to get back.'

'It was so good of you to come,' her mother says.

'I'll say good-bye.' She leans across.

I kiss her cheek.

'See you on Friday.'

'I'll see you, then.'

'He's so considerate,' her mother says, taking her arm as I turn to leave.

When I reach the porch they've disappeared; then, as I step outside, I see their heads moving past the windows towards the ward. Immediately below, in the garden, the man with the large head and the protruding eyes, is picking up twigs beneath the hedge.

I walk down to the gate and don't look back.

'I like it here.'

She leans to the curtain and pulls it back; the cathedral spire, like some dark fissure in the sky, blocks out the space above her head.

'I suppose you don't mind, in any case,' she says.

She looks across.

'Me getting into trouble.'

'Trouble and you,' I say, 'don't go together.'

'Neville's coming home at the end of the week.'

'He ought to have come home before,' I tell her.

'I mean: I can't get away as easily as I could.'

'You might ask him to be more reasonable,' I say.

'I know,' she says. She begins to laugh. 'It's so cold up here, if you're not in bed.'

Beside her clothes, on a chair by the bed, is the Jack Daniels she's brought in a silver wrapper; beside the Jack Daniels stands an empty glass; beside the empty glass, her cigarettes and the square-shaped lighter she uses with her monogram on the side and a coloured crest.

The same crest forms the clasp on her pouch-shaped bag.

She stretches her arms above her head.

'I'll arrange it soon so I can stay a night.'

'Don't you think you'll be cold?'

She shakes her head.

'You could bring your own blanket. Or something,' I tell her.

'I suppose I could.'

'Is the four-poster warm?'

'You must give it a try.'

'That'll be the day.'

'That will be the day, I suppose,' she says.

She pulls back the sheet.

She gives a yawn; she covers her face then shakes her head.

'I'd better go. I'll be falling asleep.'

She rolls on her side. Her legs stretched out, she feels for her shoes.

Her figure is dainty; the breasts symmetrical, almost like a girl's. There's a faint colouring of the skin around her stomach, and faint, bluish blemishes on the inside of her thighs. She reminds me, for some reason, in her casualness perhaps, of the fair-haired model in the life room at the college.

'I could close my eyes.'

'It would look even worse.'

'Don't you mind me watching?'

She begins to laugh. She stoops to her clothes and pulls them on.

She dresses like an athlete at the end of a race, preoccupied, intent, her head stooped, her gestures minimal, restrained.

When she's fastened the dress and pulled on her shoes she gets out a comb.

As always, forgetting, she looks for a glass.

'What a primitive place this really is.'

She looks in her bag.

'I remind myself to put one in. I always forget.'

'Just comb it straight.'

'I need to *look*.'

'I'll tell you how you are,' I say.

She stands at the window a moment, gazing out.

'If I line up on the cathedral,' she says, 'I can always see.'

She stoops to the reflection, straightens, then combs her hair.

'There's that man in the yard again,' she says.

'You could give him a wave.'

'He saw me come in. That's twice in one week.'

'He'll be getting ideas.'

'He had those before.'

I kneel on the bed.

The man is stretched out, on his stomach, doing press-ups; the back of his neck is creased, reddened. For the first time I notice the thickness of his biceps. He's dressed in shorts and a white string vest.

'Do you know who he is?'

'I've no idea.'

'Isn't he ever at work?'

'Ask him,' I tell her, 'when he opens the door.'

'You could give me a key.'

'I'll have one made.'

She stoops to her reflection; she touches her hair around her cheeks. Then, shifting her head slightly from side to side, she paints her lips.

'If I don't go now I'm going to be late.'

'Where are you going to, in any case?' I say.

'I'm picking up Beccie at the school,' she says.

I begin to laugh.

'I promised I'd pick her up,' she adds.

'That's all right by me.' I laugh again.

'I could drop in on Wilcox, too,' she says.

'And tip him the wink.'

'A tutor called Freestone ...'

'Isn't toeing the line.'

The cathedral clock booms out above our heads.

'I'd better be off.'

She crosses to the bed.

'At night,' she adds, 'I dream of this.'

'No need to take it seriously,' I tell her.

'I don't take it seriously. I just dream of it,' she says.

She kisses my lips.

'Good-bye for now.'

She goes to the door.

'I'll buy you a mirror next week,' she says.

The door is closed.

I get out of bed.

The tapping of her heels comes from the stairs outside.

I cross to the window. There's a man in the street in a trilby hat. He wears a dark raincoat, looking up briefly as he passes the door, then glancing back, a moment later, as Elizabeth herself steps out. She doesn't look up; glancing first up the street to where she's parked the car, she sets off, after a moment's hesitation, in the opposite direction.

She disappears beneath the window ledge; the street is empty. Odd lights have appeared in the valley bottom; I go back to bed, pick up the bottle, touch up the glass and, reaching for her lighter, flick up the flame and light a cigarette.

Part Four

I

Hendricks crosses to the chair and retrieves his sweater. The light now has almost gone; patches of sweat have stained his shirt; the whiteness of his shorts is blemished, stained by the ash of the court itself. His face seems grey; his eyes, from across the court, are invisible in shadow.

I say,

'Do you fancy another set?'

'Too dark, old man.'

'You played super, Mr Freestone,' Rebecca says.

She's arrived with the combat-jacketed youth, plus his dog, at the beginning of the game, standing at the net, calling the score, instructing Hendricks, if not myself – 'Oh, *super* shot, Mr Freestone,' – to such an extent that Hendricks, finally, in a rage, has lost a set.

The youth, now, has gone some distance off, calling to the dog. He's shown little interest in the game, digging his heels against the ash: but for Rebecca, and the prospect, perhaps, of watching Hendricks, he might have wandered off.

'One set each, Mr Hendricks,' Rebecca says.

Hendricks nods; he tucks a silk scarf inside his sweater.

'Fancy a drink, old man?' I ask.

'I've got to get off,' he says. 'I'm late already.' He examines his watch, stooping vaguely to the evening light.

The odd man from the hut is standing on the path outside the courts.

'Which way are you going, Mr Freestone?' Rebecca says. She's dressed in jeans, with a silk blouse and leather jacket. The blouse, unbuttoned, reveals, virtually, the full measure of her chest.

'I wasn't going anywhere,' I tell her.

'We were going for a drink,' she says. 'Mathews and myself.'

She indicates the youth who's throwing twigs now for the dog to fetch.

'That's very kind.'

'Phil,' she says. She waves to the youth who gets hold of the dog by its collar and comes across.

'Mr Freestone's coming for a drink.'

'I thought you had to get home,' he says.

'I've time for a drink, at least,' she says.

Hendricks, his tennis balls already in his string bag, has gone over to the gate.

He's limping slightly; one side of his leg is grazed. On the path outside he stoops to his racket, examining the strings; he tightens the screws on the metal press.

'I'd better say goodnight.'

'Deciding set tomorrow.'

'I'd better let this heal.' He indicates his leg.

'See you at college.'

He doesn't answer. He fastens the string bag to the handle of his racket.

'They'll be closing these next week.'

The old man comes over to the gate. He fastens the lock in a metal bracket.

Hendricks is limping off beneath the whale-bone arch.

'Goodnight, old man.'

'Goodnight.'

He waves. As he nears his car he begins to run.

'Where can we go?' Rebecca says.

'There's a pub outside the gates,' the youth has said.

'I'll take the car through,' she says, and adds to me, 'You can walk with Phil.'

The dog starts after her as she runs ahead.

Mathews calls it. I tuck in the collar of my shirt and start off with the youth towards the gates.

'Do you play tennis much?'

I shake my head.

'Apollo had an evening.'

'I suppose he had.'

'Last year he had a racket with a metal shaft. It was split into three, you see, like that.' He takes my racket. 'He left it on a bench one day and somebody soaked the neck of it in acid.' He gives it back. 'When he went to play the head fell off.' He begins to laugh. 'Here, boy! Here, boy!' he calls as we reach the gate.

The lights have gone on in the pub across the road.

Hendricks's car sweeps past, brakes as it turns to the road, then disappears quickly towards the town.

The red shooting-brake follows it a moment later. It parks in the yard at the side of the pub.

The building, in design, resembles a country mansion; casement windows are set in wood and plaster surrounds; a lantern burns inside a timbered porch; upturned barrels are set out as tables along one side of the cobbled yard.

Rebecca gets out from the car and comes across.

'I've no money on me,' Mathews says.

'I've some,' she says. 'You needn't worry.'

'We'd better sit outside.' He indicates the dog.

'Do you fancy a beer?' she says. 'Or something short.'

'I'll have a beer.' He beckons to the dog.

'I'll get them,' I tell her. I go inside.

When I come back out Mathews is sitting with his arm around her; he takes it away as I reach the table. I set down the tray and take a seat.

'Apollo, I bet, was pretty mad. Have you beaten him before?' Rebecca says.

'Once or twice.'

'You could give me a game, if you like,' she says. She looks to Mathews. 'I'm pretty good.'

'I bet,' he says, and takes his glass.

Rebecca takes hers.

'Here's to it, then,' she says.

There are one or two other groups sitting at the tables; the dog, released by Mathews, has wandered off across the yard.

'We thought it was you from the top of the hill. It's something to do with your arms,' she says. 'You were hitting the ball in a kind of dream. It's the look you have at the school,' she adds.

'Like what?'

'Like you're not really there, I suppose,' she says.

She looks to Mathews.

'What did you do before you came up here?' he says.

'Very little, on the whole,' I tell him.

'I gather you were a fighter for a while,' he says.

'For a while,' I tell him. 'Then I turned to art.'

'Representational, I suppose,' he says.

'Realist might be more appropriate,' I say.

'Realist!' he says. He begins to laugh.

Rebecca gets up; she calls the dog. Suddenly, it seems, she's grown impatient.

A man at an adjoining table, reading a newspaper, has looked across. The paper, from the headlines, is two days old.

'Art no longer exists. Only parodies, of course,' I tell him, 'and self-reflection.'

'It seems *our* time's being wasted, then,' he says.

'That's for you to decide, old man,' I say.

'We'd better be going, I think,' he says.

On the breast pocket of his jacket is a badge which says, '*I am your friend*'.

'We'll drop Mr Freestone off,' Rebecca says. 'Do you fancy another drink?'

I shake my head.

'Thanks for the one we had, Mr Freestone,' Mathews says.

We cross to the car. The man with the newspaper, a flat cap pulled down above his eyes, has glanced across.

'I'll walk back to town,' I say.

'I can easily take you back,' she tells me.

'I'd prefer to walk,' I tell her. 'I invariably do after playing tennis.'

'Some shady assignation, I suppose,' she says.

'That's right.'

She glances now to the man himself.

'Are you sure about the lift?' she says.

'I'd much prefer to walk than ride.'

She gets in the car; Mathews gets in the other side.

The dog gives a howl as the engine starts.

As she turns the car it collides with a barrel.

She glances out; an arm is waved.

'Nothing serious,' she says, and waves again.

The car turns in the road outside; to a vague revving of the engine it disappears.

The man with the newspaper has crossed the yard; having glanced down the road he taps the paper against his hand, reassures himself of the car's direction, then, with something of a gesture, follows me.

The door to the ground floor flat is suddenly opened. The man with the red moustache appears.

'Could I have a word?' he says. He glances past me to the door of the house itself. 'It won't take a minute.' He winks. 'If you could slip inside.'

He's wearing a light blue suit; he looks, for that moment, like some comedian in a thirties' farce; the red hair, the red moustache, the slightly reddened nose to match.

I step inside.

His room is furnished with elaborate care; it corresponds to the old drawing-room of the family house: there's a three-piece suite, a table that reminds me, by its age, of the one in Wilcox's dining-room, and above the marble fireplace hangs a diamond-shaped mirror in a wrought-iron frame. A pair of sliding-doors cuts off the view to the bedroom at the back.

'Fancy a snitch?'

He holds up a bottle as well as a glass.

'Damn cold these evenings: closing in.'

He sees the racket.

'Been playing tennis, sport?'

'That's right.'

'One of my games.' He indicates, in addition to a racket, a set of golf clubs propped up in a stand against the wall. 'Badminton. Squash. Might play you one evening, if you've got the time. The local technical college has a damn good court.'

He indicates a chair in front of the fire.

He waits while I sit. 'Hoping to catch you, you know, last night.'

He holds out the glass.

'Damn difficult at times in a house like this.'

He drains his own glass at a single throw, the head tossed back, the eyes half-closed.

He gives a gasp.

'Fancy another?'

I hold mine up.

'Good hunting, sport.'

He's been through several 'snitches' it seems already.

There's a line of sweat across his brow.

'Living alone?'

I nod my head.

'Same here. Only been in a couple of months.'

He takes out a cigarette case from his jacket pocket.

I offer him one of mine.

'That's very decent. Been trying to give them up, you know.'

He takes the light, puffs out for a while, then settles back.

'Keep in trim. Our age, you know, it becomes essential.'

He's nearly fifty; lines fan out from the corners of his eyes. His teeth are white, browning, however, around the edges: one or two at the back are missing. His nails are long, and neatly trimmed.

'Hear you were something of a sport yourself.'

He indicates several photographs hanging by the mirror; there's a red-haired figure in tennis shorts standing by a net; another red-haired figure, somewhat older, stands with an oar beside a boat. Another, its arms folded, poses smilingly beside a hurdle; another stands posed, a javelin in its hand, beside a wooden fence.

'Not so long ago, by all accounts.'

His eyes have grown a little brighter.

'There's a poster in one of the pubs in town. I noticed it,' he says, 'the other night. Freestone versus Corcoran. I saw him fight, you know, in London. Gave one of these American light-heavies a damn bad time.'

He swallows his drink.

'Beat him?'

'I'll have to look it up.'

He laughs.

'Can always tell a sport.' He taps his head. 'Doesn't talk about it: goes and does it. Not many of us left.'

He reaches to the bottle: perhaps my presence is all the licence he requires. He holds it out: I shake my head.

'In the same line of business still?'

'Teaching,' I tell him.

'A teacher?' he says.

He puckers his lip.

'Damn nice if you can get it, pal.'

He's had some experience of this, perhaps, himself. He swallows his drink.

'What was the word you wanted to have?'

He runs his stiffened forefinger along either side of the red moustache. For a moment, it seems, he might take it off, reveal some different character entirely.

'It's none of my concern, old man. And far be it from me to interfere.' He narrows his eyes. 'Just shoot me down if you think I'm wrong. But did you know,' he says, 'you were being watched?'

'Where?'

'In the house, old man. The flat.' He gestures up. 'And I've a damned good idea,' he says, 'in the street as well.'

'I'm being followed?'

'It's no concern of mine, old man.' He looks at his glass. 'I thought I'd mention it. Just in case.'

'It's very good of you,' I say.

He looks across.

'These H.P. people get up to all sorts of tricks. You don't have to tell me, old man. I know.'

He sips at the glass which, from where I'm sitting, appears to be empty.

'He's out here, I can tell you, every night. And I've seen him a time or two,' he says, 'during the day as well.'

'How's he dressed?'

'A trilby hat, old man. You can tell them at a glance.'

'A belted raincoat.'

'That's the one.'

He seems quite pleased. He nods across.

'Thought it was me, at first, old man.' He taps his chest. 'Not that there's anything at present, mind.'

He puffs briskly at the cigarette.

'Nowadays, you know, you can never tell. They nab you for something before they even tell you they've made it an offence.'

'I know.'

'I won't have to tell you, sport,' he says.

I get up from the chair.

'Could be the divorce, you know, old man.' He adds, 'Of course, it's no concern of mine.'

'I don't think,' I tell him, 'it could be that.'

'It could be someone else's wife.'

He waits.

'Wanting a divorce?'

'Looking for evidence, old man. I've had it happen to me, I can tell you that.'

He looks across.

'Meet some lady – quite charming; go along: make no demands – find she's after evidence, old man. When it's far too late you find you're Mr X. Subpoenaed. I've had it happen to me, old man.'

'She's providing evidence, you mean.'

'Protecting the one she really wants. I've known it happen, old man. Take my advice.'

His finger travels slowly along the underside of the red moustache.

'Doesn't say much for the husband, sport. There's always collusion in a thing like this. He's usually too high-powered to provide evidence himself. Result: gets the little lady to do it for him.'

'I see what you mean.'

'Just thought I'd mention it, old man.'

He holds up the bottle.

'Another snitch before you go?'

He pours it out.

'Once bitten in these things: you get to know. Becomes second instinct, so to speak.'

'Are you sure it's me? Not someone else.'

'Seen the way he watches the place, old man. They've no imagination, I can tell you that.'

I finish the drink.

'And the way he regards your visitors. The lady in the fur hat especially, sport.'

'I see what you mean.'

'I've seen it happen before, old man. Been the ruin of many a better man than I.'

'You think I ought to thump him, then?'

'Assault and battery, old man: get damages as well.'

He taps his eye.

'What course of action,' I ask him, 'do you recommend?'

'Confrontation, old man. It's always best.'

'With the trilby hat, you mean.'

'With the lady, old man. Take my advice.'

'Supposing she denies it.'

'They never do, old man. In too deep. Beg for mercy, and things like that.'

'The evidence's already there, you mean.'

'Precisely, old man.' He taps his head.

'I could put her onto you,' I tell him.

'Not me, old man.'

He gets up from the chair.

'I only mentioned it as a favour, sport.'

'After all, you've witnessed it,' I tell him.

'Not me, old sport. I'd deny it to anyone else.' He smiles.

'I'll have to fight it on my own.'

'I was only doing you a favour, sport. I've seen it happen before, you see.'

'So you said.'

'One sport to another.'

'I know what you mean.'

I cross over to the door.

'The difficulties start with the employers, old man. Particularly the professions. They don't like to see it happen. Not good for the firm, a name in court. Not good for the school.' He nods his head.

'It was good of you to mention it,' I tell him.

'I wouldn't see it happen to a dog, old man.'

He holds the door.

'Let me know when you're free, and we'll fix up a date.' He indicates the racket. 'Not got the shots I used to have, but I'll give you a damn good run.' He laughs. 'Not a golfing feller, I take it?'

'I can never find the time.'

'Know what you mean, old man.' He winks.

He waits while I reach the turn of the stairs.

'See you, old man,' he calls and, looking up to the landing, he gives a wave.

I wave the racket back.

He disappears.

I climb up to the room. The door's unlocked.

Rebecca's sitting on the floor inside, smoking, her head against the wall.

Her figure's lit up by the glow from the landing.

'Don't put on the light,' she says. 'I'm used to the dark.' I close the door.

'I didn't notice the car,' I say.

'I didn't park it outside,' she says.

'And the door wasn't locked?'

'I picked it with a pin.'

'Are you entitled to do that?'

'It was locked when I came. I got tired of waiting, I suppose,' she says.

A faint light, reflected from the street lamps below, comes through the window. Her figure, mounded against the wall, has begun to stir.

'Do you want a drink?'

'You've nothing in.'

'A cup of tea?'

'Your milk's run out.'

'Have I anything left?'

She shakes her head.

'You don't keep house too well,' she says.

'Won't your mother be expecting you?' I ask.

'She's often out,' she says, 'herself.'

She indicates the drawing, faintly visible on the wall, above her head.

'I see you've hung it up,' she says.

'Did you really pick the lock?' I say.

'You do it with a pin. I'll show you if you like,' she says.

She gets up from the wall and crosses to the door.

'I'll lock it,' she says. 'Then I'll come back in.'

She shuts the door.

There's the shuffling of her feet on the floor outside; a moment later the lock springs back.

Her head appears, silhouetted briefly against the landing light.

'Shall I do it again?'

'I'll never feel safe in bed again.'

She comes back in.

'It's easy with a lock like that. I couldn't do it with a new one, though.'

She shuts the door.

'The ones at college are easier still.'

'You could make a fortune,' I tell her, 'with a gift like that.'

'I've already got a fortune, I suppose,' she says.

'From what?'

'From policies. Endowments. Things like that.'

She comes over to the chair.

'I thought Mr Hendricks was funny tonight.' She sits down on the arm beside me. 'I tried to put him off,' she adds. 'With all that calling. And then that trouble with Philip's dog.'

She begins to laugh.

'He thinks he's so good. I could beat him stiff.'

'I could do with you watching every night.'

'You think so?'

'I can't beat him on my own,' I tell her.

'He's so conceited.'

'That's half his charm, I suppose,' I say.

'Has Leyland been in touch?' she says.

'Not yet.'

I wait.

'You should see his lip. When he came next day he could hardly speak.'

'It might help him with his friends,' I say.

'Mummy was pleased. It made her laugh.'

She pushes her hand against my arm.

'Did you really hit him hard?' she says.

'As hard as I could.'

'He'll get his own back.'

'I suppose he will.'

'Him and Fraser and Groves,' she says.

'They're a sort of gang.'

'With Daddy as well, I suppose,' she says.

'Will he intervene?'

'I've no idea.'

'I'd better watch out.'

'You could run away.'

'I suppose I could.'

'If you had a place outside the town.'

'They'd never find me there,' I say.

'I wouldn't tell them, honestly,' she says. 'You could live out there, and come in each day with the morning-rush.'

'And go out with the evening-rush at night.'

'They can't get you in a crowd,' she says.

'I could get up a gang,' I tell her, 'myself.'

She shakes her head.

'They've miles more people than you,' she says. 'They'd pay them more, in any case,' she adds.

'I suppose they would.'

'When his lip goes down he might forget.'

'I hope you're right.'

'He'd one or two loose teeth, you see, as well. He was going to a dentist the following day.'

'Once there,' I tell her, 'he wouldn't forget.'

'Not if he had them out,' she says.

'Time I was in bed,' I say.

'I suppose I ought to be going, then,' she says.

She leans her head against my arm.

'It's so dark up there at night,' she says.

'I thought you liked it. In the house, I mean.'

'So eerie. All those old houses. There's supposed to be a ghost in ours. The Blue Lady. I thought I saw her the other night.'

'Did you see her face?'

'It was just a haze. She was killed during the Civil War, you know. Her lover was a Roundhead. Her husband,' she adds, 'a Cavalier.'

She moves her head.

'The man who told us said he'd seen her one night when he was lying in bed. Apparently the Roundhead came to see her when her husband was away. He was calling up to the window when her husband suddenly returned. It was late at night. When he saw him there they fought a duel. The lover was killed. When the woman saw what her husband had done she opened the window and threw herself out. She was killed straight away when she hit the ground.'

'Did the husband relent?'

'I've no idea.'

'Which window was it?'

'He didn't say.'

'You better keep your lights on when you drive up there tonight.'

'Don't worry,' she says. 'I always do.'

She gets up from the chair.

'You don't mind me coming up?' she says.

'Come up whenever you like,' I say.

'There aren't many people you can talk to here.' She gestures round. 'I mean the town.'

'If you don't try their locks,' I tell her, 'you'll never find out.'

She begins to laugh.

'Honestly, you don't mind me coming in? I could easily have waited outside,' she says.

'In future I shall always knock on the door,' I say.

She goes to the door.

'And honestly, next time: I'll bring something up I can cook,' she says.

2

'This etching process,' Hendricks says, 'is scarcely used. It's all silk-screen today. That and the occasional lithograph.'

He leans over the acid bath and wipes the bubbles from the copper plate with the tip of a feather. Part of the plate has been blacked-out; there's a thin frieze of lines, each with its tiny rim of bubbles.

'In twenty years there'll not be one student in a hundred will even know the process. The whole thing,' he adds, 'is dying out.'

For a moment the tone is almost that of Wilcox; he leans on

one elbow, his shoulder pushed up, his head inclined reflectively to one side. He seems unaware of the acid fumes. The brown smock he wears is stained with acid burns; there's a broad smear of dried lithography ink, black, by each of the pockets: his bare legs and his plimsolls alone indicate that he's changed already for his lunch-hour badminton at the technical college across the way.

The room itself resembles a chemistry lab; there are long bare tables, burnt by acid, stained by inks, and, at one end, against the wall, a variety of presses. The wall opposite the row of windows is draped with rectangular sheets of paper, each one stained with an irregular blob of ink; there's a lack of definition, a vagueness about the room. The only student there is working at the silk-screen press, lowering the wooden frame and scraping on the colour.

Pollard has appeared at the opposite end, inside the door, a cigarette cupped in his hand; he smokes it quickly as he wanders by the tables, examining the silk-screen press for a moment, then coming across, wafting the smoke away with his other hand.

'It's not safe in that comon room,' he says.

He comes up to Hendricks's acid bath and peers inside.

'What's that?'

'Went in a minute ago: lit up. There was Wilcox: hiding behind a cupboard.'

'Hiding?' Hendricks says. He wafts his feather.

'Said he'd lost a paper. On his hands and knees. Half hidden, he was, by one of the chairs.'

'What did he say?'

'I nearly died. Said I'd confiscated it off one of the lads.'

He smokes it quickly, glancing at the door.

'I've been teaching in the design room for half an hour. He never went past while I was there.'

'Gestapo.'

'I think he's mad.'

'Did he blow you up, then?' Hendricks says.

'I reckon he thought I wouldn't see him.'

'He's checking up on the thieving,' Hendricks says.

'What thieving? There's nothing to thieve in there.'

'Those magazines.'

'They're twelve months out of date at least.'

Hendricks reaches into the acid bath with a pair of tongs: he carries the plate over to a sink in a corner of the room.

'You should have pretended he wasn't there.'

'I nearly passed out on the bloody floor. Just look at my hands.' He holds them out. The fingers have begun to tremble. 'It's the only safe place to smoke, is here. With all these stinks that Hendricks makes.'

'You ought to ask Freestone to intercede. He's the only one,' Hendricks says, 'who's been asked to supper.'

'And how did you get on, then?' Pollard says. 'A week gone past, and he's never said.'

'Been grafting, has he?' Hendricks says.

'I bought him his petrol: was brought home in the early hours in the back of a lorry; apart from that, pneumonia, a bout of food-poisoning, the evening passed off without incident,' I say.

'What's his wife like?' Hendricks says.

'She doesn't speak.'

'She came here, one day. Did I ever tell you?' Pollard says. 'Kendal saw her downstairs and thought she was a cleaner. Took her in the broom-cupboard and handed her a mop. Never heard anything like it. Wilcox steps out from his bloody office: finds his old lady mopping up. Heard the bloody shouts from here.' He begins to stub out the cigarette. 'Kendal'll be the next to go, don't worry. Those bloody machines of his. Can hear them whirring from the Skipper's office. He sits at his bloody desk for hours, tapping his foot and beating his head.'

Hendricks has cleaned the stopping-out ink from his plate: he turns its shiny copper surface to the light, examining the lines.

'Did he show you his pictures?' Pollard says.

'I have a faint recollection of one or two,' I tell him.

'They say he's a Pre-Raphaelite,' Hendricks says.

'A little after his time,' I say.

'Not long ago,' Pollard says, 'he brought one to the college. He hung it up in the hall downstairs. The inspectors came round one day and asked him if he thought it was wise to hang up – in such a prominent position – the more reactionary of his students' work. He took it down. When the feller was leaving he shook his hand and thanked him for his sound advice.'

'You should see him with the education committee,' Hendricks says. 'He lined the students up on one occasion, on the stairs, and as the committee left, at a prearranged signal, they clapped their hands.'

'Ever so slowly.'

'Ever so slowly. I think you're right.'

Pollard has laughed. A certain relief has come into his movements.

He cups his hand, scrapes off the debris from the cigarette which he's stubbed out on the table, and carefully pours it into the bottom of the waste-paper basket beneath the sink. He screws up a fresh sheet of paper and puts it in on top.

'What was it Kendal says: "Neurosis is infectious".'

'Contagious,' Hendricks says.

'With the Skipper it's like ever-widening ripples. He lobs in some crazy notion and we all bob up and down.'

Hendricks has crossed over to the rollers on an adjoining table. He squeezes black ink out from a tube and begins to roll it up on a metal board.

'Nobody ever knows where the Skipper lives. He takes them there at night, and sets them loose in the dark to find their own way back. At least,' Pollard tells me, 'that's what I've heard.'

'I've heard he only eats nut rissoles.' Hendricks is rolling up the ink, examining its consistency with a broad-bladed knife.

'I heard,' Pollard says, 'it was fish and chips.'

'Potato soup.' I offer him a cigarette.

'You really paid for the petrol, then?'

'Two quid or more.'

'Did you get it back?'

I shake my head.

'Deduct it from your next subscription to the "Antique and Still-Life Restitution Fund".'

'I think I shall.'

'Either that,' he says, 'or withdraw two quidsworth of stock from the artists materials and miscellaneous commodities room.'

'I'll look into it,' I tell him.

'Do you fancy a tenner on Happy Prince? I had it from a man

in town that he was held back last week at Brocksborough Park.'

'I can't afford luxuries any more,' I tell him.

'This is income, man.' He taps his chest.

The cigarette, after a moment's examination, he slips inside an already opened packet.

'*Mr Pollard*,' Wilcox says, appearing at the door. '*If you have a minute, I'd appreciate it, Mr Pollard, if you'd step outside.*'

Pollard, his back to the door, stands gazing first at Hendricks then at me as if to accuse one or both of us of some uncanny imitation of the Principal's voice.

'What's going on in here, then? Mothers' tea-party, is it?' the Principal says.

He comes inside.

'Shop-floor meeting of the layabouts union?'

He tries to laugh; a harsh, stuttering snarl erupts inside his throat.

'Annual conference of the federation of still-life exponents, is it, then?'

I have a feeling he's been listening at the door. He gives no sign.

'We were watching a new process, Principal,' Pollard says.

'For brewing up tea, then?' Wilcox says.

'Etching,' Pollard says.

He indicates Hendricks's figure at the adjoining table.

Hendricks himself looks up in some alarm.

'It's a new acid process which Mr Hendricks is investigating, sir,' he says.

'What's that then?'

Hendricks is about to transfer the ink on the roller to the copper plate, now laid out on the surface of a smooth white stone.

Wilcox crosses over; he glances at the plate.

'What's new in this, then? I can't see any difference, lad.'

'It's an adaptation of one of these old, medieval processes,' Pollard says.

Hendricks nods his head.

Wilcox stoops to the plate. 'It looks like one of Mr Freestone's poses to me,' he says, 'Straight up and down: no arms, no legs.'

'I drew it in the life room,' Hendricks says.

'I see nowt new in that, then,' Wilcox says.

'It's the acid that Mr Hendricks uses,' Pollard says.

Hendricks nods his head again.

'What kind of acid's that, then?'

Pollard looks over to Hendricks.

'It's a kind of distilled wine I've been using,' Hendricks says.

'Wine?'

'Almost a kind of vinegar, really.'

'Very acidic,' Pollard says.

'I can't see nowt different between this and hydrochloric acid,' Wilcox says. He stoops to the plate again.

'It gives it a more delicate line. Particularly with a standing nude, sir,' Hendricks says.

'I see nowt delicate in this. It looks to me like any other. A bit under-exposed, if anything,' he adds. 'You'll not get a good clean print with that.'

'More a sfumato effect. I believe that's what you were aiming for, Mr Hendricks?' Pollard says.

Hendricks, uncertain, holds the inked-up roller above the plate.

'Somebody been smoking in here, then, have they?' Wilcox says.

He lifts his head.

'Where's the wine you've been using, then?'

Pollard gestures behind him: there are any number of bottles standing on the shelves above the sink, principally cleaning fluids and diluted acids which haven't, as yet, been thrown away. 'I believe Mr Hendricks used the last of it on this.'

Hendricks, his back to Pollard, has begun to ink the plate.

He passes the roller across it several times, Pollard stooping at one point to examine the plate, even threatening to touch it with his little finger.

'A bit more there, I think.'

Hendricks stoops; he glances at Pollard then examines the plate.

He runs the roller across it lightly.

'Let's see this famous sfumato,' Wilcox says.

Hendricks eases up the plate with his fingers; he carries it across the room to the largest of the presses.

He lays it in the centre.

From an adjoining table, with his fingertips, he picks up a sheet of paper.

He lays it carefully across the plate.

'Shall I turn the handle?' Pollard says.

'I'll do it,' Hendricks says.

He lays several sheets of paper on top, then a felt cloth, then lowers the thin metal sheet and edges the press beneath the roller.

He goes to the wheel.

'First time I've heard of vinegar. What medieval process is it?' Wilcox says.

'I believe it was used in the monasteries,' Pollard says.

'When was etching invented, then?'

Pollard scratches his cheek. He glances at Hendricks.

Hendricks, his back to Pollard, has begun to turn the massive wheel.

'Quite early on, sir,' Pollard says.

'First time I've heard of vinegar,' Wilcox says.

'Most monasteries in those days made their own wine, of course, sir,' Pollard says.

'Wine's an intoxicant,' Wilcox says. 'Perverts the digestion, for a start. I can't see it being much help to an etching.'

The table of the press has disappeared beneath the roller; at the same uniform speed Hendricks draws it back.

'Let's see this famous sfumato,' the Principal says. He steps to the side of the press as Hendricks lifts the metal sheet. 'It seems no different to me. I thought sfumato was sort of blurred.'

'That's chiaroscuro,' Pollard says.

'I know sfumato when I see it. I use it in my own work,' Wilcox says. 'It's an excuse, usually, for drawing nowt clearly.' He looks at the etching in Hendricks's hand. 'And that's an example of it, as near as ought. Though why it needs vinegar to do it I've no idea.'

He goes to the door.

'Could I see you outside, Mr Pollard,' he adds. 'It won't take a minute.'

'Anything to oblige, sir,' Pollard says. He follows Wilcox out, glancing back, briefly, as they reach the door, running his hand across his jacket and dusting off the ash.

'He'll be cutting it too fine one of these days,' Hendricks says.

He looks at the plate, checks it with the etching, then takes the plate back to wash off the ink.

'He's not as foolish as he thinks.'

'Pollard?'

'Wilcox.'

He runs the tap, lays the plate on the draining-board, pours on some soap powder, and begins to scrub it.

Pollard comes in a moment later.

He crosses over to the etching, examines it, whistling, then, his hands in his pockets, comes over to the sink.

'Been invited out to dinner.'

'Who by?' Hendricks stops his scrubbing.

'The Skipper.'

'What's he after?' Hendricks says.

'I've no idea, old man. He was very much taken by my description of this process you've invented.'

'I'd have told him there was no such thing if he'd asked me directly,' Hendricks says.

'Good job he didn't in that case,' Pollard says.

'The man's not a fool, you know.'

'He's vetting the staff for loyalty,' Pollard says.

'Did he mention the smoking?' Hendricks says.

'Not a word.'

'I don't even smoke. Nor drink. Except soft drinks, occasionally,' Hendricks says.

'He's probably sure of you, Hendricks,' Pollard says. 'It's the back-sliders,' he adds, 'that he invites to dinner.'

Mathews has come in; jacketed, jeaned and booted, he goes over to the student at the silk-screen press.

When he sees me by the sink he comes across.

'There was a feller asking for you downstairs.' He takes my arm. 'Tall,' he says. 'With red hair, and a red moustache.'

'Did he give his name?'

He shakes his head.

'A friend of yours?'

'I've no idea.'

'I told him you'd be out to lunch. If I'd known you were here I could have sent him up.'

'Is he still around?'

'I saw him in the street then he wandered off.'

He watches Hendricks a moment as he rinses the plate.

'Not hiding from the feller, then?'

'Whatever gave you that idea?'

'Your expression,' he says. He shakes his head.

'I was listening to Mr Hendricks explain to Mr Pollard a new process he's discovered.'

'For doing what?'

'Mr Hendricks can tell you,' I say, manoeuvring Pollard to the table as I cross over to the door.

From the landing window I look into the street. Not only is the red-haired man standing at the corner, but not a few feet away from him the man in the trilby hat. They appear, conspicuously, to be unaware of one another, the man with the red moustache looking up the street, towards the college, the one with the trilby hat looking down it, towards the town.

I go down to the hall below, cross the corridor leading to the yard at the back, and from the yard slip out into a narrow lane backing the college, beyond the modelling shed.

A man is standing there I've never seen before; he looks up at me in some surprise, adjusts his glasses then his trilby hat, then, as I glance up at the sky, he looks up too, examines the roof of the college for several seconds and then, as our eyes meet, briefly, nods his head.

He looks one way down the street and then the other; and then, like a doorman, smiles approvingly, touching his hat, as I step back once more inside the yard.

3

'Why do we have to go this way round?' she says.

'I thought, back there, we were being followed.'

'You're mad,' she says. 'They talk like that, you know, in there.'

'Contagious.'

'I think it is.'

We cross the road. It's almost dark; the lamps have just come on: odd pools of yellowish light are strung out along the street. A pale luminosity still fills the sky.

I shift her case to my other hand.

'I suppose we've come this way,' she says, 'to avoid my mother.'

'We could hardly avoid her,' I tell her, 'if she's waiting in the door.'

'Where is the door, in any case?' she says.

She looks along the darkening street, at the decaying garden, at the Georgian terrace; it has an eerie grandeur in the evening light.

'It's the middle one along.'

I point it out, slowing in any case and looking around.

'Why should my mother follow us here? Honestly,' she says, looking round herself, 'you're paranoic.'

We reach the steps; there's no light on in the lower rooms. The hall, when I open the door, is empty. Perhaps the red-haired man, optimistically, is still waiting by the college.

We climb the stairs.

'It's very dark.'

'I'll put the light on,' I tell her, 'when we reach the landing,' yet continue climbing in the semi-darkness to the second floor.

'Which floor is it? Couldn't you have found somewhere lower?' she says.

'I was lucky to get this place, in any case,' I tell her. 'Places in this town,' I add, 'are hard to find.'

'I can't see why we couldn't have gone home,' she says. 'Gone home to my mother's house, I mean.'

'When we've got a place of our own?' I tell her.

'It's not our own. It's yours. How can it be our own, when I've never been here before?' she says.

I insert the key; the lock clicks back. We go inside. I put on the light. I close the door.

She gazes round.

'It's very small.'

'Anything larger,' I tell her, 'would cost a lot.'

I go through to the kitchen.

'Would you like some tea?'

I call to her, briefly, through the open door.

'Anything,' she says.

'You could light the fire.'

I fill the kettle, look out at the darkness of the yard below, decide it's empty, put the kettle on and light the gas.

When I go back through she's looking for the matches.

Her beret, thankfully, she's taken off; her hair, freshly washed, hangs down in a wave around her neck.

'Use this,' I tell her.

She takes the lighter; she kneels to the hearth.

'It's not very strong.'

'The pressure's very low,' I tell her.

'There's hardly any heat.'

'You could lie in bed, if you like,' I tell her.

'That's some home. You've to lie in bed to try and keep warm.'

'Some people haven't even a bed to lie in, I suppose,' I tell her.

'My mother would have a fire.'

'Is anything the matter?'

'No,' she says. She shakes her head. 'I don't know where I am.'

She begins to cry.

I lift her up.

'We're together now. That's all that counts.'

It's like holding a saint: someone in the grip of some violent, cosmic tribulation.

'Where am I, Colin?'

'You're here. With me.'

I take her head. Her eyes are closed. The mouth's pulled down in a kind of snarl.

'We shouldn't have come.'

'Just hold my arms.'

Her eyes have opened.

'I don't know where I am.'

'You're here with me.'

'I'm dying.'

'No, you're not.'

I kiss her cheek.

'I don't know where I am.'

A car goes past in the street below.

Her sobbing quietens; at one point, it seems, she might have screamed: there's the sudden convulsion of her body, then, in spasms, the tension dies.

'Help me make some food,' I say.

I take her to the kitchen; I get out the pans and set them on the stove. The food I've already bought and half-prepared.

'Can you light the gas?'

She's still got the lighter; only now, having lit the gas, does she look at it, the crown-shaped crest, then, almost absent-mindedly, she puts it down.

'I've bought some wine.'

I set the bottle down on the kitchen table.

'I haven't to drink any alcohol if I take these pills.'

'You could have a drop.'

She looks at the food, cooking; her eyes, once again, have filled with tears.

'Let's have a drop now. It'll warm us up.'

'Did my mother know we were coming here?'

She adds,

'She'll wonder where we are, if we haven't called, and begin to worry.'

'I told her we'd come straight home,' I say, yet she looks across, sensing now I've made this up.

'Do you cook here often?'

She raises her head: the lower half of the kitchen walls are painted green, the upper half a whitish yellow. A red line divides the two areas of colour. It's the line she gazes at, following it round, past the door, to the window, then over to the stove.

It's like some area of her mind she's cordoned off.

'Not often. No.' I shake my head.

I pour out the wine; I give her a glass.

'Was the crockery provided too?' she says.

'Yes,' I tell her. I add, 'Here's to it, then.'

She rests her glass against the table.

'A lot of the women in that place: their husbands get a divorce,' she says.

I put some salt in the pans. The water boils.

'They feel they can't communicate,' she says.

'With what?'

'Their wives.'

'I thought that was the wife's complaint,' I tell her.

She adds nothing for a while; there's a slowness in her movements: she looks at the vegetables once or twice. I can't think now what induced me to cook a meal: we could, just as easily, and less dramatically, have eaten out.

I get out two plates and go through to the room and set the table. The broken filaments in the fire have begun to glow. I turn out the light. A redness fills the room.

From the kitchen, bleakly, comes a sudden crash; I find, when I go back in, she's dropped a glass.

'I didn't see it.'

'It's all right,' I tell her. I sweep it up.

'I was trying to be careful. I put it out of reach. When I went to the sink I must have knocked it off.'

'Relax,' I tell her.

She stands at the sink.

'I've cut my hand.'

There's blood on her wrist.

She holds her hand beneath the tap.

'I shouldn't have come.'

'You'll be all right.'

I look for some cloth to wrap it up.

'I was looking forward to coming. I really was.'

I sit her down. By the time she's quietened the food is cooked. I serve it out in the other room.

'Are you ready?' I ask her and lead her through.

'Has the light gone out?'

'I turned it off.'

'I can hardly see.'

'Do you want it on?'

'No,' she says. 'If it's what you like.'

She eats quite slowly. Her hand is bandaged. She never looks at me directly. Only once do I see her look across, her eyes wide, startled, as if she's wondering where she is.

'Have you got my pills?'

'I can let you have them.'

'They said you should have them.'

'I'd like you to have them.'

'I'd prefer you to have them.'

She shakes her head.

'They told me to take one at night and one each morning. And one at lunch-time if I'm feeling worse.'

Something of that old, residual helplessness returns, a wanting to be absolved of her distress: she finishes the food but makes no move either to pass me her plate or get up and take it away herself.

'Are you feeling tired?'

'I don't know.'

'You could go to bed if you like and go to sleep.'

'I seem to sleep so much I don't know where I am. I've been sleeping afternoons, you know. And that's on top of what I sleep at night.'

'It's probably the pills.'

'It could be that.'

'Do you feel like managing without them, then?'

'I couldn't. Not unless they told me to.'

Perhaps if she'd carried her old convictions into her madness she wouldn't have been so bad: a determination to see it through without assistance of any kind, to let it run its course, untouched. Yet it had struck so swiftly, she'd been unprepared; the wars of the world had been undermined.

'Is there anything else to eat?'

She sits with her hands before her, resting on the table.

'Do you fancy something else?'

'Anything,' she says. She shakes her head.

I take the two plates through. I put on the kettle. In the kitchen I examine the food I've left.

There's a tin of fruit.

When I take it through she's still sitting at the table, gazing directly before her, her hands in her lap.

I put the plate down with the fruit. She picks up a spoon; she begins to eat.

She seems absorbed now entirely; I watch her as she eats, the smoothness of the brow: she pauses, the spoon raised to her lips.

'Would you like some tea?'

'I could take a pill.' She finishes the fruit. 'It's not too early, I suppose,' she says.

She looks round for a clock.

'We can wash up the plates tomorrow morning.'

Her gaze, for the first time, has been caught by the window at the back of the flat: the dividing-door to the bedroom is standing open. Visible through the window is the cathedral clock; perhaps, for a moment, she's been uncertain what it is. She half-rises in the chair.

'It's the cathedral,' I tell her.

She begins to cry; perhaps it's the shock, or a kind of exhaustion at the ending of the meal; almost absent-mindedly her eyes have filled with tears. She lifts her plate and mine and, with the same vagueness, takes them to the kitchen.

I follow her through. I find the tea-pot, put in the tea, mash it, find two cups and pour it out.

We sit by the fire. A vague wind now, in the stillness, is moaning round the house.

'Have you got the pill?'

She takes it with the tea; there's something almost religious in the way she lifts it up, places it on her tongue then flicks back her head, swallows it, then takes a sip of tea. It's some sort of ceremony, a demonstration.

'Have you had these kind before?'

She shakes her head.

I wonder, then, if it mightn't be better to toss them in the fire; or, since it's gas, failing the fire, into the yard outside. They might, after all, do the man below some good. She has a kind of fragility, a dependence; the pills, in their little plastic box, represent a kind of life, a reliance, an assertion that she's really what she is, not only in need of help, but unreliable.

I lean my head against her knee.

A moment later her hand comes down.

'I don't like it in the dark.'

'Do you want the light?'

She doesn't answer.

'We could go to bed.'

'I don't know,' she says.

'I'll sleep out here, if you like.' I indicate the chair.

'It doesn't matter.'

'Let's go to bed.'

She begins to cry. I take her hand. The window rattles suddenly, with the wind against the house.

'Where's the case?'

I put it on the bed.

'Is there a bathroom here?' she says.

'I should put on your coat,' I tell her. 'It's on the floor below.'

She goes out to the landing.

When she comes back in I'm already in bed.

She undresses slowly, standing by the bed.

'Did you drop the latch on the door?' I say.

'It shut behind me.'

'It'll be all right.'

I turn off the light. She climbs in slowly.

We lie apart. I take her hand. After a while she falls asleep.

I lie back on the pillow; I count the cathedral clock as it begins to chime.

Hours later she gives a scream; when I turn on the light she's still asleep.

I lie then like a sentinel: she doesn't stir. Her mouth is open. She scarcely breathes. I watch the faint reflection on the ceiling from the lights outside.

'Isn't that someone banging at the door?' she says.

'There's always someone banging at the door,' I tell her.

She climbs along the bed, about to dress. Having woken some time before, I've gone out to the kitchen and made some tea. It stands, steaming, on the wooden chair beside her pillow, along with the Jack Daniels which, unwittingly, I've omitted to remove.

The banging starts again.

'I say, is that you, old man?' a voice has said.

'Hadn't you better see who it is?' she says.

'I know who it is. They'll go away if we both keep quiet.'

She appears genuinely then to forget that there's anyone there at all. She pulls off her nightdress and stands for a moment looking round. The cathedral clock booms out above our heads.

The knocking starts again.

'I'd better answer it, I suppose,' I tell her.

I close the door, cross the room, and open the door leading to the landing.

The man with the red moustache is standing there. He's dressed in a raincoat and a flat, check cap.

'I'm sorry about this, old man,' he says. 'I tried to catch you, you see, last night.' He gestures behind him. 'At the college.'

He nods his head.

He glances behind me at the room itself.

'I'm busy at the moment, I'm afraid,' I tell him.

'I realize that, old man,' he says.

He examines the interior for several seconds.

'It's just something you ought to know, old man.'

'What's that?' I ask him.

He steps inside. He takes off his cap and glances round.

'I tried to catch you, you see, last night.'

'I know,' I tell him. 'You've mentioned that.'

'And the disguise, you see: it's become essential. For slipping out of the house,' he says.

'What's the important news?' I ask him.

'It's this man, old man.'

'What man?' I ask him.

'The one with the trilby hat, old man.' He narrows his eyes. 'He called at the flat.' He watches me then for several seconds. 'When I asked him what he wanted he went away.'

'Did he say what he wanted?'

'He just asked which floor you were living on, old man. When he started up I said you were out. If I hadn't have been there he'd have come straight up.'

He glances over, cautiously, towards the door.

'It's my opinion, old man, that he knew you were out. He wanted to search the flat, old man.'

'What for?'

'I've no idea, old man.' He can smell the tea: he looks over, hopefully, towards the kitchen. 'These people, you know, have methods of their own.'

His eyes, after glancing at the kitchen, have moved over in some alarm to the bedroom door.

Yvonne, for that moment, clearly, is uncertain where she is.

Quite naked, her eyes still out of focus, she gazes at the red-haired man, glances at me, and then, confused, half-smiling, turns back towards the bed.

'I was looking for the pill,' she says.

'I've got it here,' I tell her. 'I'll bring it in.'

I close the door.

'I say, I'm frightfully sorry, old man,' the red-haired man has said. He goes over to the door. 'I won't intrude.' He puts out his hand. 'My name's Ferguson, by the way,' he says.

He shakes my hand.

'Nice room you've got up here. Fresh air, and quite a view.' He gestures round. 'I haven't been up, you see, before.' He glances back to the bedroom door. 'I'll tip you the wink, of course, if he calls again.'

I close the door. I hear him hesitate the other side. His feet, slow and irregular, start down the stairs.

She's sprawled on the bed, her eyes closed, when I go back in. I get out the yellow capsules and at the rattle of the plastic box she begins to stir.

'I can't rest up here,' she says, dazedly. 'I don't like being on my own. It's cold.'

'Why don't you drink your tea,' I tell her.

'I'm feeling better now.' She starts to rise. She shakes her head. 'We could go to my mother's. She won't know where I am.'

'I thought we'd give her a miss today.'

'But there's only tomorrow left,' she cries. 'She'll be terribly hurt if I don't go down.'

'Perhaps,' I tell her, 'you ought to get dressed.'

I give her the pill. She swallows it down.

'What time do we leave?' she says.

'I'll help you on with your clothes,' I say.

She begins to dress. There's a briskness in her movements now. She packs her case.

'Are you taking it with you?'

'I thought I might.'

'Stay there for the night?' I say.

'She has a bed. She has it aired.' She gestures to the one behind. 'It'll be warmer than this. And it's easier, in any case, down there.'

She lifts the case.

'Won't you brush your hair?'

'I've got my beret,' she says. 'I'll cover it up.'

'I'll brush it for you, if you like,' I say.

'It'll be all right.'

Her coat unbuttoned, she's gone to the door.

'Do you want me to come as well?' I ask.

'Of course I want you to come.'

She doesn't look round: the case in her hand, she's stooped to the stairs, gazing down to the hall below.

I lock the door. I follow her down. Once in the street I take her hand; I take the case. By the time we've reached the end of the road she's walking briskly, her arm in mine, smiling broadly, half-intent, unaware of the crowds around – or of the man, it seems, in the trilby hat behind.

'You should have come down straight away. The bed's been ready, love. And I've baked a cake. I got food specially in, you see, last week.'

Yvonne is still sitting by the fire. Her back is straight. She looks like some retarded child, swollen, flushed with heat.

'We would have come down,' she says, for the third time now, while Mrs Sherman, sitting with her cup of tea, directly opposite, regards her face with an anxious smile.

'She so pleased to be home. She could have been here weeks ago,' Mrs Sherman adds. She gestures with her hand. 'It's obvious her home was what she'd want.' She looks across. 'Just look at her now. She's so glad to be back, amongst people and places she's always known.'

I sit down at the table. Since coming into the room, greeting her mother, then, like a deflated balloon, sitting in the chair, Yvonne herself has scarcely stirred. Her gaze, abstracted, is fixed on the mantelpiece above the fire. She seems scarcely aware of her mother at all. Behind her, on the sideboard, the photograph of her father regards her from its glossy frame, the incredulous, half-apprehensive look, like a man in pain.

'I'm sure it'll be better if you both slept here. Two hands, after all,' she says to me, 'are better than one.'

'I've got two hands of my own,' I say.

'Two *pairs* of hands,' she says. She smiles.

A train passes slowly overhead; there's the thudding of the diesel, the rattle of the trucks. Windows vibrate throughout the house: there's the rattle, somewhere, of an empty cup.

'They've so many people up there I'm sure they forget, at times, who some of them are.' She looks to the fire. 'Are you warm enough there, then, love?' she asks.

She gets up from her chair; she leans down for a moment, settles a cushion against her daughter's back, then stoops quickly forward to glance at her face.

'Would you like another cup of tea, then, love?'

Yvonne examines her mother's face; she doesn't stir.

'I'll make you a fresh one, love,' she says. 'And while the kettle's on I'll cut some bread.'

She crosses to the sink; she fills a kettle.

'If they saw her now I'm sure they'd change their minds. She's sat like that all afternoon. No trouble, you see, to anyone.'

She comes to the fire, carrying the kettle; she pokes the flames then sets the kettle down on a metal hob.

Yvonne, suddenly, has begun to stir.

Her head thrust back, she gives a scream.

The sound is huge, high-pitched. It lasts for several seconds. Her face has darkened; her tongue curls in her throat. Her body shudders. She begins to choke.

Mrs Sherman, stooping to the fire, has given a groan; she seems, for that moment, unable to rise. She turns to Yvonne as I lift her from the chair.

Her head's thrust back; her body shudders.

She screams again, her body stiffened.

'I should ring for an ambulance.'

'What?'

'Go to a phone and call one up.'

'What?' Her eyes are wide; her face is white. She holds her head between her hands.

'Dial 999. They shouldn't be long.'

Yvonne, her body arched, has screamed again.

I lift her up. I smack her face. I see the wild-eyed look behind her back.

'You'd better hurry.'

'What shall I say?'

'Tell them who you are and where to come.'

She goes to the door; she stands for a moment, gazing in, wild-eyed. I slap her again; she gives a scream.

'If you don't go now,' I tell her, 'it might easily be too late.'

She disappears.

I hold Yvonne beneath my arm: I walk her up and down.

Every few seconds her legs collapse. I slap her face; I hit her hard. I call her name. I ask her who she is.

By the time the ambulance arrives she's no longer aware of anything at all.

I carry her out to the street myself.

Her mother and I get in together.

The attendant sits by Yvonne, his hand around her mouth.

We say nothing on the journey up.

We drive between the gates and only two hours later, when I'm leaving, do they ask to see the pills. I hand them in. They count them out.

'She's only had two,' I say.

They tick the list; I go out to the hall: Mrs Sherman, dark-eyed, upright, is sitting on a bench.

I take her arm. We set off down the drive.

A street-lamp is burning by the empty gate; lamps light up the drive and the entrance to the house.

We wait by the gates for a local bus.

'Do you think she'll be all right?' she says.

'They say she'll be all right,' I tell her.

'They know what they're doing, I suppose,' she says.

'I'm not sure that they do,' I tell her. 'Not that it matters, anymore,' I add.

'Oh, but it matters, love,' she says.

The bus comes into sight.

'I can't make it out. The chances that she's had: it ends like this.'

'That's probably her trouble, on the whole,' I say. 'Not that it makes much difference. To Yvonne, I mean.'

4

'You can take it in my office,' Wilcox says.

He holds the door of the life room, allowing me to step outside then closing it carefully behind him.

As I reach the stairs leading to the hall he calls, 'If it's anything important, of course, you'll let me know.'

'Important?'

'On the phone, I mean.' He gestures irritably to the hall below.

As I go down the stairs I can hear his voice, bellowing from beyond the screens, *Is everybody gone on holiday, then? What's going on in here, then, Pollard? The annual general bloody council of the desk-top somnambulists and chair-back heelers-overs' union, is it?*

In his office, after closing the door, I pick up the telephone and hear the secretary's voice at the other end and then, a moment later, a woman's voice I don't recognize at all.

'This is Jacqueline Spencer,' the voice reminds me. 'We met briefly when you came up to the house to see Mrs Newman's picture.'

She waits a moment for this to be confirmed.

'We tried to get you over the week-end, but you seem to have been away. Mr Newman wondered if you'd like to meet him.'

'Where?'

'The most convenient place for him would be the site.'

'What site?'

'He'll send a car to pick you up. Do you have a free day at all this week?'

She waits.

'If you could give us a day he'll be very glad to fit in with it,' she says.

I tell her Wednesday.

'I've got your address from Mrs Newman. There'll be a car at your door at half-past nine.'

'What's it all about?' I say.

'The chauffeur will drive you there,' she says. 'He'll be given his instructions'

The phone's put down. I rattle my end of it for several seconds, listen, put it down, then look slowly round the office.

It's only the third or fourth time I've been inside the room. Across one wall is arranged a set of shelves, crammed full of bottles containing a yellowish liquid. A door leads off at one side opposite the window; when I try the handle I find it's locked.

I turn round to the door of the office itself and find Kendal standing there, his hands in his pockets.

'I thought it was the Skipper,' he says.

'I've been taking a call.' I indicate the phone.

'That's generous of him,' Kendal says.

He takes out a note from his jacket pocket, unfolds it and holds it out for me to read. '*Dear Kendal,*' it says, '*I'd like to see you in my office some time today. Signed: R. N. Wilcox. (Principal)*'

'He's probably inviting you to dinner.'

'You think it's that?'

'Pollard's been invited, too.'

'I can breathe more easily, I suppose,' he says.

He glances round the room.

'Anything to steal? Borrow? Anything, you think, that won't be missed?'

'I've just been trying the door.'

'It's his private wash-room.'

'Have you ever been in?'

'Never.'

He opens the top drawer on one side of the desk. It's packed to the top with india-rubbers. We both stare into it for several seconds.

'What are those for?'

'For rubbing out.'

'But why so many?'

'I've no idea.'

A footstep sounds from the hall outside. I close the drawer.

'What's going on in here, then? Mothers' meeting?'

'I've just received your letter, Principal,' Kendal says. He holds it out.

'I've just finished on the phone,' I tell him.

'From the Newmans was it?'

He gestures at the phone itself. Clearly he's inquired about the caller's identity before allowing me to answer it.

'I've been asked to a meeting.'

'Where?'

'They've asked me, at the moment, to keep it confidential.'

'With Mr Newman?' He looks across.

'That's right.'

He gazes at me for several seconds.

'You'll give him my regards.'

'I will.'

'When're you seeing him?'

'Wednesday.'

'Wednesday.'

He looks over impulsively to a calendar on the wall. For a moment I have the feeling he's going to offer to come as well.

'I'll let you know how it goes,' I tell him.

'That's good of you,' he says.

I step over, cautiously, towards the door.

Kendal, the letter in his hand, remains standing by his desk.

'I've just been complimenting Kendal on his work. I've heard one or two complimentary things about it recently,' I tell him.

'Kendal?'

'He'd be a very valuable ally,' I say, 'if we had him on our side.'

'Side?'

I close one eye.

'In reference to that scheme we mentioned.'

'Scheme.'

'Vis-à-vis,' I tell him, 'things to come.'

I gesture vaguely at the college overhead.

'I'll leave you to it.' I nod to Wilcox, nod to Kendal and, stepping outside, I close the door.

I can hear no sound at all, for several seconds; then, faintly, comes the growl of Wilcox as he begins to clear his throat.

I get out a cigarette, light it, and go up the stairs smoking, puffing out, as fast as I am able, huge, uncontrollable clouds of smoke.

'Where were you at the week-end?'

'I had an appointment,' I tell her, 'somewhere else.'

'I called at the flat.'

'I'm afraid I was out.'

'So I discovered.'

She turns over, slowly, in the bed.

'I don't suppose Beccie's been to see you.'

'Beccie?'

'Has she been,' she says, 'or not?'

'She did call, as a matter of fact, one evening.'

'I bet.' She pulls up the bed clothes beneath her chin. 'I hope you don't encourage her. To come up here again.'

'I don't know,' I tell her. 'I suppose I might.'

'Honestly. Can you imagine?'

'I don't suppose she'll mind.'

'You're mad.'

'Your husband,' I tell her, 'has invited me to meet him.'

'I know,' she says, and adds, 'I'm not surprised.'

'What's it all about?' I ask her.

'I've no idea.'

'You must have some.'

'He just wants to meet you, I suppose,' she says.

'It's very strange.'

'No stranger than some things, I suppose,' she says.

'Did you know,' I tell her, 'I'm being followed?'

'Not by a man,' she says, 'in a trilby hat?'

'You know all about it, then?' I say.

'Honestly,' she says, 'he's watching *me*.'

She smiles. Her cheeks, smooth and taut, are slightly dimpled. The grey eyes, mascara-ed, gaze out from the hollow of the pillow with an eerie light.

'It's a little insurance my husband's taken out.'

'On what?'

'On me.'

'He's having you followed?'

'You're very conceited, thinking it was just for you.'

'I'm not sure what I think,' I tell her.

'What day have you arranged to see him, then?'

'Wednesday.'

'Did he arrange that,' she says, 'or you?'

'I suggested it, I believe,' I tell her.

'That was our day,' she says. 'Had you forgotten?'

'I arranged it for the morning: I can always see you,' I say, 'in the afternoon.'

'Magnanimity!' she says.

'We could go together.'

'My darling,' she tells me, smiling, 'this meeting, I'm afraid, is just for you.'

Later, as she's leaving, she says, 'I've been asked, by the way, to give you this.'

She holds out a parcel, thin and flat, inscribed with her husband's name, which, on arrival, she's laid down on the chair inside the door.

'If you're seeing him soon I wondered if you'd mind.'

'What's this?' I ask her and begin to laugh. 'Not carrying messages, too,' I add.

'It's something he asked for.' She shakes her head. 'He's not at home, you see, at present.'

She turns to the door.

'Is our man still in the street?' she says.

When I look down at the road there's no one there.

'Probably his day off.' She laughs.

'Or perhaps his mission's been accomplished, Liz.'

She laughs again.

'But darling, it's hardly even started yet!'

I see her moments later as she steps out from the door; perhaps it's Ferguson she's aware of most: without expression she ducks her head, glances down the street towards the town, then sets off uncertainly in the opposite direction.

Seconds later the man in the trilby hat comes into view; his hands in his pockets, he wanders off, idly, not up the street, but, glancing lazily around him, in the opposite direction to Elizabeth, towards the town.

5

The car's not the salmon-pink creation I'd been expecting but a dark blue Bentley. I see its number plate from the window: N N 1. The chauffeur with the peaked cap gets out from behind the wheel; he looks up at the house, looks at the numbers on either side, then steps up to the door.

The bell rings in the hall below.

There's a murmur of voices. The bell rings again, this time in the flat.

Ferguson, his red hair dishevelled, is standing on the stairs.

'I say, old man. There's somebody for you.'

He waits, his hand on the banister, as I descend. He's dressed in a yellow and mauve striped blazer.

'The police,' I say, and nod my head.

'I say, old man,' he says. 'I'm terribly sorry.'

'I've seen it coming,' I add, 'for days.'

'I say, old man, there's nothing I can do?'

'Nothing, I'm afraid.' I shake my head.

'No messages to give?'

'They've all been given.'

'I'm sorry, old man, it's come to this.'

He comes out to the step; he sees the car. His eyes narrow; he begins to frown.

The chauffeur nods his head, turns to the rear door of the car, and pulls it open. With the flat parcel beneath my arm I step inside.

There's a second figure there: huge, massive, square-shouldered, he takes up more than half of the space available on the seat itself. He's dressed in a dark overcoat. A morning newspaper is open on his knee.

'Hi,' he says. 'Remember me? We met at Elizabeth's the other week.'

The car, with the force of his laughter begins to shake.

Outside, Ferguson, smoothing down his hair, is gazing in. I wave.

He gestures back, uncertain. There's a white handkerchief

tucked in the top pocket of his blazer. He's wearing a light blue tie, with a horse's head outlined, in a creamish colour, immediately beneath the knot.

The chauffeur gets in behind the wheel.

'Do you have the parcel, sir?'

I hold it up.

'Is that for Neville?' the broadly built man has said. I indicate the name inscribed on the dark brown paper.

'I could have taken it up myself.'

'No one knew you were coming today, Mr Fraser,' the chauffeur says.

He starts the car.

'You don't mind me cadging a lift, then?' Fraser says. 'I asked Jackie to let you know. No doubt,' he adds, 'she clean forgot.'

He gets out a cigarette case.

The car moves off.

I get out the cigarette lighter with the coloured crest.

Ferguson, still smoothing down his hair, has waved. The mauve and yellow striped arm is raised.

'A friend of yours, then?' Fraser says.

'A detective.'

'Really?'

He turns in his seat to gaze through the rear window at the disappearing figure.

'Dressed conspicuously,' he says.

'That's part of his disguise.'

'C.I.D. or private?'

'C.I.D.'

'First time I've seen one,' he tells me, 'dressed like that.'

I flick the lighter.

'A new conception.'

He nods his head.

He dips the end of the cigarette in the bluish flame, then sees the monogram printed on the side.

'Elizabeth's?'

I light my own cigarette and snap it shut.

'She left it behind,' I say, 'one night.'

The chauffeur's head has turned; it gives an involuntary jerk. Fraser, however, has glanced behind, back down the street, as if he hasn't heard.

'No one, on the face of it, could suspect him of being one, I suppose,' I say.

The figure behind us disappears.

The car dips down towards the valley.

'What branch of the C.I.D. is your friend in, then?' Fraser says.

'Murder.'

'Is there much of it goes on round here?'

'More than is generally recognized,' I say.

'What case,' he says, 'is he dealing with at present?'

'The death by strangulation of a man found on a tennis court,' I tell him.

'Hence, I suppose, his sporty get-up.'

'That's right.'

'He looked more like part and parcel of a song and dance routine to me.'

'The victim was fond of tap-dancing in his youth,' I say.

'Do you always take the piss out of everyone you meet?' he says.

'Invariably,' I tell him.

He begins to laugh.

He weighs, by my reckoning, over sixteen stone: I wonder, if he swings one over in the car, which way I ought to move: one in the belly then one in the chops, then one on the nose to make it count. He's muscle-bound, too; most of it, I suspect, has turned to fat.

'Married, are you?' He looks across.

'I have been,' I tell him, 'for some considerable time.'

'Children?'

I shake my head.

'Working is she, then? Your wife.'

'In hospital,' I tell him.

'Nothing serious, I hope.'

'Went crazy,' I say. 'She's been confined.'

He's not sure, for a moment, which way to look; the driver's eyes gleam back from the mirror then glance away.

The car turns westwards. The valley narrows; buildings creep in on either side.

Fraser, in a rather melancholic fashion, begins to bite his nails. He props one of his short, muscular legs across the other.

'You teach in the local art school, then?'

'That's right.'

'Any prospects?'

'None whatsoever.'

'Why do you stay on, if that's the case?'

'I don't intend to,' I tell him, 'for very long.'

'Has Neville offered you a job?' he says.

'None that I'm aware of. No.'

I glance into the mirror.

'He did mention, however, that he's looking for a chauffeur. He's somewhat disenchanted,' I add, 'with the one he has at present.'

'Did he tell you that?'

'Strictly between ourselves,' I say.

The car has slowed. The eyes, partly obscured by the neb of the cap, meet mine.

'Relax, Bennings,' Fraser says.

He gets out a cigarette: he offers it round the front to the driver.

'No thank you, sir,' the chauffeur says.

He taps the end of the cigarette himself: I get out the lighter, flick up the flame: his eyes, as he lights the cigarette, meet mine.

'I wouldn't mind, when the moment comes – as come,' he tells me, 'it undoubtedly will – pumping you in the mouth myself.'

'Whenever you can find the time,' I say.

'They tell me,' he says, 'you used to box.'

'On and off,' I say, and smile.

'I've done some fighting,' he says, 'myself.'

'A size like that,' I tell him, 'I'm not surprised.'

I fold one leg across the other.

'Targets of those proportions are hard to find.'

His own leg cocked up, he suddenly takes down.

He smokes his cigarette for a while in silence.

The road, a straight, concrete highway, has suddenly broadened. The speed of the car has suddenly increased. Odd trees, newly planted, have been set at irregular distances on either side.

We pass through a village. Rows of windowless cottages

appear; men with picks and hammers are working on the walls; truncated, glassless windows look out onto overgrown fields: the low white profile of a glass-roofed concrete building appears briefly on the skyline of a moor beyond.

The road dips down. Some distance further on the car turns off along a narrow lane. Immediately ahead, blocking the lane, appears a cottage. Its thatched roof with its two tall brick chimneys is surmounted by a painted metal sign, a large fist clenched around a bar of steel. The sign itself is painted red. Above it, in silver, is set the single letter L.

Two tunnels have been cut through the centre of the cottage; as we pass through the one on the left, following a large arrow, a man in a peaked cap leans out of a lattice window.

He ducks his head, glances in the car as it passes through the building, then salutes briefly as he glimpses the broad-chested figure sitting in the back.

A driveway sweeps up beyond, past a clump of rhododendron bushes and a line of trees.

It emerges at the front of a concrete mansion. A vast, pillared portico projects from its crumbled, blackened façade; much of the stone has been patched with cement. Cement too has been used to fill in the ruts and holes in the drive itself.

Across the lawns and terraces at the front of the house stand several massive shed-like structures. Bulldozers move across the edges of a lawn; the derricks of several large cranes project above a line of trees. From every direction, as the car pulls up, comes the dull, staccatic roar of engines.

The chauffeur gets out and opens the door: he opens it, deliberately or otherwise, on Fraser's side. The large man douses his cigarette and clambers out.

The pale-faced, black-eyed man I've seen at Elizabeth's appears on the steps at the front of the house.

'I'm Groves,' he says. He nods to Fraser. 'I'll take you over, if you'll follow me.'

Fraser goes off towards the house, pausing on the steps and glancing back. The car, with the small-eyed chauffeur, has driven off.

Groves waits. 'You came up with Fraser, then?'

'That's right.'

'He's jolly good company to have around.'

'Very,' I tell him. I nod my head. Fraser's large figure has turned on the steps. When I look again he's disappeared.

'There's Neville now, then,' Groves has said.

As we emerge from the trees several large buildings, windowless factory structures, have appeared on either side. On the flank of each of them is mounted the letter L, surmounted by the device of the red-painted fist clenching the bar of steel. Several trucks and lorries, stamped with the same device, are parked beneath the trees. In the furthest distance, beyond a stretch of moorland, are visible the remains of the village we passed through in the car.

Walking across the open space between the nearest building and the line of trees is a small, slight figure who, on seeing us emerge from the trees, runs his hand across his long blond hair and turns casually in our direction.

Groves, I discover, glancing round, has disappeared.

'Freestone?'

A pair of cool blue eyes examine mine.

'My name's Newman.'

He puts out his hand; the eyes glance past me now towards the house.

'They told me you'd arrived.'

I hold out the parcel.

'I was asked,' I tell him, 'if I'd give you this.'

'That's right.'

He doesn't take it. Perhaps he's wondering if Elizabeth has come.

'Is there anything in it?'

He shakes his head.

'We thought, if you had something to bring, there was more chance of you turning up.' He smiles. 'It was my secretary's idea,' he says. 'Not mine.'

He turns, his hand in his pocket, and looks back towards the moor. Trees, uprooted and dismembered, lie strewn across what at one time might have been a park. Closer at hand a tractor is filling in a dried-up lake. A balustraded bridge stands, partly dismembered, at its narrowest end, and at the other, where it disappears beyond a belt of trees, stands a roofless stone pagoda.

'What do you think?'

'I like the fist.'

'I thought you would.'

'And the bar of steel.'

'Symbolic.' He glances up.

'I suppose,' I tell him, indicating the parcel, 'I might throw this away.'

'I'll take it.'

'Shouldn't you look inside?'

He laughs. There's a faint tinge of colour on either cheek. The eyes are hard. I can see the whiteness of his knuckles as he feels the paper. On the lapel of his jacket is pinned a tiny badge with a device, in relief, I can't make out.

'I hear Fraser came up in the car as well.'

'That's right.'

'Did he tell you much about it?' He gestures round.

'Nothing.'

'It's a new industrial estate. Where that old house is now there'll be a skyscraper block accommodating, in a centralized office, over thirty or forty firms. There's even a new church if you want to look. In ten years time there'll be twenty or thirty thousand people working here. In fifteen years it might have trebled.'

'What's your job here?'

'I supervise it all,' he says.

He looks round him, sees the bridge, then, further off, the stone pagoda.

'It was quite a mess when we first arrived. In a couple of months you'll see a difference. It's all bits and pieces I'm afraid at present.'

He turns away from the trees and indicates we might walk down between the buildings immediately below us.

A tractor lumbers past; he steps aside. We follow a moment later in the tracks left by its massive tyres.

'I wondered,' he says, 'if you'd any ideas.'

He gestures round.

'We have an artist. A sociologist. An architect. An environmental psychologist. They've been with the scheme since it first began.'

I get out a cigarette. He shakes his head.

I think it might be too much to get out the lighter.

I say, 'What category do I come into, then?'

'None whatsoever.' He looks across. 'That's why I asked.'

I get out the lighter.

As far as I can tell he doesn't notice. I light the cigarette, snap the lighter shut and put it away.

He walks with his hands in his trouser pockets. His cheek, on one side, is drawn in, as if he's biting the skin inside. In profile he reminds me of those intellectual athletes, common in England before the First World War: the face is lean and slim, the eyes are calm and almost dreamy. He might, in some earlier life, have climbed the Himalayas, run the mile, high-jumped, rowed, boxed, cricketed, footballed to an almost professional level.

'I wanted the view,' he tells me, 'of someone who didn't care.'

'About what?'

'Anything at all.'

'Is that the impression your detective gives?'

He smiles. The faint touch of colour on his cheeks has gone.

'It's an impression I get from everyone,' he says.

He looks across.

'The detective's there,' he adds, 'for my own protection.'

'I thought it was for your wife's.'

He shakes his head.

'We're not together,' he says, 'at present. I need to know what's going on.'

'Aren't you getting divorced?'

He bows his head. He looks at his feet as he walks along.

We've reached the door of the nearest building; we don't go in. The track turns off towards the moor.

'Even my daughter's caught up in it,' he says.

'You could always take her away,' I tell him.

'From the college? She'd never allow it. She's as much aware of motives,' he says, 'as anyone else.'

We've turned up the track; behind us I can see Groves come out from beneath the trees. He looks over, waves, gazes over a little longer, then, with a shrug, turns back towards the house.

'Elizabeth, you see, is not unlike you in some respects. You may have found that out yourself. She couldn't give a damn about anything at times. It's almost suicidal, this impulse, in the end, to disown almost everything,' he says.

'She's got more to disown, I suppose, than me.'

'I'm not so sure.'

He kicks at the clay in front of his feet.

'I gather your wife's in hospital,' he adds.

'She is at present.'

'Is she seriously ill?'

'I've no idea.'

'Suppose she found out.'

'She wouldn't mind.'

'Do you mean,' he says, 'she doesn't care?'

'She's got past caring about anything,' I tell him.

He lifts his wrist, abstracted, then glances at his watch.

'In a way,' he says, 'I don't care much myself.' He gestures round. 'It's an act of faith, like everything else.'

'Wilcox cares.'

He shakes his head: he's not certain, perhaps, for a moment, who Wilcox is.

'He's hoping,' I tell him, 'when things materialize, you'll rejuvenate the college.'

He waves his arm: 'The whole town'll be affected by what goes on round here.' He looks across. 'I told him the college, for instance, might be expanded.'

We've reached the edge of the moor; tractors move to and fro, dragging back the turf; in every direction trenches have been dug; there are stacks of pipes standing up amongst the bracken, mounds of bricks and from further down the slope comes the clatter of a giant cement machine.

'There'll be houses right across this slope.' He waves his arm. 'Over there,' he adds, pointing in the direction of the ruined village, 'there'll be a community centre, a sports field and a running-track. There's no telling what the effect might be: colleges, schools, libraries, they'll all be needed.'

'It doesn't seem worth it.'

'Improving people's lives?'

'Hanging on to your wife,' I tell him.

'There've been men like you before,' he says.

'Have you made the same appeals?' I ask.

'It's never been necessary, in the end,' he says.

He looks across.

'I see nothing to be afraid of here,' I tell him.

'Nor anything to respect,' he says.

I shake my head.

'Then we've nothing more to say.'

He gestures back the way we've come.

'The car'll take you back,' he says. 'Just ask at the house. They'll bring it round.'

He starts off down the slope.

He doesn't look back.

By the time I reach the house it's begun to rain.

When the car comes round and I step inside, I see Fraser waiting in the porch above me, waving, his massive features lit up, despite the weather, with something of a smile.

Part Five

I

'It might be less disturbing if she didn't see anyone for a while,' he says.

He begins to pick his nose. His hand, after lying for some time on the edge of his desk, is slowly raised. The head, as if recoiling, drifts slowly to one side.

His eyes are tired; large pouches hang beneath them, each one encircled by a dark blue line.

'Does that apply to everyone?' I ask him.

'I shan't insist,' he says. 'Though with her mother,' he adds, 'I suppose I might.'

'Could I see her now?' I ask.

He's reading the papers on his desk, turning one loose sheet and then another; he tries, as he reads, to give the impression that the papers themselves have to do with her. I can see the name, however, printed on the file: 'P. D. Collins.'

'She's probably sleeping,' he says. 'You could ask the nurse.'

He's on the point, it seems, of seeing me to the door.

'I'd like to see her before I go,' I tell him.

'Okay,' he says. 'I suppose you might. It's not a prison, you know.' He begins to laugh. The sound is harsh; it raises an echo in the corridor outside.

I get up from the chair; his original intention to see me to the door has gone.

'If you'd kept her at home she'd have been all right.'

'She prefers being with her mother, on the whole,' I tell him.

'Is it something to do with you?' he says.

'I think I'm a sort of token attempt,' I tell him.

'At what?'

'To live some sort of life,' I say.

'The demands you make, in the end, might prove too much.'

'If she asks me to go I'll go,' I tell him.

'Is there anyone else?'

I shake my head.

'I've had a strange letter,' he says, 'from a Mr Newman. He wonders if the relationship you're having with *his* wife might not be having a debilitating effect upon your own.'

'Have you told him I'll sue him if he writes again.'

'Perhaps you ought to have a talk with him,' he says.

'I've had a talk with him,' I tell him.

'It's nothing to do with me.' He shakes his head. 'I just thought I ought to mention it,' he says.

He gets up, briefly, from behind the desk.

'Have you written to the college yet?' I ask.

'I've sent a note to your Principal. Setting his mind at rest. Though I can't see what he's objecting to,' he says.

He sits down once more behind the desk.

'Will you write to Newman, too?'

'I'll send him a note.' He looks across. 'Saying it's no concern of mine,' he says.

I open the door.

'If you'll see the nurse. And tell her you've got my permission. Though if Mrs Freestone's sleeping,' he says, 'she mustn't be disturbed.'

I go down to the ward. There's no one in the matron's office; when I go through to the ward itself I find all the beds are empty.

I go back to the dining-room. A nurse, working in the kitchen, has raised the window.

'Your wife isn't down here any more,' she says. She jerks her thumb towards the ceiling. 'It's the Flora Bundy Ward.' The name itself has raised a smile. 'Straight up the stairs, on the second floor.'

I go back down the corridor to the hall, climb the stairs, past Lennox's office and the corridor with the waiting patients, and go on up to the floor above.

All the windows are barred. The ward, superficially, looks like a conventional hospital interior, austere, unpretentious.

Two women without teeth are playing cards in an ante-room; a third woman, in a long dressing-gown, is standing at an open window, gazing out between the bars.

A nurse comes out of an office beside the door; presumably she's been talking to Lennox on the phone: when she sees me there she comes across.

'Your wife is awake,' she says, 'if you'd like to see her.'

She gestures off, vaguely, towards the ward itself.

'At the far end,' she says. 'We've told her you were coming.'

Whether this is true or not I've no idea; Yvonne, when I get to the bed, shows no expression at all.

She's sitting up, her back supported by pillows, gazing vacantly before her. She seems, suddenly, to have acquired more weight; her cheeks are fatter, her face is red. There's some sort of magazine lying on the bed, open, as though it's being read by someone else.

I call her name; she seems unconcerned, nodding slightly as if at the end of some hour-long conversation.

'More open up here.' I point to the windows. 'A better view.'

'Have you brought some flowers?'

Her hands hang down, limply, on the cover of the bed.

'I haven't,' I tell her.

'I thought they said you'd brought some, then.'

'How're you feeling, then?' I say.

'I feel all right.'

'You're looking much better,' I say, 'already.'

'They give you good food,' she says, 'I'll grant you that.' She looks along the ward; one or two other figures are lying in the beds, a woman with white hair, a woman without any teeth, and a woman with bright red lipstick and brightly rouged cheeks who's smiling now in my direction.

The nurse I've spoken to at the door comes down the ward.

'And how are you today, Yvonne?' she says.

'All right.' She glances at the nurse, then looks away.

'She's just woken up from a good night's sleep.' The nurse consults a watch pinned to her tunic. 'That's thirteen hours,' she says. 'She'll be setting a record if she keeps it up.'

'What's the record?' Yvonne has said.

'I'll have to look it up,' she says.

She moves on, calling to the women as she passes by the beds.

'Are you allowed to smoke in here?'

'I don't know,' she says. She shakes her head.

'Do you know any of the other patients here?' I say.

She shakes her head.

The woman with the make-up on has left her bed. She's half-way down the ward already: 'How are you feeling today?' she says.

'All right,' I tell her. I nod my head.

'I saw you yesterday, you know,' she says.

'I wasn't here yesterday,' I tell her.

'I saw you,' she says. She begins to laugh.

She has on a pink dressing-gown, pinned at the neck.

Yvonne, stiff-backed, upright, has fixed her gaze on the opposite bed.

'I have a boy-friend,' she adds, 'like you.'

'Does he come here every day?' I ask.

'He's always here.' She gestures round. 'He's up here now, as a matter of fact.'

We both look round.

'He's just talking to the doctors. He'll be coming back.'

The nurse, at the far end of the ward, has turned.

'He's bigger than you. You should see his chest.'

She pushes out her own and hits it soundly with either fist.

'I'd better keep out of his way,' I tell her.

'He'll find you,' she says. She laughs again.

'Mr Freestone wants to talk to his wife,' the nurse has said. She takes her arm.

'I was telling him he'd better look out,' she says.

'Oh, he knows that well enough,' the nurse has said.

She leads her back towards the bed.

'I've seen him here before.'

'Oh, he'll be coming up quite often,' the nurse has said.

Their conversation drones on for a while from the other bed.

'Is there anything you need?' I say.

'I've got everything in the cupboard,' she says.

I open the door of the cabinet beside her bed.

Her clothes are folded up inside, though not her dress.

There's no sign, either, of her coat or shoes; her slippers

have been tucked beneath the bed. There's her handbag, a toothbrush and a torn-up packet of cigarettes. On top of the cabinet is a cup of cold tea standing in a saucer.

'Do you need any washing done?' I say.

'They've taken it away.'

She waves her hand, vaguely, towards the door.

'You've put on weight.'

'What?'

'The food.'

'I don't eat much.'

She glances down the ward.

'Did my mother say she'd come?'

The shadows darken around her eyes.

'I haven't seen her yet,' I tell her.

'Will you see her tonight?'

'I can give her a message.'

'I don't know why she doesn't come,' she says.

'Have they been up to see you from the ward below?'

She shakes her head. Her thoughts, it seems, have wandered off.

'I wrote her a letter. I can't remember when it was,' she says.

She rubs her head.

'It wasn't long ago.'

The nurse, smiling, has wandered back.

She widens her eyes, still smiling, then nods her head.

'Time for your husband to go,' she says. 'He's been granted a special privilege, you know. Visiting at this time. You realize that?'

I lean over Yvonne and kiss her cheek.

The nurse, still smiling, pats down a pillow.

She pulls up the covers; Yvonne slips back.

'I'll come up soon,' I say. 'And bring some flowers.'

'She's so much better,' the nurse has said.

When I reach the end of the ward the woman with the make-up waves. Yvonne herself is lying on her back, her face hidden now by the angle of the pillow.

I wave in any case, get another wave back, and go out through the door to the stairs to the sound of women's laughter.

The bracketed light that normally burns above the rear

entrance of the college has suddenly gone out. As I lock the modelling-shed door I hear a step in the yard itself and turn round to see a figure, its arm raised, standing immediately above me. I hit out instinctively, the keys still in my hand.

The figure moves back: it goes on one knee; a second figure materializes from the darkness by its side. There seem, in that instant, to be four or five.

I move back against the wall; I swing my fist. The keys fly off.

Somebody's boot comes up between my legs.

There's a flash, like a sheet of lightning, inside my head. It comes again. A moment later I'm lying on the ground. Other boots appear. A club comes down.

A light goes on across the yard; feet run off. An engine starts in the street outside.

Hendricks is standing on the steps; he holds the door open behind him, the light shining out across the yard.

'What's going on?'

'I've fallen down.'

He flicks the switch. 'The light's gone out.'

'That probably explains it.' I indicate the steps.

'Can I give you a hand?'

'I was locking up the modelling shed,' I tell him. 'I've gone and lost the keys.'

'I've a torch in the car,' he says. 'I'll look around.'

A few minutes later a pale beam of light starts wandering round the yard.

'Got them,' he says.

He comes across.

'Are you all right?'

He holds my arm.

'You could sue the college, you know, for that. They're responsible for lighting the steps,' he says.

He holds the door.

One of my eyes, it seems, is closed; the other's half-obscured by a swelling below.

'My God,' he says. He gazes at my face in the corridor light.

'I'll go into the bogs,' I tell him, 'and wash it up.'

I step into the toilets and fill a bowl; in the corridor outside, as I wash my face, I can hear Wilcox talking to one of the cleaners then, seconds later, Hendricks's voice: 'Mr Freestone's fallen down the steps, Mr Wilcox. The light doesn't work.'

'What light?'

'The outside light, Mr Wilcox,' Hendricks says.

'It worked all right a minute ago,' the Principal says. 'I switched it on myself.'

I'm aware of his figure, vaguely, as he stands inside the door.

'I've been telling him he ought to sue the college, Mr Wilcox,' Hendricks says.

'He'll do no such bloody thing. I can tell you that.'

'If he's fallen down the steps and the light doesn't work, it's the college's responsibility,' Hendricks says.

'Are you trying to blame me, then, Hendricks?' Wilcox says.

'I thought you'd be on our side. Against the college,' Hendricks says.

'I *am* the college, Hendricks,' Wilcox says.

There's a moment's silence. The white-tiled room with its row of basins, its two glaring figures, seems slowly to be spinning round and round.

'There's a first-aid kit in my office,' Wilcox says.

'If Hendricks can take me home,' I tell him, 'I think I'll be all right.'

'Are you sure, then, Freestone?' Wilcox says. He sounds relieved.

He watches me move out to the corridor and then, feeling the wall, along the corridor towards the door.

Hendricks, after a moment, holds my arm.

'I say, shouldn't you go to the hospital?' he says.

'You don't want the hospital brought into it, Hendricks,' Wilcox says. His voice is reasonable, cajoling. It's developed, almost, a kind of whine. 'A lot of fuddy-duddies there. Fuss about nothing, I can tell you that.'

'I'll be all right, old man,' I tell him.

He holds the door.

Once in the car my mind goes blank; there's an aching in my head, a blur of light, then Hendricks is leaning over me and saying, 'We're there, old man. You'll be all right.'

I catch a glimpse of Ferguson's moustache; a lighted stair.

A clock booms out. I count the hours.

Elizabeth, when I wake, is sitting by the bed.

'Why didn't you call me?' she says. 'I could have come yesterday, if you'd only got in touch.'

She kisses my one good eye, hesitates over the other, then runs her lips, circumspectly, across my cheek.

'Was it Nev?'

'Or Leyland.'

'Did you see his face?'

'There were four of them, at least,' I say.

She kisses my mouth, my hand: she presses her lips once more against my eye.

'I'd have thought,' she says, 'it would have been Leyland.'

'I can't understand,' I tell her, 'what they hope to gain.'

She draws back her head; her eyes are dark; recently, it seems, she might have been crying.

'Do you think it's Nev?'

'I don't really mind. One or the other. They're two of a kind.'

The cathedral clock begins to boom. It's almost dark. The eerily-lit face of the clock glows out, yellowish, from the darkness of the building.

She hasn't, as yet, removed her hat; her coat she's already taken off. Underneath she wears a dark brown dress: the sleeves are transparent and, like nearly all her dresses, buttoned at the wrist. There's a small brooch, in the shape of a silver wing, pinned beside her collar. She's on her way, I imagine, to some other appointment: she wears no make-up; even her eyes, usually masked in with mascara, she's left untouched.

She goes to the kitchen. There's a tinkle of a glass: a bottle's opened; when she comes back in she offers me a drink.

She watches me then for a while from the angle of the door.

'Would you ever leave him, Liz?' I say.

'Neville?' she says.

She shakes her head.

'Has he got too much?'

She begins to smile.

'He's hoping, I think, to get me fired.'

'I don't think,' she says, 'he's got much chance. You've nothing to lose. You'll keep your job. You have my promise on that,' she adds.

She moves to the window.

'They've changed our man.'

She's gazing down.

'The one we have now has got red hair. Just like the man below.'

She turns to the bed.

'I suppose it's all a game,' she says.

'For me,' I tell her, 'it's a way of life.'

'You don't know what he's like. He hates to be crossed. He can't bear to lose. He'll never let me go whatever I do.'

She sits on the bed. For a moment, faded, she's poised there like a child, slender, antagonistic, her arms thrust out.

'He'll never release me.' She glances down. 'It's something he almost seeks,' she says.

She stays the night.

The following morning, as we're lying in bed, the door bursts open and Rebecca comes in.

For some time I've been listening to the lock, to the key being turned, to a piece of wire; only as she enters do I call out from the bed.

She says nothing for a while. I think, for several seconds, she doesn't recognize her mother at all; only slowly does she come across.

Elizabeth lies back.

Her eyes half-closed, she gazes over at Rebecca and shakes her head.

It's like waiting for a child, impatiently, to be taken from a room.

Rebecca turns to the door; I get up from the bed.

By the time I've reached the landing she's half-way down the stairs. There's a vague, 'Anything I can do, Miss?' from Ferguson in the hall, and the outer door of the house is closed.

I see her from the window, crossing to the car; she climbs inside: the door's pulled to.

'I never knew she had a key,' Elizabeth says. She lies back in bed.

'She's got in the habit,' I tell her, 'of picking the lock.'

'Hasn't the lock been changed?'

'I never saw the need.'

The car drives off.

I go back to the bed.

'Have you got a light?' she says. She reaches for her bag, releases the catch, takes out a cigarette.

I flick the lighter.

'My God, you've had it all the time,' she says.

She holds it in her hand.

'Honestly,' she says. She slips it in her bag.

She smokes for a while; I begin to dress.

'Is there somewhere you have to go?' she says.

'I've an appointment,' I tell her, 'to see my wife.'

'Is she going to get better?'

'I don't think,' I tell her, 'she'll ever get well.'

'Do you mind a great deal?' She turns her head. 'You could even divorce her. Nowadays, incompatibility isn't difficult to prove.'

When I mention Rebecca she begins to smile.

'Honestly, what can a mother do? Should I take precautions? It's a wonder we don't have bulletins pinned up outside.'

She begins to laugh.

'It's the only thing Neville will never countenance,' she says. 'I'd love to be there when he gets his report.'

'I'll see you tonight,' I tell her, 'if you've time to pop in.'

'There's a party at the house,' she says. 'For Beccie.' She adds, 'It's her birthday, you see: I thought you knew.'

'That's probably why she came,' I say.

'An invitation!'

She begins to laugh.

'And would you have gone, supposing she had? Invited you, I mean,' she says.

'I might.'

'You're a glutton for punishment: I'll grant you that.'

She puts up her arms.

'I'll see you,' she says, 'as soon as I can.'

I can still hear her laughing as I close the door.

Ferguson comes out of his room as I reach the porch. I keep

on going when I hear his door and am round the corner before I hear his shout.

I get on the bus and climb upstairs: with one eye closed and the other half-shut I watch the outskirts of the town pass by, and it's not until the asylum's reached that I realize, in my present state, I might do more to alarm than reassure and, having paused at that empty gate, gazing in myopically towards that fettered house, set off back, on foot, towards the town.

2

'I don't know what they've been doing to her,' Mrs Sherman says. 'She scarcely seems to know me. On top of which, she's put on all this weight.'

She sits beneath the armorial reliefs, unaware of the fur-coated figures at the adjoining tables; she hasn't, as yet, removed her scarf which, in addition to being fastened at her throat, is pinned to the top of her head with a metal brooch. Her handbag, the size of a small suitcase, she's placed on the table beside her plate. The waitress, when she comes across with her tray of coffee, is at a loss for a moment where to put it. Finally, with a kind of groan, Mrs Sherman picks up the bag and sets it on the floor beside her.

She rubs her hand across her nose, half-weeping, then searches in her pocket.

'I had one with me,' she says. 'I don't know where it's gone.'
I hand her mine.
She blows her nose.

'She's changed out of all recognition. She's never had all that weight. Not even as a girl. I didn't recognize her, you know, when I first went in.'

She gazes at the coffee, picks up a spoon, stirs the cup, replaces the spoon then gazes vacantly before her.

'I'm sure, now, she shouldn't have come out. She wasn't well enough. If we'd only been patient she'd still be in that admission ward. You can see into the garden you know, from there. From where she is now, it's like a prison. I felt so awful when I first went in. And all those other patients.' She runs the handker-chief across her mouth.

She wipes her eyes.

'Have you seen Doctor Lennox at all?' she says.

'It was over a week ago,' I tell her.

'I asked to see him. They said he was busy. If you want an appointment, they told me, it'd take three weeks. She might be dead by then. Or so ill from seeing those people around her she'll not recover.'

'She's already much improved,' I say.

'But she doesn't know me. When I talk to her she doesn't listen. I try to imagine at times what she must be thinking. But it's all a blank. It's like talking to a wall, or somebody you've never seen before. There's no contact between us, and we've been so close before. Particularly since her father died. She's been such a good daughter to me. She really has.'

'I should drink your coffee.'

She wipes her nose. She screws up the handkerchief, then hands it back.

'You lose your appetite for food when you've been in there. I've hardly eaten anything these last few days. I get it ready, cook it; but when it's there I just think of her, you know, and cry.'

She looks across with tear-filled eyes.

'You've been so good to her, I know. But I honestly think, Colin, she's getting worse. It's a disease of the mind. It's not like a broken arm. There's nothing to mend. It's all inside. And now, you see, she's grown so fat.'

She lifts her cup. She presses it for a moment against her lip. She doesn't drink.

'I've been in here, you know, before. Yvonne brought us, when she got her degree. We came here afterwards and had a meal. You should have seen us then. It makes you wonder why you live at all. All that effort.' She begins to cry.

I hold out the handkerchief.

She searches for her own. The heads, at the surrounding tables, begin to turn.

She feels down to her bag, lifts it up, knocks over the coffee: a brown stain seeps out across the table.

The waitress comes across.

'Will there be anything else?' she says as if she's watched this charade go on now long enough.

'If you've got a bill.'

She puts it down beside the cup.

Mrs Sherman herself seems unaware that anything's occurred; she roots inside the bag, still sobbing, taking out a bag of oranges, a bag of apples, a box of chocolates and some envelopes and paper: gifts these, which, at the hospital, inexplicably, her daughter has refused.

'I must have dropped it.'

I offer her mine.

She takes it in her hand, examines it for several seconds, finds a spot unmarked by lipstick, and wipes her cheek.

The waitress, having deposited the bill, is mopping up the table. I replace the chocolate, the fruit and the writing material in Mrs Sherman's bag.

I get up from the table. I pay the bill.

When we get to the stairs leading to the street she takes my arm.

'I don't see any point,' she says. 'If somebody you love ends up like that what's the purpose in going on? All she's ever wanted in life is to help other people and do some good. You read every day of criminals who get unpunished, of people, who never do anything with their lives at all: and there's Yvonne, a heart of gold. And she ends up in a ward like that. Some of those women.'

She shakes her head.

When we reach the street she takes the bag.

'You got its number, then?' she says, and adds, 'This car, I mean, that knocked you down.'

'They're trying to trace the owner now,' I say.

'You want to sue them for a lot of money. You could easily have been killed with a thing like that.'

We reach the stop. A queue has formed.

'What'll you do with the fruit?' I ask.

'I've no idea.' She wipes her eyes.

'I'll take it with me, if you like,' I say.

'You can have it all for me.'

She plunges her hand inside the bag.

She lifts out the envelopes, the box of chocolates. She takes out the fruit.

By the time she's finished my arms are full.

When the bus pulls up she climbs aboard; a hand is raised; the bus moves off.

As I turn up the street I see Hendricks walking towards me with a canvas cricket bag. He's dressed in plimsolls with short white ankle socks, a raincoat thrown over his shorts and the white, scimitar-crested sweater. He sees me himself a moment later and glances back, hastily, the way he's come.

He's already moving off by the time I catch him up.

'Just the man I want,' I tell him.

'I say, I heard you'd been in hospital,' he says. 'I called at your flat, you know, last week. That man on the ground-floor with the red moustache said he thought he'd seen you taken off.'

I hold out the fruit. 'I was just wanting a bag,' I tell him, 'to hold all this.'

'I'm just on my way to give him a game, as a matter of fact. Did you know he was the Surrey Hardcourt Champion in 1946? Or was it seven?'

'I'd deem it a very great favour if you could relieve me of it all,' I say.

He opens the bag.

'Did you have your hand X-rayed?' he says.

'And chest.'

'Was anything damaged?'

'A couple of ribs. I've broken two fingers, it seems, as well.'

'Wilcox, you know, made me write a report. The bulb in the light, apparently, had been taken out. And this last week, while you've been away, someone's lifted one of these stuffed birds from the natural history shelf. There's only that otter and that squirrel left. You should have seen Wilcox. Went quiet as death.'

He gazes at his bag, now stocked with fruit.

'Is your wife improved at all?' he says.

I shake my head.

'Wilcox was telling the Major you mightn't be coming back.'

'When?'

'It was something he mentioned, I believe, this morning.'

'I wrote him a note.'

'Perhaps Wilcox never got it.'

'Perhaps he's fired me, after all,' I say.

'He went to see Newman the other day.'

'I hope,' I tell him, 'you win the match.'

I watch him walk off.

When he's got some distance away he suddenly turns.

'What shall I do with the fruit?' he says.

'Anything you like,' I say.

'I'll eat it,' he says, 'if that's all right.'

'That's quite all right by me,' I add.

He nods his head.

Weighted down by the bag, he sets off down the street.

Lightened, I set off, more slowly, in the direction of the college.

'Just look at this, man,' Kendal says.

He's standing in the door of Wilcox's office: beside him are two of the cleaners, leaning on their mops.

On the desk itself stands one of the bottles which usually occupies one of the shelves on the office wall.

'Guess what's in it?'

The cleaners, grimacing, shake their heads.

'They've just knocked one of them down,' he says.

A bucket of steaming water stands by a pile of broken glass in the middle of the floor.

'Acid?'

'Urine.'

'Dirty bugger,' the cleaners say.

I step inside.

'Every one of them,' he says. 'You can have a look.'

He runs his hand along the wall.

'We knocked one of them down,' the cleaners say. 'All these years we've been mopping up.'

One of them stoops down; she collects the glass, sweeping it up beneath her mop.

With their bucket and the debris they go out to the hall; their voices, complaining, drone on a moment later from the corridor beyond.

'I heard them in the door when I was working in my room.

When I came in here they were taking all the stoppers out. They're acid bottles from the etching room. Would you believe it? What a terrible pong.'

Kendal, entranced, has rubbed his hands.

Rebecca has appeared on the stairs outside.

A moment later she comes over to the door.

Unaware of Kendal, she steps inside the room.

Kendal, standing by the door, looks up.

'I shouldn't come in here,' he says.

Rebecca, startled, has looked across.

'I wondered if I could have a word with you,' she says.

'Just look at this, then,' Kendal says. He indicates the bottles glinting on the wall.

'Would you like to open a door?' I say.

'What door?'

'The door to Wilcox's lavatory,' I say.

'Have you something I could open it with?'

'I'll get you something,' Kendal says.

'Isn't Mr Wilcox here?' she says.

'He's out,' Kendal says. 'I won't be a minute.'

He crosses the hall to the door of his room.

The two of us, for a moment, stand in silence.

'I'm sorry about bursting in,' she says.

'Look before you leap,' I tell her.

'I should have known. Only I never thought.'

'Will you tell your father?'

'I shouldn't think he needs to be told,' she says.

'Have you seen your mother yet?' I say.

She shakes her head.

'She'll not be disturbed,' she says. 'It's happened before. I just never thought of it. Not on this occasion, at least,' she adds.

Kendal reappears in the hall outside.

'I've a piece of wire. Some metal. A pair of pliers. Whatever you like.' He holds them out.

'I'll try the wire,' she says.

She goes over to the lock. She tries the door.

Kendal stoops beside her as she feels with the wire inside the lock.

A few moments later the door swings back.

I feel inside for a switch on the wall.

The light goes on.

There's a hand-basin immediately opposite the door, a toilet, and a wooden cupboard.

The entire room, however, is packed to the ceiling with dismembered statues, with pieces of pottery, easels, stuffed animals, palettes; with lumps of coke and coal and clay; with picture frames and prints and magazines; with miscellaneous boxes, packages and chests. I recognize the Cupid, an Apollo Belvedere; a broken 'cello stands, its bodywork eroded, in the sink itself. There's an atmosphere of dust and damp. On the lavatory seat stands a plaster cherub; on the floor beside it lie the dismembered limbs of an articulated wooden horse. A skeleton, a hook embedded in its skull, hangs from the topmost link of the lavatory chain.

'My God,' Kendal says. 'The man's gone mad.'

Rebecca gazes in, wide-eyed, from the open door.

'But it must have taken years,' she says.

'Even longer, I imagine,' Kendal says. 'It's a work of art.' He rubs his hands. 'He puts his refuse on the wall, where his culture belongs, and the relics he confines, don't you see, to his bloody bog. Wilcox is an artist. A man of his times. He could exhibit this wherever he liked. A bloody genius.'

'It looks more like kleptomania to me,' I tell him.

'To an outsider,' he says, 'I suppose it might.'

He steps inside. He examines the pieces.

'I should leave it,' I tell him. 'The shock of it being discovered might prove too much.'

'What about the bottles?'

'I should leave them, too.'

We go outside.

'Can you lock the door?' I ask Rebecca.

'I'll have a try,' she says. 'It's more difficult than opening.'

She feels inside the lock with the piece of wire.

'I'm not sure what's more amazing,' Kendal says. 'Wilcox, or the girl herself.'

The door itself has given a click.

'I'll see you home, if you like,' I say.

She gives Kendal back his piece of wire.

'I wouldn't mind going for a drive,' she says.

'Will you tell Apollo and the Major?' Kendal says.

'I should keep it,' I tell him, 'between ourselves.'

'Until the opportune moment.' Kendal smiles.

He gives a wink.

'It's as safe as a dicky-bird with me,' he says.

He goes to his room; he turns on his light. We go out to the hall and close the door.

The cleaners are in the rooms upstairs; there's the rattle of buckets and the banging of mops.

'There's this party tonight.'

'That's why I came.'

'To the college?'

'I was hoping to find you.'

'What time does it start?'

'We've a couple of hours.'

We go down the corridor; I hold the door.

'Wasn't it strange? Finding all that stuff.'

She steps down to the car. She opens the door.

'Can you control it?' she says. 'A thing like that.'

'You can control almost anything,' I say.

'You sound like Daddy.'

'I'm beginning to feel like him,' I say.

'But you're not like him at all.' She laughs.

She starts the engine. We move out from the yard.

'I hope it's not going to be *too* bad a night for you,' she adds.

It's dark. Immediately above us looms the low stone wall separating the overgrown garden of the ruined house from the heath itself: the battlemented roof with its balustrade shows up against the moonlit sky beyond.

'They're sort of demons, I suppose,' she says. 'Daddy has his girls. Mummy has her men. Most of them,' she adds, 'like you.'

She climbs the wall.

We move between the overgrown mounds towards the house.

'Wherever we go it gets like this. At first, you see, I was away at school. But recently, coming back, I've seen it all.'

We step into the drive. The jagged outline of the roof and the tall, rectangular blacknesses of the house's mullioned windows loom about our heads.

'Do you think it's spooky?'

She takes my arm.

The heath, below us, is full of shadows.

'With you it's different, I suppose,' she says.

'Why's that?'

She shakes her head.

Two figures, silhouetted, have stepped out from the trees.

Silently, they pass down the garden, the way we've come.

'It's a kind of circus. Leyland. Fraser. Groves. They hang around. They all have parts, you see, as well.'

The gate, surmounted by the stork, appears ahead.

'I'm not sure what you hope to gain from it,' she says. 'From getting involved, I mean, with me. And them.'

She gestures round.

A bird flies off from the shadows of the gate; on one of the posts is the lower half of the metal stork; the silhouette of the other stands out against a luminous bank of moonlit cloud.

'Do you hate all this?'

She indicates the village; perhaps she's been mistaken about the time of the party: the road across the green is lined with cars. More cars are parked in the driveway of the house and around the gates. Others, as we come out from the overgrown driveway, are being parked in rows along the verges of the green itself.

'It's just an excuse.'

'For what?'

'For junketing, I suppose,' she says. 'Do you want to come in? I'll slip in the back. I have to change.'

She lets go my hand. We start across the green.

'I'll leave the car where it is,' she says. 'Afterwards, if you like, I'll take you home.'

Other figures are moving across the green; there are shouts and cries from the garden of the house.

'I suppose it's mischievous, in the circumstances, inviting you,' she says.

'I'd have preferred to have come in any way,' I tell her.

'No wonder that Mathews approves of you,' she says.

She begins to laugh.

'His father's a bus-driver, you see. He feels you haven't sold out.'

'To what?'

'To people like me, I suppose. Like Mummy and Daddy.'

Groups of figures are drifting up the drive; all the lower windows of the house are now alight; there's the sound of music coming from the open doors. There's a burst of laughter: a window in one of the upper rooms has opened: a voice calls down to the drive below.

'You remember Eddie? The one with the factory.' She shakes her head. 'He's the only decent one there is,' she says.

Pettrie is standing in the porch.

He comes down the steps as he sees her in the drive, folding back his hair. He's wearing a suede jacket, with a thin, string tie.

'Your mother's been going frantic,' he says.

He leans down to Rebecca, kisses her cheek, then gives her a small parcel he's holding in his hand.

'Honestly,' she says. 'I've just been rounding up my guests. You remember Colin.'

Pettrie puts out his hand.

There's a cry from the porch; other figures emerge from the lighted door.

Rebecca disappears; I see her being greeted inside the hall: figures intervene. A couple dance slowly to and fro in the shadow of the porch.

'Let me get you a drink, then,' Pettrie says. 'It's a case of grabbing what you can. I've tried a couple of times,' he adds, 'already.'

The thin-faced chauffeur is standing in the hall; he's examining invitation cards from the people flooding through the porch. Beside him is the close-cropped, grey-haired secretary; she smokes a cigarette, scrutinizing each face as it comes in through the door, looking up in dismay as she recognizes mine.

'Mr Freestone hasn't got a card, Bennings,' Pettrie says. 'Rebecca rounded him up herself.' He takes my arm.

We move off towards the lounge; there's a small orchestra playing in one corner of the room; several couples are dancing; other groups stand against the walls: most of the furniture in the room has gone. Over the fire-place, however, still hangs the 'View of Delft'.

'I shan't be a second,' Pettrie says. He disappears amongst the crowd.

A waiter passes carrying an empty tray.

I go back across the hall. The secretary herself has gone: I nod at Bennings. In a room beyond the hall a bar has been set out; a frieze of glittering bottles and half-filled glasses lines the edge of a narrow table above which hangs Elizabeth's triangulated abstract picture. Immediately beneath it, by the bar itself, stands Wilcox, a glass of fruit-juice in his hand.

He looks over quickly, blinks, then looks again; he regards me, as I cross the bar, with widening eyes. He's dressed in a dinner-jacket, with a black bow-tie.

'Freestone.'

'Been here long?'

'I've just been having a word with Mr Newman.' He holds up the glass, perhaps as an indication of his pacific intentions. 'I thought you were in hospital, then.' He looks at my face, glances at my bandaged hand, then looks over at the barman as I call for a drink.

'I'll be back at college next week,' I tell him.

'That's something,' he says, 'I meant to talk to you about.'

I take the drink as the barman passes it across; I take another from a tray of drinks already on the counter. I swallow them down. I take a third.

I say, 'Have you done any dancing yet?'

'My wife couldn't come this evening, I'm afraid.' He makes some attempt to move away. I take his arm. Figures press in on either side.

We move over to the door. Immediately ahead of us Pettrie reappears.

'You've got a drink. Good show.' He taps my back, moves past, his figure swallowed up amongst the groups behind.

'You've been here before, then?' Wilcox says.

'Several times.'

'I had an invitation from Newman,' he says, 'the other day. I went out to see this new place he has.'

'A bit of a mess.'

'It'll mean big changes in the town he says.'

He looks towards the stairs; Elizabeth has appeared; she wears a red gown: her hair's piled up above her head. Her neck and arms are bare. She moves off, without seeing Wilcox or myself, towards the lounge: there's a cry from inside followed, a moment later, by a roll of drums. An announcement's made; people stand on tiptoe, gazing in.

'The party-girl's been found, then,' someone says.

'Apparently Rebecca wasn't here when the party began.' Wilcox gestures towards the door itself. 'I saw her at the college, earlier today. She's taken up, you know, with that trouble-maker Mathews. I've been half in a mind, in the past, to pitch him out. He's started one of these student action groups. Actually came up, you know, with a signed petition: said he wanted to participate in the planning of next year's curriculum. Plus, I might tell you, representation on the Board of Governors.'

Leyland's red head appears, stooping at the door of the library at the rear of the hall; he's seen me already for he calls into the room behind then comes forward, forcing his way between the crowd.

His pale blue eyes have lighted. He puts out his hand, sees the bandage, and begins to laugh. 'Not run into a wall, then, have you?'

'Just about,' I tell him.

He laughs again.

'Left hand as well?'

I hold it out.

'Terrible eye.'

'Fell down a flight of steps. Damn lucky he wasn't more seriously injured,' Wilcox says.

'Always say: "look where you're walking nowadays",' Leyland says.

'A damn good motto, if you want my opinion,' Wilcox says.

'Enjoy yourself, then,' Leyland says. He slaps my back. 'We've got the steps out here well lit.'

'He'll watch his step here, I'm sure of that, Mr Leyland,' Wilcox says.

Leyland disappears towards the lounge.

'Met Leyland,' Wilcox adds, 'the other day. He showed me round some of those buildings when Newman himself was called away.'

I see Neville myself a moment later; he's standing at the door of the library, a cigar in his mouth, talking to Fraser whose broad, bulky back is turned towards me. He glances round, smiling, as Neville points me out; he bows his head, briefly, allowing the look to linger on my face; then, the smile broadening, he turns away.

When I glance back to Wilcox I find he's disappeared.

I turn back to the bar.

Pettrie, a drink in his hand, is returning to the door.

'There are quieter conditions,' he says, 'upstairs. If you get a chance I'll meet you there.'

He disappears to the hall outside.

I stand at the bar. I empty another glass; I pick up another. I drain it slowly. I light a cigarette. Through a window directly opposite the bar I can see into the drive outside; other groups are still arriving: lights show up across the green. A phone is ringing somewhere in the house; from the lounge across the hall comes a second roll of drums.

Mathews materializes in the space beside me.

He's still wearing his American combat-jacket.

'You're for it, aren't you?'

'Me?'

'I've heard all about it,' he says, 'from Bec.'

'What have you heard?'

'Enough,' he tells me.

'Don't count your eggs,' I tell him, 'before they hatch.'

'Yours are all cracked,' he says, 'if half of what she says is true.'

'I believe,' I tell him, 'in the true democratic processes of the British constitution, emulated and admired throughout the world.'

'Bollocks to all that,' he says.

I finish the glass I've already started, pick up another and start to empty that.

'Haven't you had enough of that?' he says.

'I've hardly even begun,' I tell him.

'Have you got a fag?'

I hold one out.

'They try and undermine you first by attempting to rouse in you feelings of common decency,' I tell him. 'Failing that, they clobber you, if they can, on top of the head. Failing with that, they compromise you, if they can, entirely, by offering you positions not so easily distinguishable from the ones they hold themselves.' I tap my head. 'I've got it screwed on, you see, all right. The one thing you can refuse them is co-operation, until the whole system, with a bit of luck, collapses of its own volition. I don't give a sod for any of them, Phil.'

Rebecca appears beside me. I kiss her cheek.

She wears a frilled white blouse; her hair's been fastened back beneath a ribbon.

'You've not got him plastered,' she says, 'already?'

'I've scarcely spoken to him,' Mathews says.

'There's Mummy and Daddy in the other room. They're about to make the presentation, if you want to come through and see it all,' she says.

'What presentation?' Mathews says.

'It's my birthday, darling,' Rebecca says. She takes his arm.

Glass in hand, I turn to follow them as they move across the hall.

The crowd has thickened.

A gap opens as we reach the lounge; someone begins to clap. The orchestra starts up. There's a brief fanfare, a roll of drums; the lights in the room go out, replaced by the glare from a single lamp.

Newman and Elizabeth are standing by the fireplace, caught by the light, smiling, looking round; the crowd in the room have begun to sing.

'Happy Birthday, dear Beccie, Happy Birthday to you.'

Rebecca steps forward into the pool of light.

There's a round of applause, a cheer; the music from the corner veers off into another fanfare.

Newman, smiling, raising his hand, steps forward.

'I was just wanting to say thank you,' he says, 'to all you good people for coming to our celebration. It was very good of you to find the time.'

There's a roar of laughter; a cheer; a burst of applause.

'I know how busy you are.'

Another roar.

'It was just an informal affair which we thought we'd ask you to participate in. Being, as we are, newcomers to the district, so to speak.'

There's another burst of applause.

Groves is standing beside me, his pale face even paler in the glare from the single lamp, his dark eyes, if anything, even blacker.

On my other side, his broad shoulder against mine, is Fraser. Mathews, like Wilcox before him, has disappeared.

'We're the harbingers, if you like, of history. Certainly of progress. We don't stay long, unfortunately, in any place; like a fairy godmother, we spread enlightenment on every side.'

'Here, here,' comes Wilcox's voice from across the room.

'We bring glad tidings of another world, less hidebound, more energetic, more enterprising than the one we're hoping to replace.'

'Here, here,' comes a voice from the door behind.

'The new town we're building, we hope, will enhance the old; revitalize it, provide it with a new stimulus; reinforce its old traditions, by, we hope, defining new ones: draw sustenance from it in the same way in which the old town we hope will draw sustenance from the new.'

There's a burst of applause.

'I don't wish to go on making speeches. It's the first opportunity, however, that Elizabeth and myself have had of meeting all our new friends at one time, and in one particular place; we'd like you all to enjoy yourselves, to have a glimpse of what *our* home life is like and trust that it's not too much unlike your own.'

There's a burst of laughter.

'And we'd like to take the opportunity, since this is a gathering of friends, to present to our daughter, Rebecca, a little token of our esteem on this, the occasion of her eighteenth birthday.'

He takes his hand from his jacket pocket.

There's a fanfare from the corner.

He presents Rebecca with a satin-covered box.

There's a burst of applause, a cheer; Rebecca, red-cheeked, has taken the box; she kisses her mother, kisses Newman, then, to calls from the crowd, she opens the lid.

She gazes inside.

She holds up what appears to be, from across the room, some sort of pendant, a wing-shaped brooch.

There's a gasp; the spotlight shifts over to a screen at the side of the room: a vast cake, glittering in the light, is revealed to the crowd. There's a second cheer, a roll of drums.

Rebecca, her arm held by Newman, comes into the light.

She's presented with a knife.

The next moment there's a flash of light; the blade is raised, a moment later it's plunged, heavily, into Newman's chest.

A stream of blood is ejected across his shirt, the redness glistening against the white. A table's overturned; a cry, like a groan, has filled the room.

'My God. There's been an accident,' Wilcox says, his voice calling, half-wailing, as if some dietary blunder is being announced.

At least, I endure this sensation for several seconds; when I look again Rebecca is pressing the knife into the top of the cake: she eases it down. There's a flash of light.

She cuts the cake. There's a burst of applause.

The lights come on.

There are several cheers.

A dance tune recommences in the corner of the room.

Food is being served from a table by the door. I take another drink from a passing tray.

'I hear you've had an accident.' Fraser smiles.

'I'm amazed at the interest it's aroused,' I say.

'We've so little to entertain us with round here, that an accident like that,' he says, 'despite its seeming triviality, inevitably stands out.'

'Maybe this'll stand out, too,' I say.

I hit him on the nose; from all around me come screams and shouts.

I hit Fraser so hard with my other hand that I can hear his teeth break up inside his mouth. I hit him once again, feel more stitches come apart, and continue to the door.

There's something like a space around me; there's a figure I fail to recognize; then someone, with a shout, has caught my arm: there are lines of feet. There's a rush of air. A fist comes down.

A blackness, darker than the night, descends.

We're sitting in a car. Elizabeth, a coat wrapped round her

shoulders, is sitting beside me. Her gaze, aloof, remote, is fixed on some point in the road ahead.

Only as I open my eyes a little further do I see that she's sitting directly behind the chauffeur; her head is silhouetted against the light from the headlamps of the car.

'Are you all right?' she says.

I'm covered in blood. I can feel it on my hands and round my cheek.

'Where are we?'

'We're going to Eddie's place. He's gone ahead.'

'What time is it?'

'I've no idea.'

The chauffeur stirs.

'It's just after twelve, Mrs Newman,' he says.

I lie back in the seat for a while.

'Do you want a cigarette?' she says.

She gets one from her bag; there's the click of her lighter.

'What happened at the house?' I say.

'I should just lie there,' she says, 'and rest.'

'Is Rebecca all right?'

'Of course she's all right. She's gone with Eddie.'

The car gives a lurch.

'A fox. Or a badger,' the chauffeur says. 'This road is full of them,' he adds, 'at night.'

I pour out a cloud of smoke; my head has cleared.

'I should, by all rights, I suppose, have seen a doctor.'

'Eddie's calling his,' she says.

Her voice is hard, discordant; it's as if, seconds before, she might have been shouting. Her hair, mounted above her head earlier in the evening, has been allowed to fall down around her face.

'Are you feeling all right?' She glances down.

'I feel I've had my arms torn out.'

'Put your head against this,' she says.

She lowers her arm.

My head, a moment later, is cushioned by her breast.

Seconds later, it seems, the door has opened.

There's a light outside; a glimpse of trees, a pebbled drive: a white, nail-studded door is slowly opened.

We cross a white, monastic-looking hall. A panelled door

swings back. I catch a glimpse of Rebecca's face, then Pettrie's; then an older, bearded face is gazing down. My eye-lid's lifted; a hand taps at my fingers. Darkness follows. There's the sound of birds.

'Honestly, if you hadn't have been brought here you might have been arrested.'

'He would have been arrested,' Elizabeth says. She and Rebecca are sitting on the bed. The walls of the room I'm in are painted white. A window looks out onto a leafless tree. Beside the door is a wooden cabinet; porcelain figures, dancers in crinolines and men in breeches, stand on top. Immediately above it hangs a picture: a house, long and flat, glimpsed distantly at the summit of a hill.

'Phil,' Rebecca says, 'got hit as well.'

'I asked Mr Wilcox,' Elizabeth says, 'to take him home.'

'I bet he was pleased at that,' I say.

'He had no choice, I'm afraid,' she says.

'What happened to Neville while all this was going on?' I say.

Elizabeth, her eyes shielded by dark glasses, glances at her daughter.

Rebecca gets up.

'I'll leave Mummy to explain all that,' she says.

She crosses to the door.

'I'll have to go into college, in any case. Eddie's taking me in. I'll see how Daddy is when I call tonight.'

The door is closed.

The room is tall; the shadow of the tree outside falls in a strangely tremulous pattern across the wall. It agitates the figures of the dancers, and the picture of the house above their heads.

Elizabeth is dressed as she was the night before: her arms are bare: there are four faint bruises beneath her lip.

'Neville called the police,' she says. 'Or said he did. Whether they arrived or not I've no idea.'

'What happened to the boy?' I say.

'He tried to join in. He jumped on Fraser's back.'

She leans over the side of the bed and opens her bag; she gets out a lighter and finds a cigarette.

She gets out another; she lights them both.

I get up from the bed.

'Your finger needs resetting. Perhaps both of them. I've to take you in to the hospital. Eddie's doctor called last night.'

I take the cigarette.

I climb out from the bed. My right hand, it seems, I'm unable to use.

I go over to the window.

The pebbled driveway of the night before I now see as a narrow, rutted track winding off between clumps of trees to what, in the distance, looks like a tall stone wall; there's a pebbled courtyard immediately below, a small pond between the courtyard and the nearest clump of trees and, beyond a wooden fence, a system of hedged fields stretching away to a line of hills, their summits at the moment lost in wreaths of mist.

'What's happened to Neville?'

'I've no idea.'

'Did he call last night?'

She shakes her head.

'What happened,' I ask her, 'when we left the house?'

'We had a row.'

'With everyone there?'

'I was standing in the drive; Neville was at a window. He came out onto the porch when they got you on the lawn. I must have gone berserk.'

She removes the glasses.

'I put these on while Eddie was here.'

Her eyes are swollen. She gets out a handkerchief. She holds it in her hand.

'Shouldn't you go back home?'

'I suppose I should.'

'I'll get a bus to town,' I say.

'You won't from here. We're miles from anywhere. That's why we came.'

'Have we got a car?'

She looks at her watch.

'They're sending one from town. It'll take an hour.'

The fingers of my right hand are blue and swollen, the

knuckles disjointed. The strapping on my ribs has been renewed.

I can see my face reflected in the window; my nose is swollen; cuts have re-opened above my eyes and nose.

'Does Neville know we're here?'

'I suppose he must.'

'Who got me to the car?'

'Bennings did, I suppose,' she says.

'What happened to Groves?'

'He was lying in the hall.'

'What happened to Fraser?'

'He was lying on the lawn.'

'Did you see what happened?'

'Not all of it.' She wipes her eyes. 'What started it off, in any case?' she says.

'I can't remember.'

'Do you imagine these provocations,' she says, 'or are they real?'

She waits.

'Most of them are real.'

'You only have one reaction to anything,' she says.

'It's more honest, I suppose, than most.'

'I'm not so sure.'

She gets up from the bed.

'I think I'll have a wash. I've been talking to Eddie half the night. There's a woman downstairs, called Mrs Bowen. She'll get you anything you want.'

She goes to the door.

'When the car arrives,' she says, 'I'll let you know.'

The door is closed.

The house is silent.

My clothes are folded on a chair beside the bed. The shirt and the coat are covered in blood. The trousers, when I pull them on, I find, are torn. My tie has disappeared.

There's blood on my shoes; there's blood, too, I notice on the bed.

I pull on my shirt; I go to the door.

Outside, a broad, white-walled corridor with a bare wooden floor runs down to a landing; from the banister rail I gaze down to the hall; there's a wooden table, a wooden bench, long and narrow, in the centre of the floor: there's the inside, too, of the metal-studded door. Other doors open off on either side.

Plates and cups and saucers have been set out on the table; a woman in a white overall is clearing some of them away.

She glances up.

'Is there anything I can get you, sir?' she says.

'I'm looking for the bath,' I say.

'It's the second door along.'

She turns back to the table.

I go back up the corridor towards the room.

The second door is already open; there's a bath inside, a shower.

I'm standing under the shower a moment later when Neville appears inside the door.

He stands there a moment, dark-eyed, then says, 'I'll see you downstairs as soon as you've finished.'

I begin to laugh.

My arms have begun to shake.

He's dressed in a dark blue suit; he has a clean white collar; there's a white handkerchief showing out of the breast-pocket of his jacket.

I step out from the shower and begin to dress.

When I go down to the landing I see Groves and Leyland and Fraser waiting in the hall. There are two men I've never seen before standing by the door: they both wear suits, one with a flower in his button-hole, the other with a handkerchief sticking from his pocket.

I go down the stairs and fasten my shirt.

I pull on my coat as I reach the hall itself.

Neville is sitting at the table; the others stand around the room. The woman in the white overall has gone.

Neville's hair is neatly combed; the light, which comes from windows high in the walls, shines, glistening, along the parting. His hands, small, neat-fingered, he rests before him on the table.

'We weren't expecting you,' I say.

'That's all right.'

He points to the cups.

'Do you fancy some coffee?'

'I wouldn't mind.'

'We've had some already,' he says. He adds, 'You must help yourself.'

Leyland has taken a seat against the wall. His eyes seem almost luminous, brilliant beneath the redness of his hair, his skin, if anything, even paler now than that of Groves.

Fraser has one eye closed; maybe I'd been mistaken about his teeth; he doesn't smile.

Groves, apart from a small bruise on his cheek, appears unmarked.

I pour out some coffee from a metal jug.

The two men by the door have moved over to the table. One of them, perhaps, I recognize; a vague impression of a face I've glimpsed in the unlit yard at the back of the college.

'Elizabeth's upstairs,' I say.

'That's all right,' he says. He nods his head.

'There's a car coming shortly. She's taking me to the hospital.' I hold up my hand. 'My eye needs some attention, too,' I add.

'We wondered,' he says, 'if you wanted a job.'

'What doing?'

'We normally have an adviser to our architect,' he says. He unfolds his hands. 'Usually it's an artist of some repute. Though it's not essential, if we feel, for instance, that his temperament is right.'

'I have a job,' I say 'at present.'

'I think, when you get to work,' he says, 'you'll find you haven't.'

He's begun to smile.

'Do I get your wife as well?' I ask.

The smile has faded.

'I should just knock his teeth in,' Leyland says.

He comes over from the wall; he sits down at the table.

Fraser, too, has come over to the bench, easing himself down at the opposite end.

'My wife herself,' he says, 'will have to answer that.'

He looks to the banistered landing overhead.

Elizabeth, evidently, is standing there.

One hand on the banister, she comes slowly down the stairs.

'I shouldn't take his job,' she says.

She comes over to the table.

'He's no intention of giving you one, in any case,' she adds.

I begin to laugh.

I see her eyes, grey, hooded, almost invisible, the strands of hair: Neville has caught her arm; he gets up from the table, pushing her back.

'Are you ready, Elizabeth?' he says. 'We're about to leave.'

She doesn't answer. Leyland has begun to laugh; Fraser smiles: one of his teeth, at the front, is missing.

'Do you really want her?' Neville says. He looks across. 'Is she worth all the effort you've been putting in? She isn't to me,' he says. 'I can tell you that.'

The others, it seems, have scarcely moved.

It's like some familiar routine; Leyland, as if reassured, has begun to tap his fingers against the table.

Groves, expressionless, still stands against the wall. He has a bandage, I notice, on one of his hands.

The man with the flower in his button-hole has a broken nose; the other one, with the handkerchief, has cauliflower ears. His hands are bruised. There's a recently healed cut above one eye.

Elizabeth turns back to the table; she begins to cry.

Neville, as if antagonized, with an almost boyish alarm, hits her suddenly on the side of the head.

As I get up from the bench I find, suddenly, I'm being held down.

I begin to shout.

He hits her with his fist. He hits her then with the back of his hand. She falls on her knees. He lifts her head and hits her once again. She begins to scream. Leyland and Fraser have begun to smile.

She lies on the floor. I get up from the bench.

'Don't move,' someone says, 'you'll be all right.'

Elizabeth, swaying, has climbed back to her feet.

'Get in the car,' Neville says. She shakes her head. 'Get in the car,' he says. 'I'll be out in a minute.'

A moment later, moaning, she moves over to the door.

Groves, it seems, has opened it for her; his black eyes, briefly, glance towards the room.

He follows her out.

'Do you want the job, then?' Neville says.

'No,' I say. I shake my head.

He begins to smile.

'That's why I thought I'd take the precaution of removing you from the other one,' he says. 'You'll not work round here,' he adds, 'again.'

He buttons his coat.

'I don't suppose we'll meet again.'

He nods his head towards the door.

I sit at the table. I don't look up.

The man with the button-hole is the last to leave.

There's the sound of car engines starting up in the drive outside.

The engines fade.

The woman in the white smock has appeared at one of the doors.

'Will there be anything else?' she says.

I lean on the table. I shake my head.

'If there's nothing else, then,' she says, 'I'll clear the table.'

'Did you hear all that?' I ask her as she comes across.

'No, sir,' she says. 'I was in the kitchen.'

I get out a cigarette; I begin to laugh.

'I'll call you when the car arrives,' she adds.

I get up after she's gone and wander round.

I look in the other rooms; there's a library with other porcelain figures mounted on the shelves; a window, sheathed in curtains, looks out across hedged fields to a mansion on a hill.

In a field immediately below the house groups of figures are running to and fro: pitches have been marked out and posts set up.

Pettrie, when I turn round is standing in the door.

He folds back his hair, slowly; then, with two dogs at his heels, he steps inside the room.

'I thought I'd come back,' he says. He gestures behind him. 'I saw them on the road. I dropped Beccie off,' he adds, 'at the college.'

He strokes the dogs.

'Did anything happen?'

'Elizabeth left.'

222

'I thought she would.'

'It's a regular circus.'

'They're very odd.'

He crosses to the window.

'I'll drive you to the hospital. We needn't wait for the car. I'll leave a message with Mrs Bowen.'

'I'd appreciate a lift,' I say.

'Would you like a drink,' he says, 'before you go?'

'I wouldn't mind.'

'I'll get you one,' he says. 'I shan't be a minute.'

The dogs stay in the room. They're both retrievers, perhaps relatives of the ones the Newmans have.

He comes back in with a half-full glass.

'I shouldn't have more,' he says.

I drink it off.

'You might run out, you mean?' I tell him.

He laughs.

'I'm thinking of last night,' he says.

He gestures to the window.

'That's the family house. Or was. It's run now as a teacher's college.'

He indicates the figures, running to and fro in the field below.

'The one we're in now's the dower-house,' he adds. 'If you ever have time, I'll show you round.'

He runs his hand across his head.

'I suppose we better get off,' he says.

A car with a folding hood is waiting in the drive outside. In its general proportions it's not unlike Wilcox's vintage Armstrong Siddeley.

He opens the door; as I climb inside he gestures at the house.

Low, one-storeyed, it stands in the shadow of several trees; dark branches are coiled above its broad-angled roof. It reminds me of the Newman's house. Its yellow stone-work has begun to crumble. A single flight of steps runs up to the metal-studded door; white-painted sash-windows are arranged in pairs on either side.

The dogs have followed us to the car; Pettrie calls out as the white-overalled figure of his housekeeper appears at the door.

The dogs run back towards the house.

We turn to the drive; I can see the house more clearly as we reach the trees; it's like a massive boulder, pale, symmetrical, a quaint facsimile of the larger mansion on the hill above.

The white figure at the porch, with the two dogs, has disappeared.

'Did Neville say anything to you?' Pettrie says.

I shake my head.

'He offered me a job.'

He begins to laugh.

We reach a pair of gates; there's a coat-of-arms mounted on a plinth on top of each of the posts: I catch a glimpse, in relief, of a bear, standing upright: to its left are grouped three feathers.

'Did he say what it was?'

'A consultant. In a wholly artistic capacity of course,' I add.

He laughs again.

The car, having passed between the gates, turns into a walled lane the other side.

The walls, after a while, give way to hedges. I catch a distant view of the house on the hill, the glitter of its windows, a vague impression of jerseyed figures running to and fro in the field below.

Pettrie's hands are long and thin, the knuckles crested white as he grips the wheel.

'Will you be seeing Elizabeth again?' he says.

'I've no idea.'

'Did he beat her up?'

'Has he done it before?' I say.

'It's the one thing, it seems, that keeps them going. That and the provocation necessary, preceding it,' he says.

He concentrates for a moment on the road ahead.

It runs along the bed of a shallow valley. Low, pine-covered hills have appeared on either side; we pass through a village of low, stone, terraced houses: a larger house stands back from the road amidst a clump of trees; an asphalt drive leads up towards it.

The road dips down; it crosses a stream.

Further on we reach a junction.

A lorry lies on its side; one of its wheels is still revolving; men with shovels and a hosepipe signal us past. There's a van with a flashing light. The front of the lorry has embedded itself in the trunk of a tree. Pieces of glass are strewn across the road.

Further on, parked in a lay-by, is the Newmans' Bentley. The upper half of it has disappeared. We're almost past it before Pettrie, seeing it, calls out.

He turns into the side of the road and stops the engine.

'My God: I believe that's Neville's car,' he says.

He doesn't look back.

'I came the other way,' he adds. 'It's quicker. If I'd come back this way I might have seen it.'

He seems more concerned with this than anything else.

I open the door, climb out, make sure that he's no intention of following, then walk back along the verge towards the wreck.

The seat at the front is spattered with blood; blood runs, too, in a great gash across the bonnet.

A policeman comes across from the direction of the lorry.

'Would you mind,' he tells me, 'moving on.'

'Was anyone injured? They were friends of mine.' I indicate the car.

'The driver of the lorry's been killed. And one occupant of the car,' he says, 'is seriously injured.'

'Which one was it?'

'Do you mind giving me your name?' he says.

He writes it down.

Pettrie, when I glance back, is still sitting in the car, his gaze still fixed on the road ahead.

'It was a gentleman, sir,' the policeman says.

'Do you have his name?'

'I'm afraid I haven't. You could get it at the station,' he tells me, 'when I send in my report.'

I glance back down the road.

'What happened to the rest of them?' I ask.

'They drove on to town, sir, in another car.'

He waits.

I look down at his pad.

'Between ourselves, it's the chauffeur in the car who's injured. The rest of the occupants, I'm glad to say, appear to be unhurt.'

I go back down to Pettrie.

'Is anybody hurt?' he says.

225

'The driver of the lorry,' I tell him.

'Seriously?'

'Dead,' I tell him.

He nods his head.

He adds nothing further.

I get back in the car.

We drive in silence.

The traffic, after a while, begins to thicken. The first buildings of the town appear.

'It's always the innocent with them,' he says, 'who suffer. That's why, in the past, I've been so keen on protecting Bec.'

'Is she innocent?' I ask.

'I think she is,' he says.

He adds nothing further.

On the far horizon the cathedral spire appears; the road dips down towards the valley: the town, like a mound of rock, rears up, strangely inhospitable, on the opposite side.

We cross the river.

He drops me off at the hospital gates.

'If there's anything I can do,' he says, 'you must let me know,' but seems in no mood to wait for any answer.

I watch the car move off, then, scarcely aware of anything any longer, I turn up the drive to the hospital door.

3

'They were very lucky,' Wilcox says. 'They might, very easily, have all been killed.'

His fingers, short, stubby, drum unrhythmically on the surface of his desk.

'They'd drunk far too much, for one thing, to be driving around in cars. Newman himself, in my opinion, wasn't fit to be outside the door.'

'I've had a letter,' I tell him, 'informing me that my services will no longer be required after the end of the Easter term.'

'That's right. Three months' notice either side. It's the normal procedure in a case like this.'

He glances at the door behind my head.

All the bottles on the wall have been removed; but for a tea-cup standing in a saucer all the shelves are bare.

Even the door to his washroom is standing open.

'It gives no reason,' I tell him, 'for my dismissal.'

'You don't have to give reasons, you know,' he says.

Some unreasonable demand is being made.

'Is anyone else included in this clearing-out?' I say.

'I've told Mathews there'll no longer be a place for him when the Easter term commences,' he says.

'What about Kendal?'

He glances at his desk. As if preparing for a battle its entire surface has been cleared; the ink-wells, pen racks, blotters, diaries and miscellaneous bric-à-brac have been removed.

'I don't see what concern one teacher's professional life should be to another. Mr Kendal's work here is a matter of concern only to Mr Kendal and myself,' he says.

'All I want to know,' I tell him, 'is whether Mr Kendal is staying or leaving. For some better post, perhaps.'

'Mr Kendal is staying at the present,' he says. 'If a better opportunity happens to come his way I shan't stand in his path,' he adds.

'I'm prepared,' I tell him, 'to do a deal.'

'We don't have bargains here, you know.' He rubs his head; the wreath of greying hair appears to have turned appreciably whiter over the past few days. The skin at the top of his head has slowly reddened.

'I don't mind leaving here myself,' I tell him, 'providing, that is, that Mathews stays.'

'The enrolment, or otherwise, of students,' he tells me, 'is my affair. That's why I've got the job; it's one of the responsibilities I have in running the place.'

'I want you to ensure that Mathews stays in the college until another place is found for him elsewhere, or he leaves,' I tell him, 'of his own volition.'

'I'm not quite sure what you're getting at,' he says.

'To put it another way: if you want to stay in the job you've got to make sure that Mathews doesn't leave and that I,' I tell him, 'leave only when I find it convenient to do so.'

His eyes have widened. The redness from the top of his head spreads slowly downwards across his face.

I glance behind him to the open door.

'I've applied, on Mathews' behalf, to a college in London. With a bit of luck, next year, he'll be going there.'

'London? There's nothing that goes on in London that we can't do just as well up here.'

'I just want your assurance that he'll go on doing it,' I tell him, 'until he leaves.'

'I'll not stand in his way,' he says. 'If you've applied, you see, to a school already.'

'What happened to all the refuse, then?'

I gesture to the door.

'There were one or two pieces of bric-à-brac,' he says, 'that Mr Kendal offered to remove. They've accumulated there, you know, over a number of years. These things mount up if you don't keep watch.'

'I'll be leaving,' I tell him, 'at the end of the week.'

'I thought you said next term.'

'You can tell the Governors,' I say, 'I'm indisposed.'

I get up from the chair.

'For all effective purposes,' I go on, 'I've left already.'

'I shouldn't let this Newman business overwhelm you, you know,' he says, 'too much. I know he's a powerful man. But powerful men can have their limits.'

'It's more my limits I'm thinking of,' I say.

I go over to the door.

I light a cigarette.

'I gather that smoking in the staff-room has recently been allowed.'

'Well, as long as it's kept within limits, I suppose it can be allowed.'

'And that Mathews has acquired representation on the Governors' Board.'

'I haven't heard about that,' he says.

'Nevertheless, it's something you'll have to pursue,' I say.

I blow out a cloud of smoke.

I wait.

'I'll always listen to reason,' he says. 'It's these wild emotional forays I take exception to.'

'I'll keep in touch,' I tell him.

'I'll always look forward to hearing how you've got on,' he says.

'Are the plans for a bigger college still under way?' I ask.

'Oh, they're still being very much talked about,' he says.

'The bigger the better.'

'That's what I think in a thing like this.'

He stands up briefly behind the desk; I let the door swing to.

The glare of coloured lights comes from Kendal's room.

I cross over to the door and step inside.

Mathews is working at one of the benches with a soldering iron; Kendal himself, a mask on his face, is welding a sheet of metal across the room.

As the glare from the torch subsides he looks across.

He lifts up the mask, smiling, puts down the apparatus and comes over to the bench.

'I hear you had dinner with Wilcox recently,' I tell him.

'Two nights ago, old man.' He rubs his hands. 'I expand my work in here, he expands whatever he has to expand out there, and never the twain of us shall disagree.'

'Did you offer to clear his room?' I say.

'That was part of the arrangement, you understand. Some of it in any case,' he says, 'has come in useful.'

I can see the 'cello with its partly dismembered body standing in the corner; the skeleton, an anatomy torso, and the remains of what appears to have been the Apollo Belvedere are scattered across a bench.

'Mathews and myself are doing a sort of assembly of the more enigmatic pieces in the Wilcox collection. We thought of calling it "Skipperania", a hitherto unknown cultural syndrome characterized by an aversion to all known forms of artistic expression in favour of a collection of one's own excreta, usually displayed in one's place of work in forms that aren't, at first sight, at least, immediately recognizable.'

Mathews looks across.

'How's your eye?'

'All right.'

'Need any stitches?'

'One or two.'

He goes back to his soldering iron.

'Has Wilcox spoken to you yet?' I say.

He shakes his head.

'Whenever he does,' I tell him, 'let me know.'

He doesn't look up. I go over to the door.

'If you'd like to make your own contribution,' Kendal says, 'you're very welcome. The whole conception, you see, is essentially a communal gesture. Not the prerogative of one particular man.'

'I've made my gesture already,' I tell him.

'I've even kept one of the bottles,' Kendal says. 'Vintage 1912,' he adds.

I go out to the hall.

Pollard is mounting up the steps, consulting a newspaper; a cigarette he's smoking, as he hears my steps, he hastily puts out.

'It's you, old man.' He folds the paper. 'I've just been given a tip,' he says, 'by this friend of Hendricks. I don't know whether you know him.' He twirls his hand above his head. 'A large moustache. Bright red. Says he rode Agamemnon in the National in, what was it now; one of those immediate post-war years.'

'1946.'

'That's right.'

He stabs the paper.

'Fancy a gamble, then, old man?'

'Had all I want for the present,' I say.

'I know what you mean, old man.' He taps his nose. 'Had dinner, you know, the other night. Boiled fish plus a rendering of "Hail, Thou Wandering Spirit" by the Skipper's better half.'

He goes on up the steps.

From Kendal's room comes the whirring of electric motors, the flashing of coloured lights.

I push open the glass doors and go down to the street; I glance up at the black, tall-windowed building, at the sign above the door, 'Municipal College of Fine Arts and Crafts', then, with my collar up, my hands thrust in my pockets, set off down the road towards the town.

A boot, perhaps thirty feet high, stands in the centre of the yard. Where the eyelets might have been there are coloured lights; the lace itself is a coloured rope: the heel, it seems, is made of glass: the figures moving past are divided into two, the smoothness of the heel itself reflecting the legs and feet, the curve of the boot above the upper half of arms and heads.

The whole structure, it appears, has begun to shake; the black texture around the lace and the ankle begins to glow.

A rocket streaks across the college roof, exploding against the evening sky; a low humming emerges from the boot itself; white smoke emerges from an opening at the front; it drifts across the yard in a bulbous cloud, changing colour above the upturned heads: a tongue lolls out, a brilliant red. The lights, too, around the eyelets have begun to twinkle; the lolling tongue at the front begins to shake; a tune emerges, muffled, from the interior of the boot itself.

Yvonne, red-cheeked, watches now with widening eyes; her head's turned up, shrouded in a scarf: she holds the edge of the scarf between her teeth, her lips drawn back: she begins to smile.

The whole boot, as if antagonized, begins to sway; the upper half, as if impelled by an invisible foot, contracts, expands; the one bulbous half, beginning to vibrate, bursts finally with a roar of rockets. The edges of the boot begin to crumble: the lace itself is a coil of flame; smoke drifts up in clouds from around the eyelets.

Wilcox, transfixed, is gazing up at the glittering edifice with his wife on one side and Hendricks on the other; Pollard, his hat on the back of his head, is standing with his wife and a crowd of children, too numerous to count, in the open door of the modelling shed; a shower of sparks cascades across the yard: the crowd have screamed. Kendal crouches on the steps at the back of the college: he manipulates a series of knobs and levers on a board before him, his face lit up, gleaming, as he gazes at the boot itself: the thirty foot edifice begins to crumble.

The neck of the boot falls in; the crowd draws back. Yvonne herself has caught my arm; a cloud of smoke and flames obscures the college: standing at the gate are Rebecca, Mathews and Elizabeth. Mathews, seeing Kendal, has crossed over to the steps; a crowd presses in from the road outside. Sparks drift off across the roofs.

The large salmon-coloured car is parked against the kerb.

Elizabeth, bare-headed, her hands in the pockets of her coat, has looked across.

Yvonne is laughing; she glances back towards the yard.

Elizabeth doesn't stir; Rebecca, her back to the car, is gazing over to where Mathews, on the steps, is talking now to Kendal.

I go across. Her face, vaguely, has caught the light reflected from the yard.

'A farewell visit,' she says. 'I thought you'd left.'

'I have.'

'Come back for the celebration.'

Her face is thinner, hard, the hair pushed over now entirely to one side.

'I heard about the chauffeur.'

'He died,' she says.

'That's what I heard.'

'Neville was driving. The poor bastard, I'm afraid, was sitting beside him. The other way around,' she says, 'and it mightn't have been so bad.'

She looks over to Yvonne.

'Is that your wife?'

'Would you like to meet her?'

She shakes her head.

'Is she out of hospital yet?'

'For a couple of days.'

'She looks quite well.'

Yvonne, suddenly aware of my absence, has glanced across.

The boot has vanished. An anonymous mound of burning debris now occupies the centre of the yard.

'We're leaving in a couple of weeks. I suppose,' she says, 'I should say good-bye.'

She reaches up; she kisses my cheek.

Abstracted, half-smiling, she glances back towards the yard.

'Is Neville still here?'

'He'll keep popping back, I suppose, for the next two years.'

'Is Rebecca staying?'

'She'll be coming with me. We'll be living in London for a while. She'll probably, if she wants to, go to a college there.'

She turns away, slowly, towards the yard.

'Give my love to the flat,' she says.

Not only are there the drifts of coal dust which have fallen off the lorries, the refuse, the bits of paper, the droppings from the horses, the twigs and leaves and lumps of clay from the heath itself, but these hardened packs of ice which have accumulated beneath the wheels of the passing traffic. I loosen them with the shovel, sweep up the rest of the refuse, and drop the whole load in the metal bin; having swept one side of the road, I wheel the bin over to the other side and start sweeping up the debris there.

A car passes down the road, from the direction of the village. It slows as it draws abreast of the bin and, a little lower down, pulls over to the side.

A man gets out in a trilby hat; he stamps his feet, turns up his collar, and comes back up the road, blowing in his hands.

'Your name Freestone?'

He has bright red cheeks; thin veins run in patterns across his nose: it too is red, the eyes above dark brown. The whites show up as a dullish pink.

'That's right.'

'Used to fight: what was it, now?' He glances at my jacket with Urban District Council printed in luminous letters across the back. 'Light-heavy.'

'That's right.'

'You were pointed out to me,' he says, 'the other day.'

He looks at the brush, the shovel, at the dustbin on its metal trolley, then stamps his feet against the cold.

'Fallen on hard times.'

'I believe in the principle that you should pay people,' I tell him, 'not to work. Then the ones who do work would do it for purely equitable reasons. I believe in a society built upon that principle,' I add.

He shakes his head. 'You'd find a lot of loafers, then. There'll be nobody in the factories. Nor down the mines. Nor anywhere, if it comes to that.'

'I think you'd be surprised.'

'At what?'

'The sort of society that that principle might produce,' I say.

'I could get you a job, if you like.' He gestures at the shovel. 'Better than this.'

'I don't know of any job,' I tell him, 'better than this. This is a job I've chosen,' I go on, 'of my own volition.'

'A man like you?' He stamps one foot and then the other.

'Think about it,' I tell him, 'when you get back home.'

'I've thought about it already, lad.'

He tries to laugh.

'Then think a little harder. If you had a job like this,' I tell him, 'you'd find you had the time.'

'You married, then, or just looking to yourself?' he says.

'I'm married,' I tell him.

'Euphoria,' he says. 'You'll find it pass.'

'I'm too old for euphoria,' I tell him.

'Aye, well,' he says. 'I'd better get on.'

'It'll not wait for you,' I say. 'I can tell you that.'

'What won't wait?'

'Your kind of time.'

He goes back to the car.

He gets inside.

It moves off slowly down the road, quickening then, appreciably, as it nears the town.

The snow drifts down.

Across the valley, like a ligament of rock, stand the buildings of the town, black, crested white, the cathedral spire thrust up like a fissure into the greyness overhead.

I pick up the shovel and start again.

More About Penguins and Pelicans

David Storey

This Sporting Life

This is an exceptional first novel in these days, because
the characters are concerned with expressing themselves
in physical, not emotional or intellectual, terms.

The world in which the story is set is that of professional
Rugby League football in an industrial northern city. It
covers several years in the life of the narrator,
Arthur Machin, from the day of his inclusion in the local
team to the match when he begins to feel age creeping up
on him and his feet failing. David Storey recounts the
fortunes of his gladiator hero with little sentimentality and
with all the harsh reality of grime, mud, sweat, intrigue,
and naked ambition.

Flight Into Camden

Acclaimed as a remarkable young writer for his first novel,
This Sporting Life, David Storey was awarded the 1961 John
Llewellyn Rhys Memorial Prize for *Flight into Camden*.

This moving story is recounted by Margaret, the daughter
of a Yorkshire miner, who falls in love with a married
teacher and goes to live with him in a room in Camden
Town, London.

'A love story written with seriousness, sensibility, and
intensity' – *Observer*

David Storey

Pasmore

A young university lecturer is in the grip of a nervous
breakdown, struggling to resolve a disintegrating marriage
in a chaotic and meaningless world.

'Swift clean and painful . . . as good as anything he
has done' – Michael Ratcliffe in *The Times*

David Storey

Radcliffe

The story of a passionate relationship between
two men and its tragic and terrible consequences.

'It tears viciously at you one moment and sets you
shivering the next', commented the *Observer*. 'A
brainstorm of a book; it boils in the mind long after
it is done', wrote the *Sunday Times*. 'Comparable with
another classic rooted in Yorkshire, *Wuthering Heights*',
said *The Times Higher Educational Supplement*, whilst
the *Daily Telegraph* paid tribute to 'an astonishing
achievement', adding that *Radcliffe* established David
Storey as 'the leading novelist of his generation'.

David Storey

Saville
Winner of the 1976 Booker Prize

'One of the finest and truest novelists of his generation' – *The Times*

The passionate conviction and almost physical impact of *Saville* confirm David Storey as the outstanding writer of his time. The novel is an overwhelming and evocative saga of a Yorkshire mining family – at its centre, Saville, a boy whose growing-up in the forties and fifties forges a powerful conflict in his nature and a destructive resistance to his environment.

It is a theme that recalls the preoccupations of Thomas Hardy and D. H. Lawrence; but the writing, the imaginative scope and the constant tension of the narrative all mark *Saville* as a magnificent and wholly original epic.

'Certainly a major achievement . . . a definitive and liberating statement' – *The Times Literary Supplement*